The Pack's Alpha

The Pack Series Book Three - Part II: Claiming Her Birthright

Cooper

Author Cooper

Author's Note

First and foremost, this is a work of fiction. In the world of supernatural shifters, there is advanced healing, heightened senses, increased strength, and an overall resistance to germs and infection (once you get your wolf).

In my world of werewolf shifters, gestations are five months long. I chose a middle ground between wolves (two months) and humans (nine months). So, all stages of pregnancy are advanced and occur much sooner than they would in a human pregnancy.

I'm putting a general trigger warning here. There are scenes of violence and coercion in this book. Those chapters will not have specific trigger warnings included.

I hope you enjoy the book and happy reading.

~Cooper

Contents

Chapter 1: Alpha Michael

Yorick

My first week back after being gone a week was hectic. Alpha Nevaeh was right that I'd missed a lot. I underestimated how much time it would take to catch up and try to keep up after missing only a week. However, my sweet mate helped me through.

Sparring is the only class where I feel like I didn't fall behind. And now that Alpha Leo is gone, I feel like I'm really starting to learn better fighting techniques. I have a lot of fighting knowledge already and unlike some in this class, including my mate, I've fought in real battles. I know firsthand that what you learn in class comes in handy, but you can't assume that everything will be as easy as it is in a controlled environment. People die on the battlefield. My sister Wendy was almost one of those casualties two years ago.

Having learned from two men who fought in a lot of wars, my father and Quirin, I feel like sparring is my best and easiest class.

On Wednesday morning, Alpha Nevaeh walks into the dining hall before sparring class and calls for quiet. Beside her is an older man, obviously an Alpha. He's large, looks like he's never smiled a day in his life, and he emits a dangerous aura, as if all he's ever done his entire life is fight. Based on the multiple scars that I can see on his body, including the one that slices through his eyebrow making him look like he's constantly frowning, I'd say my assessment is correct. He reminds me of an older Quirin if he'd never mated with my sister.

"Everyone, this is Alpha Michael. He is a new instructor here at the Academy. He will be taking an active role in sparring class and will be teaching the Art of War and Battle Tactics next semester. Alpha Michael has experience with multiple real-life battles and he will bring that experience to our Academy. We are very lucky to have him. He will be assessing your skills over the next couple of days and he, like me, will have a say in who becomes eligible for the elite fighting groups at the end of the year. Many of you saw one of those teams when Alpha Leo was removed from the school. There are currently three such teams that work for the Council and as members retire, they need to be replaced. There are two positions that will become available this year. You are the elite. Alpha Michael and I will make you the elite of the elite."

I look around the table. Unlike Wendy who has a penchant for technology, I've always been a fighter. In some ways, I'm glad that Connor is the first-born son. It's left me open to follow a path that I wanted, not one that was laid out for me. Connor has the responsibility of the entire pack, not just mentally and physically, but also financially. His job is a lot more paperwork than I would ever want. Becoming an elite fighter, however, sounds incredible.

I can see that the others at our table, other than Cyra, look excited at this possibility as well. Cyra's path is in her pack, and that thought makes me pause. If she is going to be Alpha of her pack, is there a possibility of me becoming an elite fighter? What happens when Cyra begins having our pups? Could we put that off for a few years while I was fighting? Would I be able to be away from her for long periods of time while I was completing a covert operation? And what would happen to her if something happened to me?

Almost as if she can sense my thoughts, she reaches out and takes my hand, squeezing it and smiling at me. I pull her hand to my lips and kiss her knuckles. My path lies with Cyra, no matter where that takes me.

On our way out to sparring class, everyone talks excitedly about the possibility of becoming an elite fighter.

"You need to go for that," Cyra says quietly as we walk out.

"We need to talk about what that means for us," I tell her.

She smiles but continues watching the others around us. "I know what it feels like to not be able to follow your dreams. I saw the look on your face, Yorick. You love the idea of being an elite fighter and you'd be good at it. Don't hold back because of me."

I stop and pull her to a stop with me. "As I said, we need to talk about what that means. We still have a lot of other things that need to happen between now and then, not the least of which is getting you out of the alliance bond with Stellan. I'll do some research to find out what kind of operations the teams run and how long that would keep me away from you. But I have no intention of spending my life away from my mate. I want pups, I want a life, with you, in case that wasn't obvious. Once you've been instated as the Alpha of your pack, we'll see what options are open to me."

"You're not listening to me, Yorick ..." she begins.

"No, you're not listening to me, Cyra. I want you, more than anything else in this world, more than being a fighter, more than traveling around the world. Is my future following a different path than I thought it would with you? Absolutely. But that doesn't mean that I don't want it."

"I don't want you to ever have regrets or feel like you gave up your dreams for me, Yorick."

"You are my dream, Cyra. You, our future, our pups, our life together," I say, holding her gaze.

She presses her lips together in a firm line. "Let's see what the elite teams look like. Maybe you can be part of one of those teams. Maybe they are divided into different skill sets or timeframes for operation completion."

"See, it's already working out," I say, smiling and leading her onto the sparring field.

"Before we start today, a show of hands, how many of you have been in an actual battle?" Alpha Michael asks.

I raise my hand as does Zach, Megan, which surprises me, and one other warrior.

"You four, with me," he says. I kiss Cyra quickly before stepping aside with Zach and the others.

"Name?" he asks Zach.

"Zach Mont, Alpha."

"Alpha Zane's boy?" Alpha Michael asks.

"Yes sir."

Alpha Michael turns to me. "Name?"

"Yorick Hill, Alpha."

"Alpha Warren's boy?" he asks. How the hell does he know our parents?

"That's correct."

He turns to Megan. "Name?"

"Megan Alston."

He raises an eyebrow. "You're Alpha Cory's daughter?"

Megan lifts her chin defiantly. "I am."

"I'm surprised he let you come here."

"He doesn't expect me to succeed," she says, the muscle in her jaw ticking.

"Prove him wrong," Alpha Michael says, making Megan blink. I'm surprised when the defiance falls away.

"Yes sir."

He nods and turns to the last person.

"Name?"

"Carlos Sanchez, Alpha."

"Warrior?" Alpha Michael asks.

"Yes sir."

"What's your Alpha's name?"

"Alpha Atticus, sir."

Alpha Michael grunts. "He's been in a lot of battles lately."

"Yes sir, he has. It's how I got accepted to the Academy."

He nods. "Spread out. You're all going to attack me at once."

The four of us look at each other.

"Sir?" I ask.

"Do I look like a man who hasn't been in a lot of battles, young Alpha?"

"No sir."

"I've been in more battles than the four of you combined, I can promise you that. I was on one of the elite fighting teams for twenty years. Believe me, four young fighters, even those with minimal experience, are nothing to me."

We spread out around him. Once we're in position, we look at each other. Alpha Michael doesn't move, but the aura around him becomes even more dangerous.

I look at the others and nod. Almost as one, we attack.

He swings fast and hard, knocking Megan aside, before landing a punch to Zach's gut. I hear him wheezing as he drops to the ground. I duck from the punch headed toward my own gut and take the hit on the shoulder. Pain erupts across my torso, but I don't let it stop me. I continue to drop and as I see Carlos flying through the air, both Megan and I go for Alpha Michael's legs. She uses the same punch that she used on Cyra, landing the punch on Alpha Michael's inner thigh as I swing my leg, ready to take him down. I hear him grunt at her punch and he shifts his weight to the leg nearest to me just as I swing my leg behind his, knocking his legs out from under him.

As I spin around, I see him going down, but by the time I've spun all the way around and popped back up for another attack, he's back on his feet, somehow having swiped Megan's feet out from under her.

Zach is getting up, having finally regained his breath and he goes for Alpha Michael's gut. Alpha Michael takes Zach down, elbowing him in the chest, before agilely hopping back to his feet in a move I've never seen in someone his size. My moment of distraction is all he needs to get the better of me. As he takes me down, I manage to land a punch to his kidney. I hear him grunt just before I land on the ground, the air in my lungs punching out of me and making it impossible to breathe for a few seconds.

When I finally suck in air, Alpha Michael has called a halt to our fighting.

"You two fight clean. That's good in class, not good on a battlefield," he says to Zach and Carlos.

"You fight dirty. Good on the battlefield, not good in class. You need to work on your form. You have good skills, but improving your form will put power behind those skills," he says to Megan before turning to me.

"How did Warren Hill's son learn to fight dirty?" he asks me.

"My sister is mated to Quirin Bishop," I say. Quirin is the person who taught all of my family members to fight dirty. He's already teaching his daughters Kendra and Kaylee to fight dirty and they're not even three yet.

"Bishop? As in Alpha Harold Bishop? I thought he only had the one son."

"Alpha Harold adopted Quirin after the death of his father, Alpha Quinton Harris," I tell him.

He raises that eyebrow at me. "Your sister is mated to the man whose father was killed by her father?"

"How do you know so much about our packs?" I ask him, not sure I like how much information he has about my family.

"Rule number one of being an elite fighter - always know who you're fighting. If you make it to the elite fighting squad, learning about every pack on the continent will be one of the most important classes in your second year. You all have some work to do if you're interested in becoming elite fighters, but having some experience behind you gives you a leg up against the others in the class. Get back into formation."

I stand beside Cyra, watching Alpha Michael. I have no idea if I can make it work being an elite fighter while living in a pack, but I know that I want it more now than I did at the start of class.

Chapter 2: Mentors

Hacker

While Tracker has been away, Hijack and I have taken turns watching over Sphinx. Neither of us expect that she will get into trouble before she comes to the Academy, but sometimes trouble comes looking for you. Since all of us like to be proactive and cover all our bases, we agreed that we'd monitor Sphinx when we could. Having been the ones who put the security system into her brother Connor's pack, it's a lot easier for us to monitor what's going on in that pack.

This morning, I'm watching her in warrior training. I smile. She's good. Really good.

Until she isn't.

I frown, turning up the volume on the security system. It doesn't help. There are too many other warriors on the field talking and giving instructions. Sphinx and Alpha Connor, who is talking to her, are on the other side of the battlefield.

I watch her nod, then see the look on her face like she knows she's disappointing her brother. Having seen them in person, having had Shakespeare basically threaten Hijack and I even knowing that we're the ones helping to get his mate out of her situation, says a lot about the love this family shares.

Sphinx is no different. She looks devastated.

I watch Alpha Connor pull her into a hug, still talking to her. I watch her nod again against his chest and when he steps back, he continues talking to her until she gives him a small smile. Then he chucks her under the chin and moves on.

I continue to watch her until sparring is over, then I get back to work, waiting to hear the notification that she's back at her computer. As soon as I hear it, I turn to our chat.

Me: Good morning.

Sphinx: Good morning to you.

Me: What was that in warrior training this morning?

Sphinx: What do you mean?

Me: I was watching you. You were incredible, until you weren't. What happened?

Sphinx: You were watching me? That's not at all creepy.

I've started to realize that distraction is her way of avoiding topics she doesn't want to discuss.

Me: The Council gave us a directive to ensure that nothing happens that will keep you out of the Academy next year. We take that seriously. Stop avoiding the question.

When she doesn't immediately respond, I growl at the computer. I wish I could see her. Is she upset or avoiding me? Did she walk away to use the bathroom, or did she leave so she doesn't have to answer me?

Sphinx: It's too much to write here.

I switch to my earbuds and grab my phone, hitting video call. She answers with a huff.

"Seriously?"

"Yes, seriously. You have a weakness. Weaknesses can be exploited, especially ones that you're trying to hide. Talk to me," I say.

She looks down, the shame that I saw on her face earlier returns and she grits her teeth.

"I nearly died in a battle a couple of years ago. I haven't been able to get past it," she says softly.

"Tell me what happened," I say, keeping my voice soft.

She shakes her head, and I see the tears welling in her eyes. Whatever happened to her may have happened two years ago, but she's still feeling it like it was yesterday.

"Why were you in a battle at fifteen?" I ask her, trying to give her a starting point.

She swipes a tear off her cheek but still doesn't look at me. "It was my brother-in-law's pack. We were attacked the night of Kennedy's Luna ceremony. I knew my father and brother would have ordered me into a safe room, so I waited until they were outside before I joined them. I'd never been in a battle before and the moment I got outside, I realized I was in way over my head. But by then, it was too late. I was trying to find one of them when Connor realized I was in the battle. Then I saw my brother Yorick but before I could get to him ..."

She cuts off and her body shakes with the sob she's trying to keep inside.

"Take your time," I purr at her. Damn, I've never wanted to hold someone like I want to hold her right now. I have a nearly desperate need to wrap my arms around her and rock her until she's back to her strong, sharp-witted self.

She takes a deep breath. "He was a Beta from the attacking pack. I should have been able to take him but ..."

"You were a pup. He was a grown man, an experienced fighter," I say, keeping my voice steady. Inside, I'm anything but calm. I don't have to know the rest of the story to know that she's lucky to have survived. Why the fuck would a Beta go after a pup on a battlefield?

She nods. "Anyway, his wolf slashed Dasha deeply. He was coming in for the kill. If Henry hadn't gotten to me when he did ..."

Her voice cuts off again and her body shakes as she fights her sobs.

So, that's the bond between them. I'd seen the bond they share outside the Council chambers. Henry saved her life. She idolizes him and he feels even more protective of her because of what happened.

"Even with his intervention, I almost bled to death. My mother, for the first time in her life, lost it. My sister Kennedy was the one who had to sew me up. She said I nearly died several times. Everyone in my family and some of the other warriors in Quirin's pack gave blood so I could get a transfusion."

Fuck! She really did almost die if she needed a transfusion. I'll look up the medical records later, but right now, I need to help my partner.

"Look at me," I say. She shakes her head, unwilling to look up. She swipes the back of her hand over her cheeks, but I can still see the tears dripping onto her desk.

"Look at me, Wendy," I say gently.

She sniffs and when she looks up, her shattered look nearly breaks my heart. But I don't let that show on my face.

"You didn't die. You survived. Do you know why?"

"Because my sister is an incredible doctor-in-training?" she asks.

I smile at her. "I'm sure that's part of it. But you survived because you're strong, Wendy. You are stronger than you're giving yourself credit for."

"I don't feel strong," she says softly.

"But you are. Look at you. You're still out on that training field every day trying to push through. You're here, helping your brother and his mate so they can be together. If it wasn't for you, it might have taken us years to find out about Alpha Leo."

She shrugs. "A lot of that was Yorick."

"Stop giving credit for your work to other people, Sphinx. You are an incredible woman. If you weren't, we wouldn't have told the Academy to put you on our team. Do you know how often that's happened in the three years I've been here?"

She looks at me, giving me a ghost of a smile. This one is more real than the one she gave Connor earlier.

"Once?"

"Once," I confirm.

She wipes her cheeks again and this time, they stay dry.

"Thanks, Hacker. I've never told anyone that story before," she says frowning.

"How do you feel?" I ask.

"Better," she says, nodding and this time I get a nearly full smile.

"Good. I'll be watching you from now on. Get out of your head and listen to your brother. He's a good fighter. Not as good as Yorick will be when he's done with this year, or you will be when you're done with your first-year next year. But for now, he'll do."

She snorts. "I probably shouldn't mention that to him."

"Probably not," I say, hearing one of my alarms go off.

"What's that?" she asks.

"Tracker's back. We're meeting with your brother, Cyra, and your family to go over the next steps in an hour. Hijack is ready to pull the trigger and buy out Alpha Christer's debt."

"That's awesome!"

"Are you part of that meeting?" I ask her.

"I haven't been invited to attend," she says.

"Well, you're invited now. You are part of the Tech Team, and this is a learning opportunity for you. Although, remember that this is Hijack's work, it's boring shit that you would never want to do," I tell her, making her laugh.

"I'll keep that in mind."

"Okay then, I'll see you soon."

She nods, but just before I hang up, she stops me.

"Hacker?"

"Yeah?"

"Thanks again. I really do feel better."

"Anytime, my little Padawan," I say, making her smile again before I hang up.

As soon as I disconnect, I pull up her medical records. When I see the gashes on her body, the extensive number of stitches that were required to put her back together, I understand just how lucky she is to be alive. It's no wonder she's still holding on to that fear.

I should tell the others. This is a weakness that we should all be watching for. A weakness in one of us is a weakness in all of us. But I feel protective of Wendy. She said she's never told anyone what happened before, but she told me. Yeah, I pushed, but she still told me.

I decide to keep an eye on her in warrior training. If she doesn't start to improve, I'll have no choice but to tell the others. Hopefully, though, she'll listen to what I said and start finding the strength inside herself that I see in her.

Raptor POV

"You didn't have to drive me to the Academy," my mate says, as I pull her hand to my lips for a kiss. Damn, I can't get enough of this woman. I've already had her three times this morning and I want her again.

"It gives me more time with you. Since I'm not working today, I'll go sign the lease on that apartment after I hit the gym," I say.

After we'd marked each other, we'd talked to the Council about being mated and how we could make it work. As

I expected, they want both of us to continue in our careers, so they agreed that I could move farther away from the elite fighter's base and Jaelynn could move off the Academy's campus.

We've alternated over the last couple of days between thoroughly exploring each other's bodies and finding a new place to live. Rather than spending any time apart or rushing into buying something, we agreed on an apartment that we could lease for a year while we decide on something more permanent.

Since she is still in school and I still have work, we're not planning to move her off campus until this weekend. Between now and then, I'm staying with her. We each have our own car, but I'm reluctant to leave her. Hopefully that will get easier with time since I won't have a choice when my squad is running operations.

I grab my bag out of the back of the car with the clothes I'll need for the next couple of days and then take her hand as we walk into the Academy. I can smell the scent of young warriors and breakfast coming from the dining hall.

"Raptor? What are you doing here?"

I turn, surprised to hear the familiar voice. "Steel? What am I doing here? What the fuck are you doing here?" I say, hugging my previous commander and slapping him on the back just as he does with me.

"I'm the new instructor here at the Academy," he says, grinning wickedly.

I burst out laughing. These poor cadets don't know what's about to hit them.

"Honestly, that's a good thing. You'll make sure that whoever gets promoted to the elite squad is more than qualified," I say, stepping back to put my arm around Jaelynn.

"Steel, meet my mate, Tracker."

He raises an eyebrow. "Tracker? You must be new."

"Yes sir. This is my second year."

"She tracked The Wily Fox," I say proudly. Now Steel's eyes go wide.

"You did? We searched for that bastard for three years!"

"You didn't have a Tracker," she says, smiling at him.

"Obviously. Congratulations you two," he says.

"It was nice meeting you," Jaelynn says to Steel, then turns to me. "I have to go, Kit."

I turn, taking her mouth in a passionate, fiery kiss that promises more of what I gave her this morning. She returns the kiss with just as much passion.

"Take care of my mate," I growl at her.

"You take care of mine," she growls back before turning and walking away. Even the way she walks is sexy as fuck.

"So, how's my squad?" Steel asks, pulling my attention back to him.

"MY squad is good," I say, making him grin. I took over the squad when Steel stepped down two years ago.

"Have you had breakfast yet? I'd love to hear about what's been going on since I left," he says.

"I can always eat," I grin. "And I'd love to hear your impressions of who you think might be able to fill Lace's position. She and her mate have decided to settle down and start having pups."

"Ahh, I was wondering whose position needed to be filled on that squad," he says as we begin walking and talking.

Two hours later, I reluctantly say goodbye to my previous mentor as he walks out to sparring class. It was good talking to him again. And now I feel much more confident that whoever he chooses as Lace's replacement will be perfect for our squad.

Chapter 3: Purchasing the Debt

Cyra

Yorick and I got up early to get breakfast so we could meet with the Tech Team before Sparring class. Hijack apparently has information to share with all of us.

Rather than meeting in the library, we're meeting in Hijack's room. When we arrive, I realize that third year students have much larger rooms than we do as first years. However, even with the added space, Hijack's room is filled with so much computer equipment, it's still difficult to find a place to sit. His bed is shoved against the wall like it's an afterthought for someone who forgets to go to sleep and needs a place to fall into when they're so exhausted they can't stay awake any longer.

While the room is cluttered with equipment, it's spotless and there's an almost perfectionistic structure to it. I have no doubt that Hijack knows where every bit of equipment is and could access it within seconds if needed. From the look of it, he's already set up the video equipment and turned a monitor to face the room. I'm guessing that's where we'll be interacting with Yorick's family.

Tracker and Hacker are there when we arrive. They've set up their own stations with their own computers on either side of Hijack's desk. Once Yorick and I are seated, Hijack connects to the video call. On the monitor in front of us, the faces of Hacker, Tracker, and Hijack instantly show up. We can't see Hijack over the mountain of computer equipment that he's sitting behind, but it's weird to see Tracker and Hacker on screen and in my peripheral vision.

"Testing one, two," Hacker says. I hear his voice through the monitor and in the room.

"I can hear you," Wendy's voice says a moment before her face shows up on the screen. "Good morning, everyone."

"Wendy, does Dad know you're on this call?" Yorick asks.

"She's part of the team. We've been instructed to keep watch over her and we're training her so she's ready to start working with us next year. This is a learning opportunity for her and doesn't interfere with her school schedule," Hijack says as if this explains it all and Wendy's Dad isn't part of that equation. I glance at my mate, knowing how protective he is of his sister. Hijack lifts his head over the equipment to look at Yorick, making sure there's no further argument.

"She's learning what we do. She's not participating in any part of this that crosses legal lines. We won't have her start that until she's officially on campus next year," Hacker says.

"I get to do illegal stuff?" Wendy asks excitedly.

I watch both men's lips twitch while my mate growls softly. "Wendy, you're not helping," he growls just as three other videos connect to the call; Alpha Connor, Alpha Quirin, and Alpha Henry. Alpha Warren is sitting beside his son.

"Wendy? Where are you?" Alpha Connor asks as he joins.

"In my room. I was invited to join," she says defensively. Oh boy.

"Are we ready to begin?" Tracker asks, cutting through the argument that was no doubt about to begin.

Connor looks at their father, but neither says anything more.

Tracker turns to Hijack and nods.

"Okay, I have been in contact with the loan shark, who goes by the ridiculously boring name of Sharky. He doesn't care why we want to buy out the loan as long as he gets his money."

"Has Alpha Christer paid off any of the principal?" Alpha Quirin asks.

"Not quite fifty thousand dollars," Tracker says.

"That's it?" Yorick asks.

"That's a lot considering how much interest he's paying," Quirin says.

"So, what's the plan?" I ask. "You buy out his debt and then what?"

"A lot of that will depend on you, Cyra," Alpha Warren says.

"The first thing I think we should do is call the note on Alpha Christer," Quirin says.

"What does that mean?" I ask.

"It means, I tell him he has to pay me what he owes on the debt effective immediately. I'm assuming since this was created through a loan shark that the note can be called at any time?" he asks.

"That's correct," Hijack says.

"Do we have the terms of the buy-out agreement?" Henry asks.

"I'll send it to you now," Hacker says. "But Hijack and I have combed through it making sure that there wasn't anything that could be held against you or us in this buy out. Just as long as it's a one-time, complete payment, it's clear. Is that going to be a problem?"

"Not a problem," Quirin says distractedly. It looks like he's pulling up the agreement and looking it over.

"What are you doing, Daddy?" I hear a little girl's voice ask. Without glancing away from the screen, Quirin picks up a gorgeous little girl around three years old and puts her on his lap.

"Daddy's taking down a bad man, Kaylee. Want to help?"

"YES!" she says excitedly.

"Say hi to everyone," he says, his tone still distracted as he reads through the agreement.

"Hi Wen-Wen! Hi, Gwanpa! Hi Connor. Hi Henwy. YORRIE! Uncle Yorrie's on the TV, Daddy!" she says excitedly.

"Hey beautiful. Are you sparring hard? I want to see your new moves the next time I come to visit," Yorick says to her.

"Yes. Who's that?" she asks, pointing to the screen. Quirin's eyes flit to where she's pointing.

"That's Alpha Cyra, Uncle Yorrie's mate," he says, before going back to reading.

I swear I feel sweat breaking out on my temples as the little girl assesses me through the video monitor. I wave at her, but she doesn't wave back.

"Do we like her?" she asks her father in a whisper that everyone can still hear without taking her eyes off me.

Now it's Connor, Warren, and Henry's turn to hide their smiles. Quirin doesn't bother to hide his.

"Yes, we like her. Well, I love her," Yorick says, pulling me into a hug and kissing the side of my head. "You're going to love her too, Kaylee."

"When do I get to meet her?" she asks seriously, like she needs to see me in person before she makes a final assessment about me.

"Damn," I hear Tracker murmur.

"Next time I visit, I'll bring her with me," Yorick tells her.

"Who are they?" Kaylee asks, probably asking about Hijack, Hacker, and Tracker. Quirin does a quick round of introductions and when he gets to Hacker, he grins at her.

"You should think about a career in the Council, young Alpha. They like people who can interrogate others like you can," he says to her.

"I'm a warrior, like my Daddy," she says seriously.

"Yeah, you are," Quirin says proudly, kissing the side of her head.

"You know when the Council gets wind of her, they'll be putting her on the 'to be watched' list as well," Hacker tells Quirin.

"I'm sure she and her twin, Kendra, will both be on their list. But my daughters will always be allowed to choose their own path in life. I'm good with this agreement. Henry?" Quirin says.

"It looks good to me too," he says.

"Connor? Warren? Any concerns?" he asks.

"None for me," they both say.

"Okay, pull the trigger, Hijack. I'll set up the wire transfer right after this call."

"Who's the bad guy, Daddy?" Kaylee asks, watching her father as he types out something on his computer. I can hear Hijack typing as well and I'm assuming they're setting up the buyout.

"A man who is trying to keep Alpha Cyra away from Uncle Yorrie," he says, still distracted by what he's doing. I'm impressed with his ability to multi-task work while talking to his daughter who, at such a young age, seems like she's following along pretty well.

I hear her soft, pup's growl. I know it's meant to be fierce, but it's one of the cutest sounds I've ever heard in my life. "Then it's a good thing she has us," she says, confidently.

Quirin smiles at his daughter again and kisses the side of her head. "Yes, it is. We protect our own, don't we, baby girl?"

"Yes, we do," she says, crossing her arms over her chest in a way that looks so similar to how Alpha Quirin stands that I know she's picked it up from him.

"Cyra, I know you have class this morning. Hijack and I will get this done. Do you have any problem with me calling the note on Alpha Christer?" Quirin asks.

"What happens if he can't pay it? Twenty million dollars is a lot of money," I say.

"Then we bankrupt his pack, or he uses it to pay off the loan. How far away is his pack from yours?" he asks.

I shrug. "It's the next pack over from ours. There's a land gap in between, but ..."

"That land is sitting idle. We could look into who owns it and you could buy it out, giving yourself a larger pack land," Hijack says.

"Larger pack land?" I ask.

Yorick turns to me. "If Quirin bankrupts Alpha Christer and buys out the pack, it belongs to him. We could buy it back from him and if we buy the land in between the two packs, that entire area would become your pack land after you take over as Alpha."

"I don't have twenty million dollars," I say, frowning at him.

"Once you and Yorick are mated, you'll be family, Cyra. We'll figure that part out. But Yorick is right, you could expand your pack lands, increasing the wealth of your pack after we remove your father from his position," Quirin says.

"It's a lot to consider," Yorick says, watching me as my mind spins with the possibilities. He turns back to the video monitor.

"Can you hold off on calling the note, Quirin, give Cyra time to think through all of this?" he asks.

"Of course," Quirin says. "Let's plan to talk later tonight."

"In the meantime, we'll begin erasing the documents that Christer and Stellan have on your father so that when you do call the note, he has nothing to hold against you or your father to force the alliance bond. If anything, he'll be desperate to enter into an agreement with you where he can maintain his pack lands and his Alpha title," Hijack says.

"He doesn't deserve that title," I growl.

"No, he doesn't," Connor agrees.

"You're right, Daddy," Kaylee says, as we're about to end the call.

"About what, baby girl?" he asks, pulling her in for another kiss.

"I think I like Alpha Cyra."

For some reason, earning Kaylee's acceptance makes me feel like I've just passed a major hurdle.

Chapter 4: Becoming an Alpha

Yorick

"You've been awfully quiet today," I say to Cyra. She's been in her own world of thoughts since our call this morning. In class, I had to nudge her several times to help her stay focused and now that classes are done for the day, she's back to being in her own head. What I wouldn't give to have my mark on her neck so I could follow along with whatever she's thinking.

Okay, I just want my mark on her neck, but it would definitely help right now.

Cyra looks at me and smiles. "You know, Kaylee is the scariest pup I've ever met in my life."

I burst out laughing. Quirin would be so proud to hear that.

"She and her twin, Kendra, are something else. Wade calls them the Double K, Triple Threat, because they have learned to fight together and even at a young age, they're pretty powerful. I wasn't there, but Quirin loves to tell the story of how his two-and-a-half-year-old daughters dropped one of his warriors."

"Dropped him? You mean took him down?" she asks, her eyes going wide.

"More or less. It wouldn't have been a win on the sparring field, but they knocked him to his knees. He was being cocky and teasing them about being pup warriors. They reminded him that they are not only Alpha females, but also Quirin's daughters."

"How?"

"As I understand it, the two tag-team very well, so while the warrior was focused on one twin, Kaylee I think, the other came behind him in a sneak attack. When he turned to take on Kendra, Kaylee punched him in the inner thigh hard enough that it distracted him while Kendra kicked out his knee and brought him to the ground. Then they leaped on him until Quirin got them off. Quirin's one of the strongest fighters I know, which is saying something since my father is a powerful fighter as well. But it wasn't until I started fighting with Quirin that I became the strong fighter I am now. Dad is an incredible technical fighter, but Quirin fights dirty. I've gotten the best of both teachings, and the girls are getting that same instruction from a much younger age."

"So, my instincts were right. She is scary," Cyra says as we sit in her room before dinner.

"Yes and no. They also have a lot of Kennedy in them. They are fiercely loyal, you saw that this morning, and extremely protective of each other and our family."

"I saw that too. She wants to make sure I'm worthy of being your mate," Cyra says, chuckling.

I pull her into my lap. "What's really on your mind, my mate."

She leans her head on my shoulder, and I rub her back, waiting for her to tell me what she's thinking.

"I don't know the first thing about being an Alpha, Yorick. I realized that today. Your father, Connor, Henry, and Quirin all seem to know exactly what they should be doing to make this work. They all seem to have a plan that they inherently agree with, and I feel like I'm on the outside looking in with no clue what I should be doing. My father never included me in any of the pack dealings. I've learned more about being an Alpha in the short time we've been at the Academy than I ever did at home, and they're not teaching us to be Alphas here. They're teaching us how to use the skills an Alpha has to be better. If we overthrow my father, whether I challenge him or the Council removes him from his position, am I really the person that should lead my pack? I don't even know how to manage pack finances. You've seen me in finance class. I'm still struggling to understand the hundreds of lines of incoming and outgoing finances, much less tracking the financial trails to where they go."

"All of those things that you just mentioned can be learned, Cyra. What you have that your father doesn't is compassion and a willingness to do the right thing for your pack. The rest is just knowledge," I say to her.

"Yeah, but who is going to teach me? Who is going to make sure that I don't run my pack into the ground months after taking it over? You're brilliant, Yorick, and you have obviously been more involved in pack decisions and conversations than I have in my life, but you weren't raised to lead a pack either. And based on what I've seen in the last few days, that's not what you want anyway."

She lifts her head to look me in the eye while we're talking. I can see the frustration and torment in her eyes as she struggles to figure out how she can be the Alpha that she wants to be for her pack.

I take her face in my hands. "My family will help you, Cyra. You're right, the idea of pouring over financial ledgers makes my eye twitch," I say, making her smile, but it fades quickly.

"They have their own packs to run, Yorick."

"My father doesn't," I say, the idea flashing like a light-bulb being turned on in my head.

"I'm sure your father has better things to do than teach me how to be an Alpha," she says.

"Actually, he doesn't. He struggled a lot when Connor took over as Alpha. He spent a year helping Quirin clean silver powder out of his pack lands because he needed something that would make him feel useful. My mother still has the medical school, but he doesn't really have anything that is permanent. Honestly, I bet he'd jump at the idea. We should call him before we talk to the others tonight," I say excitedly. "My dad is a fantastic Alpha. He's confident, knowledgeable, and he's a patient teacher. Plus, he might be willing to oversee the pack while you finish out your year here at the Academy, Cyra. You could learn everything you need to know here while still learning how to run a pack. We could spend weekends at your pack while you work with Dad, and then when the year is up, we'll figure out next steps."

"Do you really think he'd be interested?" she asks.

"Let's call him right now and find out."

Warren POV

"ARGH!" I say, holding my side and falling to the ground in mock pain.

"Are you okay, Gwanpa?" Kendra asks, bending over to check on me like I knew she would.

"Of course I'm okay!" I growl, grabbing her around the waist and pulling her to the ground as she squeals. "What's the first rule of battle?"

"Never lose focus," she says, obviously aggravated that I tricked her.

I kiss her head. "That's right but thank you for checking on me. You pack quite a punch, Ken," I say and I mean it. Kendra and Kaylee are natural born fighters. They absorb the instruction that others give them and use it in their sparring training. Even at a young age, they're already putting the full force of their body behind their punches making them much more effective than any other pup their age and even most pups three to four times their age.

I get back on my knees which eliminates my height advantage, ready to take her on again when I hear my phone ring.

"Hold that punch," I say, standing and going to grab my phone. I'm surprised when I see Yorick's name on the caller ID since we're planning to talk later tonight.

"Hey son, is everything okay?" I ask as I answer.

"Hey Dad. I have Cyra here with me. We wanted to talk to you about something before tonight."

"Okay, what's up?" I ask, grabbing a towel and wiping off the sweat and grass as I sit, watching Kendra walk over to fight with her sister against Wade. I smile as he raises his hands as if the two of them together are too much for him to take on, making both girls laugh.

"You obviously know that Alpha Arden doesn't think much of Cyra," he says.

"That's obvious, he basically sold her off like chattel. No offense, Cyra."

"No offense taken, Alpha. You're right about that."

"Well, the thing is, Alpha Arden never taught Cyra anything about being an Alpha. He never expected to give the pack to her and she's nervous, now that we're about to start moving forward, that her lack of knowledge could be a detriment to her pack," Yorick says.

I smell my mate walking up behind me. Since I don't smell anyone else with her, I quickly turn and pull her into my lap, kissing the side of her head while I talk. She wraps her arms around my neck, kissing my throat and making Arric purr before she turns to watch our children and grandchildren sparring.

"I think that's a very proactive way of thinking. Many young Alphas who didn't know how to manage a pack have run their packs into ruin, whether through financial collapse or battle-weary defeat from other Alphas attacking repeatedly to take over the pack. What can I do to help?"

It's quiet on the other end and Yara turns to look at me, obviously listening in to the conversation.

'It must be important if they're taking so long to ask,' she mumbles in her mind. Goddess, I love this woman. I kiss her nose while I wait for Yorick or Cyra to respond.

"How would you feel about teaching Cyra to run her pack, and possibly maintaining her pack while she finishes this year at the Academy, Dad?"

My eyes snap to my mate's. I know she feels the excitement swell inside me. I've found a way to keep myself busy, raising my pups and spending time with my grandpups. But lately, I've still felt like something was lacking in my life. Never in my personal life, my life with Yara and our pups is amazing. But not having a purpose in life has started to eat at me again.

"What do you think of that, Cyra?" I ask, watching a smile spread across my mate's face.

"I know it's a lot to ask, Alpha. But I need someone I can trust to teach me how to manage a pack, someone who has the time to do it. I would understand if managing my pack while I finish the Academy was too much for you, that's asking a lot. But I would be grateful if you could teach me how to run my pack so that I can be the kind of Alpha that I see in you and Alphas Connor, Henry, and Quirin."

'Could we make it work?' I ask Yara in our mind link.

'Of course we'll make it work. So will our pups. You need this, Warren. It will be good for you, and it will be good for Cyra and Yorick, too,' she says, caressing my cheek.

"I would be happy to teach you anything and everything you need to know about being an Alpha, Cyra. And if you need me to manage your pack while you finish the Academy, I'm happy to do that as well."

"Really?" she whispers.

"I told you, Cyra. You are family now. Family is every-thing. I won't let you fail, and I won't let anything happen to your pack while you're finishing your studies," I tell her.

I hear her soft sob.

"See, I told you he'd be willing to help," Yorick says to her softly.

'My son is perfect, just like his father,' Yara mumbles in her mind.

I suddenly have an almost desperate need to be inside my mate.

"Let's talk more about this tonight. We'll make a plan of how this can work, and when and how we plan to remove your father from his position. Once all of that is settled, Yara and I can talk about moving to your pack. It would be better to do that when you can be there so we can address the pack together and let them know what is going on.

I'm sure they'll test both of us, but you didn't get into the Academy without being a good fighter."

"My father's warriors know they can't defeat me," she says, sniffling.

"They're your warriors now, Cyra. You need to start thinking like an Alpha. The pack is yours. The warriors are yours. All you're doing now is making a plan to reclaim what rightfully belongs to you as their Alpha," I tell her.

"Thank you again, Alpha Warren."

"We're family, Cyra. Call me Warren."

"Thank you, Warren."

"You're welcome. We'll talk soon," I say, hanging up as I stand, keeping my mate in my arms.

She laughs as I begin walking her inside. "Where are we going?"

"I'm feeling the need to show you just how perfect a mate I truly am," I growl, before taking her mouth in a possessive kiss.

I don't stop until I've gotten to our room, shredded our clothes and walked into the shower where I press my mate against the wall and bury myself inside her, reveling in the sound of her sweet moans and my name echoing around the small room as I make her come again and again.

Chapter 5: Confidence

Cyra

"I know you're still struggling to understand that you're not alone anymore, Cyra, but you aren't," my mate, my sweet, amazing mate says to me.

He's right, I don't know what it means to not be alone, but I'm getting a crash course on what it's like to have family, a real family, surround you with their love. Looking at my mate, seeing the pure and absolute love in his eyes, makes me realize several things all at once.

First, no matter what, I want his mark on my neck and mine on his. Second, I want to be the kind of Alpha that a man like Yorick will be proud of, someone he would want to follow, but would also be willing to stand beside and lead our pack together. And finally, no matter what it takes, no matter how difficult it might be for me or for us, I want him to follow his dream and become an elite warrior for as long as he wants that life.

Since I'm already in his lap, I turn, straddling him as I take his mouth in a passionate kiss. His response, as always, is instant. Now that my decision is made, I want to start making it happen right now, all of it. We have a plan, a plan that we can make work. I'm ready to start this life, my new life with Yorick, right now.

When I pull back, he frowns slightly, his arms stroking over my hips and thighs. I'm not sure what he sees on my face, but he smiles.

"Did you want to skip dinner?"

"How much studying do you have to do tonight?" I ask.

"That depends on what my mate has planned," he says, watching me intently.

"Can you give up one night of studying?"

"For you? For you, I can give up anything," he says.

"No," I say, pressing my fingers to his lips. "Not your dreams. Don't ever give up your dreams for me, Yorick."

"What is this about, Cyra?"

"I want tonight to be about us. Just you and me. I want to show you how much I love you and appreciate you, to show you how much I want you," I tell him.

I watch his sexy smile spread across his face. "Hmmm, let me think. Reading over financial ledgers or making love to my mate all night long. Is that really a question?" he asks.

I slide my fingers through his silky black hair. "I'm going to show you just how much I love you tonight, my mate," I purr at him.

"I like the sound of that," he says, nipping at my chin then kissing me again. "Let's go eat, so we can have our call with the family and then start our night of passionate, mind-blowing sex," he growls, making me laugh.

He doesn't know what I'm planning, but I'm pretty sure he'll agree. If he doesn't, then I'll wait. Goddess knows he's waited for me.

We have dinner with our friends and for the first time in a long time, I feel like I can just relax and enjoy being with them. We quietly update them on what's going to happen with Alpha Christer and the loan, and when we finish dinner, Yorick and I head to Hijack's room for the call.

"That was a lot of whispering. Are you about to get another instructor fired, Yorick?" Megan asks as we walk out of the dining hall.

"Stop being petty, Megan. Really, if you want to be treated like an Alpha, you should start acting like one," I say to her, my newfound confidence shining through.

"Look who grew a pair," she says.

"The only thing I needed to grow was my self-confidence. You should try it," I say, before walking away. Since I'm holding hands with Yorick, I lead him away with me.

"Okay, that was sexy as fuck. Can we skip the call and go straight to the sex?" Yorick growls. The sound flows through me sending waves of heat and desire straight to my core.

I flash a grin over my shoulder. "If you're good and come to the meeting, I'll make sure I was worth the wait."

He tugs me back to him, pressing his warm body against mine. "You're ALWAYS worth the wait," he says seriously.

"Damn," I murmur before kissing him passionately, but quickly. "I can't wait to get you in bed later."

"That makes two of us."

When we get to Hijack's room, it's set up the same with Tracker and Hacker in the same seats they were sitting in this morning like they never left. Hijack dials into the video call and within minutes, everyone is on. This time, Alpha Warren is sitting beside Alpha Quirin.

"Good evening, everyone," Hijack begins. "Just to make sure we're all on the same page, the loan shark has been paid off. Alpha Quirin now holds the note that Alpha Christer took out to blackmail Alpha Arden into the alliance agreement. We are here to talk about next steps. Alpha Cyra, I believe you needed some time to think about what you wanted to do," he says, looking over the wall of computer screens to look at me.

"I've had some time to think about how I want to proceed and I agree with calling the note. I want out of this alliance agreement effective immediately. I want Alpha Christer and Alpha Stellan out of the picture, and I intend to contact the Council tomorrow to submit the information that the Tech Team has accumulated about my father and have him removed from his position as Alpha by this weekend."

Everyone stares at me. Only Yorick and Warren smile, knowing where my new confidence has come from.

"Spoken like a true Alpha," Warren says. For some reason, his praise makes me feel special, like I've made him proud of me. It's the praise that I've struggled to obtain from my own father for years but could never achieve.

Alpha Quirin looks at Warren, then back at the monitor. "Forgive me, Alpha Cyra, but you seem different than you did this morning. This confidence isn't something I've seen in you before. Granted, I don't know you well, but what changed since this morning?"

I smile at Alpha Warren and lift my chin. "My biggest fear was that I am not prepared to take over a pack as Alpha. I have no training or knowledge of how to do that. I spoke to Alpha Warren earlier today and he has agreed to not only teach me how to run a pack effectively, but he is also willing to manage my pack so that I can finish my year here at the Academy. He'll train me on the weekends when I go home, and I'll take classes and study during the week."

"You didn't mention this earlier," Quirin says, raising an eyebrow at Warren.

"I was busy," he says shrugging.

Quirin snorts, making me wonder what Warren was 'busy' doing.

"Well, I can attest that you have one of the greatest mentors possible to teach you how to be the best Alpha you can be, Cyra. Congratulations," Connor says.

"Yes, congratulations," Alpha Quirin says, getting a very menacing look on his face and rubbing his hands together excitedly. "So, do I get to pull the trigger?"

"Are you ready to go to war if that's what it takes, Q?" Alpha Henry asks him.

"Yeah, and I'm bringing you with me. You could use the battle experience," he says, grinning at his brother. Henry just shakes his head.

"We've done an assessment on the strength of Alpha Christer's pack compared to the three of yours," Tracker says, making all the Alphas turn their attention to her.

"Excuse me?" Connor says.

Tracker looks at the screen. She's an intense woman anyway, but now that intensity is warring with arrogance on her face.

"We do this sort of assessment for all the elite fighting teams so they know what they are getting themselves into before they attack. My colleagues and I thought you would appreciate the same sort of assessment before you potentially go to war. However, if you don't want our assistance ..."

"I'll take whatever you have," Quirin says quickly. "Thank you."

"Is there anything your team doesn't know?" Connor asks them.

"Anything we haven't looked into," Hacker says with a negligent shrug. "But if we're working with someone, especially if we're working with the Council, we have their approval to dig as far and as deep as necessary to get answers. We're a big reason we don't lose many of our elite warriors."

"It's a good thing your brother and sister are going to be working for them, right Connor?" Warren asks.

"I guess so. It's just more power than I realized any one group had over the packs," he says.

"That's why we go through annual assessments. We, this team, check each other to make sure that we're all staying on the correct side of the work that we're doing. It's rare, but Tech Team members have been ejected from the group in the past," Hijack says.

"Because of the power that we have, it's important that we always do things for the right reasons. It's also why, when we find talent that we think we can trust, we alert the Council to invite said talent to receive early admission to the Academy, or to actively seek them out to apply for admission," Tracker says, smiling at Wendy who sits up straighter in the chair beside Connor. Sphinx is obviously part of their 'in' crowd.

"Okay, we have a plan. Alpha Quirin, will you let the group know after you've spoken to Alpha Christer? There is a possibility that he and Alpha Stellan may go after Alpha Arden and his pack, but if he doesn't know that you're working with Cyra, then he probably won't put the pieces together, at least not until they realize that all the paperwork they had on Alpha Arden has been wiped clean," Hijack says.

"It won't matter after tomorrow anyway," I say. "I'll be submitting all of that to the Council so even if Alpha Christer does have anything on my father, he won't be able to use it. If anything, it will make him an accessory to the crime, since he didn't tell the Council when he found out," I say.

"Someone's been paying attention in Battle Strategy," Hacker says, smiling at me.

"Yes, I have. Warren, I'll be in touch with you tomorrow after I speak to the Council, but my intention is to remove my father this weekend. Does that give you enough time to prepare to join me at my pack?"

"It does. Call me after you speak to the Council and we'll talk about next steps," he says.

We say goodbye and Yorick and I walk back to his room.

"You're amazing, you know that?" he asks once we're inside his room.

I wrap my arms around his neck, leaning into him, and just looking at him for a moment. Then, I smile. "Amazing enough that you're willing to complete our bond tonight?"

Chapter 6: Threat

Quirin

"Did you want to listen in?" I ask Warren when we hang up from the video call.

"I think it's always good to be reminded of how truly vicious you can be, Quirin," he says, just as the people in my life who have taken that viciousness out of me knock on the door.

I stand and walk to the door. Before I reach it, it's pushed open, and my gaggle of girls comes flooding into the office.

"DADDY!" they all say rushing toward me. I've learned from one of the best fathers out there how to manage a large group of children, so without breaking stride, I reach down and scoop up all four of my quads, as I continue walking toward the woman who has given me everything I've ever wanted in life and so much more.

I lean over the girls in my arms and my son in her arms and kiss my mate, drawing her into the kiss since I don't have any arms to pull her to me.

When I pull back, I growl softly, letting her know that I'll be finishing that later tonight. She gives me her sweet, naughty grin that sends desire straight to dick, making it swell painfully in my pants.

"It sounded like you were off the phone and the girls wanted to come say goodnight," she says.

"We just finished," I say, kissing the side of each girl's head in my arms one at a time. Raif begins purring at all of them, knowing it will help them fall asleep.

"Did you take out the bad guy, Daddy?"

"I'm about to, Kaylee."

"So, everything went well?" Kennedy asks as Warren walks up with my twins in his arms. They were sleeping in here with me while Kennedy managed the quads and Harold.

"It did," I say, kissing the tops of my twins' heads once they're close enough.

"Can you read us a story, Gwanpa?" Quinlee asks him.

"Grandpa is going to watch your Daddy take down a bad man and then I'll come up and read you a story," he says, kissing the heads of the four girls in my arms while Arric purrs at the two in his.

"Can we watch?" Kaylee asks.

I look at Kennedy. She's better at navigating these sorts of things than I am.

'How bad will it be?' she asks in our mind link.

'I'm sure there will be nasty words and threats, but I'm not going to war over the phone,' I tell her.

"Pwease, Mommy?" Kendra asks her. I know my pups are still young, but Kendra and Kaylee are already so much like me that it's scary. Scary in a good way, in a way that makes me proud. Thankfully, I have family now who can help make sure that they grow up able to manage the fight and darkness inside them, unlike me.

"You will sit with your grandfather, and you will be quiet," she says to my girls, just as Luna Yara walks up.

"Did I hear something about a story before bed?" she asks, smiling at her mate.

"Oh, can we hear the one about the wabbit doctor again, Gwanma?" Quilla asks. Those two twins are growing up in the hospital with their mother and grandmother. I expect they'll be just like both women when they grow up, and it makes me so proud.

"I have a new one," she says excitedly, taking Quiana and Kyla from Warren. "It's about a grasshopper surgeon."

"YAY!" Quinlee and Quilla say excitedly. I put my quadruplets down, kiss my son on the head, then kiss my mate with enough passion to let her know I want her naked in our bed when I get upstairs. Then I say goodnight one more time before closing the door and walking over to where Warren is already getting Kaylee and Kendra settled on his lap across from my desk.

I crouch down in front of them, making sure I have their attention.

"Daddy is going to be talking to a bad man, someone who was trying to keep Uncle Yorick away from his mate," I begin. Both my girls growl their cute little pup growls. Warren smiles and kisses the tops of their heads again.

"Daddy is going to yell and probably curse. Raif will probably growl and snarl, but I want you to know that none of that is aimed at the two of you. I don't want you to be scared. If you get scared, grandpa is here. Just remember, who do I love more than anyone else in this world?"

"Mommy," they both say instantly.

"That is true. Who else?"

"Us," Kendra says.

"Family," Kaylee says.

"Exactly. Family is always first. So, no matter how mean Daddy seems, I still love you more than anything else in this world. Right?"

"Right."

"And no repeating any bad words that Daddy says, or you won't be allowed to listen in ever again, okay?"

"Okay, Daddy."

I go to my desk and put my ear buds in. Warren will be able to hear both sides of the conversation, but my girls will only be able to hear mine.

I dial the number that I got from the Tech Team and when someone answers I ask for Alpha Christer.

"Who's calling?"

"Alpha Quirin."

"One moment please," the person says, and I wait. While I wait, I wink at my daughters whose attention is completely focused on me.

"This is Alpha Christer."

"Alpha Christer, my name is Alpha Quirin."

"Alpha, what can I do for you?" he asks.

"I'm not sure if you're aware, but I have purchased the loan that was previously funded by the loan shark named Sharky," I tell him.

I get nothing but silence for several beats.

"Why would you buy out that loan?" he asks.

"I have my reasons. The point is, I'm calling the note," I say.

"You can't do that," he growls.

"I assure you, I can."

"And where am I supposed to get twenty million dollars?" he snarls.

"That is not my problem. It's yours. You owe me twenty million dollars, minus the forty-eight thousand dollars that you previously paid Sharky, and I want it paid in full within three days," I say, keeping my tone neutral.

"I don't have that kind of money. If I did, I wouldn't have needed the loan shark."

"Again, not my problem."

"And if I don't come up with the money in three days?" he growls.

"Then I will take your pack, which you put up as collateral, instead."

"You fucking piece of shit. I dare you to try to take my pack from me," he snarls.

"Oh, Alpha Christer. You've never heard of me, have you?" I ask, my tone becoming menacing.

"Should I have?"

"I am the most feared Alpha in the country. Any Alpha worth his title would know that. But since you're the type of Alpha who uses his pack as collateral for a loan he can't afford, I'd say you aren't worthy of the title and I'll be happy to take your pack off your hands."

"How scary can you be if I've never heard of you?" he asks arrogantly.

"Look me up. Quirin Bishop. I'll wait," I say.

I hear the keys on his computer keyboard typing. Then silence.

"Why are you doing this?" he asks with less arrogance in his tone.

"Maybe I just like the idea of acquiring land from Alphas who don't deserve their titles. You have three days, Alpha. On the third day, my warriors and I will be there to take what is owed to us. I'd prefer not to kill your pack members, that is needless killing. But it wouldn't be the first or last time I kill to get what I want," I say, the last part coming out in a snarl.

"FUCK YOU!" he snarls.

"I have a mate for that, but thanks for the offer."

"Maybe I'll come for her then," he snarls.

The darkness consumes me in an instant and everything around me goes black as I snarl, Raif's claws sliding out of my knuckles.

"You just made the worst mistake of your life, Alpha. You do not threaten what is mine. When I come for you, I will string you up and I will kill you slowly and painfully. I will make you suffer, and I will put your suffering on display so everyone can see that no one, NO ONE, threatens what is mine. You just lost your window of opportunity because of your insolence. My money or your pack tomorrow," I snarl, then disconnect the phone.

I sit there fuming, remembering what Echo and Kennedy looked like after Jasper took them.

I smell her citrus and mint scent before I see her. I reach out to her blindly, pulling her into my lap.

"I'm right here. I'm safe. Your family is safe," she says, holding my face in her hands.

"He threatened you," I snarl.

"As if he could get to me. As if he could ever get past you, my love. He's a fool, Quirin, a stupid, desperate fool."

I pull her against me, feeling her inside my mind, pushing my darkness away. I wrap my arms around her tightly and breathe in her scent.

"Come on girls, let's let your mommy calm your daddy down. We can go read that story before bed," I hear Warren say. I don't release Kennedy as I hear them get up and walk to the door.

"Our daddy's a badass," Kendra says.

"A big badass," Kaylee agrees.

"Yeah, he is," Warren says.

As soon as the door clicks closed, I shred my mate's clothes, shoving everything off my desk before laying her on it, ripping off my own clothes, and thrusting inside her.

She wraps her body and her mind around me, the darkness inside me lifting with each orgasm I give her until I finally empty myself inside her, roaring my release as her bright, cheerful light blasts the last of my darkness away.

I collapse over her, pressing my forehead to hers. "He threatened you, Kennedy. He dies for that," I growl.

"I know," she says.

I lift my head and look at my sweet, beautiful mate. "You're not going to fight me on that?"

"If he's a threat to me, then he's a threat to our pups as well. No one hurts our family, right?"

I don't know how I got so lucky to have a woman like Kennedy as a mate, but I send a silent thank you to the Moon Goddess before I take my mate again on the desk. Then I take her upstairs to our room where I take her several more times before falling into a calm, restful sleep.

Tomorrow, I fight, but tonight, I let my mate heal me in the way that only she can.

Chapter 7: The Truth

L^{ila}

"Baby, you know I want to be with you as much as you want to be with me," Stellan says. He pulled me into an empty room in the packhouse when I confronted him once again about getting out of the agreement with Alpha Cyra.

Ever since that woman, Piper, called me, I can't get the thought out of my head that what she said might be true. But every time I say something to Stellan, he has a good reason why he can't get out of the agreement.

"What if she finds her fated mate at the Academy, Stell? Maybe she will and that will be that," I say, remembering that Piper told me Cyra did find her mate and he's the one who punched Stellan.

"She didn't, baby. I told you, when I was there, she refused to release me from the alliance bond. If she had met her mate, she'd have told me. She'd have been as eager to get out of this alliance bond as I am," he says, running his fingers over my cheek and tucking my hair behind my ear.

Now I don't know what to believe.

"You know I only want you, right?" he says, leaning in to kiss me.

It took that call from Piper for me to pay attention, but I've finally realized that this is how he gets me to stop asking questions. He moves our conversations into sex and by the time we're done, I don't want to drag up the argument again.

He has just pressed his lips to mine when he jerks back.

"Stellan?"

"Christer just sent me a mind link. I have to go see him. We'll finish this later, okay? Promise," he says, stepping away from me.

He doesn't wait for me to respond but turns and makes his way out of the room quickly. I only wait a moment before I carefully follow him. Maybe now I can get some answers.

I make my way to Alpha Christer's office. There's no one else here at this time of night, so I find a dark corner and tuck myself into the shadows. The door to Christer's office is slightly ajar, and since he's yelling and banging around, it's not hard to hear him.

"Some Alpha named Quirin bought the loan and is calling the note," Alpha Christer growls.

"Who the fuck is Alpha Quirin?" Stellan asks.

"Fuck if I know. Some mega-powerful, mega-wealthy Alpha according to the pack logs."

"What loan did he buy?" Stellan asks.

"What loan? WHAT LOAN? The loan that I took out so we could blackmail Arden, and you could become an Alpha, Stellan! That's what loan!"

I slap a hand over my mouth to hold in the sound that my mouth wants to make as I feel my heart breaking. Bree, my wolf, begins howling in my head as our mate's betrayal hits us like a brick. I know that Alpha Arden is Cyra's father. Christer and Stellan are blackmailing him so Stellan can become an Alpha?

"He has to give us time, right? He can't just expect us to come up with twenty million dollars," Stellan says.

"The terms of the loan were that it could be called at any time. At the time, we only had a year before Cyra turned eighteen and you took over as Alpha. I had enough money to pay the interest for that year. Then you had to go and agree to let her attend that fucking Academy for a year!" Alpha Christer screams.

I slide down to the floor keeping myself pressed against the wall. Piper was right. Stellan has been lying to me all along.

"So, how long do we have?" Stellan asks.

"Until tomorrow. He's coming here, planning to take my pack from me. I'm not losing my fucking pack because I listened to your stupid idea of taking over Arden's pack," Christer growls.

It was Stellan's idea? All of it? I feel like I'm going to vomit.

"Fine, I'll drive to the Academy tonight. I'll force Cyra to complete the bond. Then we can get our hands on the money and pay back the loan," Stellan says.

"You'd better be ready for a fight, Stellan. If her mate finds out that you're there to force your mark on her, he'll kill you."

"He can try," Stellan snarls. "That money is ours. That pack is mine."

"Before you leave, call Arden. Tell him that if we go down, he goes down with us, so he'd better get his warriors here tonight and be ready for a battle tomorrow," Christer growls.

"What are you going to do?" Stellan asks me.

"I have to prepare to defend the only fucking pack we currently have," he snarls. "Now call Arden and get the fuck out of here. Whatever you have to do, you better put your fucking mark on that girl. Did you get her birth control replaced with placebos?"

"Yeah. I did that before she left," Stellan says.

"Then make sure you fuck her long enough to put a pup in her, so there's no choice but for her to accept you," Christer says.

I hold perfectly still as the door swings open and Stellan rushes out the door and down the hall. I feel bile rising in my throat. He not only lied to me, but he's going to force Cyra into a mate bond she doesn't want so he can become an Alpha.

'Hey baby. Something has come up. We'll have to put that make up session on hold until tomorrow. Sorry, baby,' Stellan's voice says in the mind link.

'Sure. No problem,' I say, feeling like my entire world is collapsing around me. I've been such a fool. He played me and I fell for it.

I was worried he'd realize something was wrong, but the link is closed before I finish talking.

I hear something crashing against the wall in Alpha Christer's office a moment before our Beta and Gamma go rushing inside. When the door is closed, I rush out of the hallway, careful not to run into Stellan. Then I race to my room and grab my phone.

I had intended to delete her number, but something inside me, some instinct in Bree, told me to keep her number. I'm glad I did.

I dial the number, hoping that she answers. It rings several times, then goes to voicemail. I hang up and dial again. When it goes to voicemail again, I try one more time. If that doesn't work, I'll leave a voice message and hope she gets it in time.

This time she answers, sounding aggravated.

"What?" she growls.

"Piper, this is Lila. Do you remember me?"

I hear her shifting. "Yes, I remember you. Is everything okay?" Her tone is gentle enough and Stellan's betrayal is so raw that my eyes fill with tears.

"No, but that's not why I'm calling. You need to warn your friend, Alpha Cyra."

"Warn her about what?" she asks, her tone turning menacing.

"Something is happening. I don't know exactly what. Something about some Alpha buying the loan that Alpha Christer and Stellan used to blackmail Alpha Arden. The Alpha is threatening to come here tomorrow to get his money or take our pack. Stellan is going to the Academy tonight to force Alpha Cyra into a mate bond. You have to warn her."

Piper snarls.

"Get up, Zach. We need to warn Cyra and Yorick," she says. Yorick. That must be Alpha Cyra's fated mate.

"Lila, what's your rank?" she says, and I hear her moving around quickly, probably getting dressed.

"I'm a warrior, why?"

"Don't fight tomorrow. I'll let Yorick know that at least one warrior needs to be protected. Hopefully they'll give everyone a chance to stand down," she says.

"Who is Yorick?" I ask.

"Cyra's fated mate and the brother-in-law of the man who is calling the note on your Alpha," she says.

Holy shit! I know Alpha Christer and Stellan don't know that.

"I have to go, but Lila?"

"Yes?"

"Thank you. If you ever need anything, call me."

"Thank you."

I hang up, wondering if I will survive tomorrow. Then I think about Stellan's betrayal, and I wonder if it even matters.

'It matters,' Bree says, the ferocity of her tone tainted by the pain of betrayal. 'He lied to us, but that doesn't mean that we will lay down and die for him. We are stronger than that.'

Yes. Yes we are.

Chapter 8: Alerts

Arden

I'm just getting up from my desk to go to bed when my phone rings. When I look at the caller ID, I growl. What does that little prick want now?

I put the phone to my ear. "Alpha Stellan, I've already cancelled the payment for the Academy. Cyra should be home soon," I tell him.

"Soon isn't soon enough, Arden. The note for the loan we took out to save your fucking ass was bought. The Alpha who bought it will be here tomorrow to take our pack as payment. You need to rally your troops and get them over here. I don't have to tell you what happens if we go down."

He's such an arrogant little shit.

"What Alpha bought the loan?" I ask.

"Alpha Quirin. He's supposedly very wealthy and powerful."

I pull up the name on the pack log, then run a search on him frowning when the search doesn't go through.

"Arden, did you hear me?" Stellan asks.

"Yeah, I heard you," I murmur, typing in an override to do the search. Nothing.

"Where are you?" I ask distractedly, putting in a different override.

"I'm on my way to get your daughter. I'm going to force my mark on her neck and take over as I should have done already."

"That was your decision, not mine. Good luck getting past her mate. Didn't he already break your nose once," I say snarkily, getting frustrated that I can't get past whoever has blocked the search on Alpha Quirin.

"Rally your warriors and get them to Christer's pack tonight. Alpha Quirin will be there tomorrow. If you don't, Christer will send everything he has to the Council and he won't be the only one without a pack. We're all in this together, Arden, so get your ass moving," he snarls before hanging up.

I hang up distractedly, still trying to override the search for Alpha Quirin. Is this guy some sort of tech genius that has locked down my ability to search him?

Rather than searching for data on Alpha Quirin, I begin digging into who is blocking his information. Maybe I can find him that way.

I've just found the code, when it switches. Switches? That's impossible!

The numbers and letters begin alternating so fast that I can't read any of them. Who the fuck is protecting this guy?

I sit back, thinking through Stellan's demand. If this Alpha Quirin is as powerful as he thinks and from what I can get on the pack logs, he is, then there's a good chance that Christer won't survive the battle. It depends on how honorable this Alpha is. But how honorable is an Alpha that buys a twenty-million-dollar loan and calls it almost immediately threatening to take over the pack?

I've spent nearly twenty years dealing in risks, measuring them, calculating them, betting on them. Granted, that backfired when Christer found that I'd been skimming off the company, but otherwise, I'd say I'm pretty damn good at playing the odds.

And the odds tell me that Christer won't survive the battle tomorrow. Eliminating him and Stellan will eliminate all my problems. Hell, maybe this Alpha Quirin would like to take Cyra as a mate. I could create an alliance bond with him and then figure out who is protecting him and why.

Fully intending to ignore Christer's demand for my warriors, I get back to digging into who is blocking me from getting information on Alpha Quirin.

Hacker POV

The alarms had gone off the moment Alpha Arden tried to search for Alpha Quirin. I'd been chatting with Sphinx at the time, showing her how I was hacking into someone's pack information to get something for the Council.

Sphinx: What's happening?

Her message comes in at the same time my phone rings. Hijack.

I put the ear buds in and answer.

"Yeah, I got the alarm," I tell him.

"Is someone going to tell me what the alarm is for?" Sphinx asks. I realize this is a conference call and Hijack called all of us.

"It looks like Alpha Arden is trying to do a search on your brother-in-law, Alpha Quirin," Tracker says as I switch the screen I was sharing with Sphinx to the one I'm pulling up on Arden.

"Does this mean Quirin called the note?" Sphinx asks.

"Probably. He said he was going to, but he was supposed to call us after it was done," Hijack says distractedly.

"Thank goodness you thought to override the override, Hacker," Hijack says as we watch Arden try to bypass my override.

"You put another one on top of mine, right?" I ask.

"Two, one with Sphinx's code as well."

"I put a fourth on there and then put a scrambler on it too. You're welcome," Tracker says.

"Damn, I thought being newly mated would distract you, but it's made you even more deadly," I tease, watching Arden try to bypass our overrides.

"Being mated to a deadly man makes one more deadly," she says seriously. Of the three of us, I'm the least intense. It's a tie between Tracker and Hijack who is more intense. Sphinx will add a nice balance to our group next year.

"Congratulations, Tracker!" Sphinx says. "Do I get to meet him?"

"The next time you're here, Sphinx. You actually saw him in court. He was one of the men in the group guarding Alpha Leo."

"The one who couldn't stop looking at you?" Sphinx asks, making me smile. For someone so young, she's very observant.

"That's him," Tracker says, just as her scrambler goes into effect.

"Damn, Tracker. That's impressive," Hijack says.

While the others work to keep Arden away from Quirin's information, I begin hacking into Alpha Christer's phone. Something happened if Arden is searching for Alpha Quirin and I want to know what it is.

Once I'm in, I connect it to the video feed that we're watching, splitting the screen and putting the audio alongside the video of Arden's attempts to override our override.

"Now you're just toying with him, Hijack," Tracker says, but I can hear the smirk in her voice.

"He'll be here tomorrow. I've got Stellan calling Arden. He'll be here sometime tonight or early tomorrow morning before this fucking Alpha arrives," Alpha Christer is saying to whomever is in the room with him.

"Where is Alpha Stellan?" an unknown voice asks.

Tracker sends me the coordinates for the phone so I can start hacking into whatever is nearby to watch Christer when another alert pings.

"I've got it," Tracker says as Hijack continues to play with Arden. I'm surprised he's wasting his time until I realize that he's using this as an opportunity to teach Sphinx. I bite back the growl. Sphinx should learn everything she can and honestly, she's absorbing everything we're giving her like a sponge.

A moment later, our screen splits again, and Tracker mutes my audio feed as I continue searching for a camera that I can use. I find it on Christer's computer, just as the audio comes in from Piper's phone.

"Something is happening. I don't know exactly what. Something about some Alpha buying the loan that Alpha

Christer and Stellan used to blackmail Alpha Arden. The Alpha is threatening to come here tomorrow to get his money or take our pack. Stellan is going to the Academy tonight to force Alpha Cyra into a mate bond. You have to warn her."

All of us snarl at that.

We listen as Hellfire tells Nickname to get up, that they need to warn Aphrodite and Shakespeare.

"Raptor and I will go find Hellfire and Nickname. We need to alert Alpha Nevaeh," Tracker says.

"I need to call Yorick!" Sphinx says.

"No, Tracker and Raptor will handle that," I tell her.

"I at least need to tell Connor or Dad," she says.

"You're in Connor's pack, right?" I ask her.

"Yes."

"Mind link him," Hijack says as he cuts Arden off, completely disconnecting him from the internet before muting us to call Alpha Nevaeh.

"Connor is calling Dad. He's in Quirin's pack. Hopefully he'll answer," she says. I get the feeling she interrupted her brother and his mate and she's worried that her father and brother-in-law won't answer for the same reasons.

"Do you know why Alpha Quirin is attacking tomorrow?" I ask Sphinx. That wasn't the plan.

"No, but if I had to guess, I'd say Alpha Christer threatened our family, or maybe Kennedy or the pups. If he did, Quirin will kill him. He's intense on a normal day, but when someone threatens his family ... you don't want to be anywhere near him. I've never seen it, but I heard about what he did to the Alpha who kidnapped Kennedy a couple years ago," she says.

Yeah, I did too. I was in my first year when the Council was called in after two Alphas were killed. Since their packs had already been absorbed into other packs, they didn't do anything further. But I'd seen the pictures of Alpha Jasper after Quirin had attacked him. It was obvious that someone else had killed Alpha Brogan. His death was quick, Jasper's wasn't.

"Alpha Nevaeh is waking Alpha Michael. They are meeting the others at Cyra and Yorick's rooms to alert them and come up with a plan," Hijack says coming back to the group.

"Is it me, or was Alpha Arden in no rush to pull his warriors together to go to Alpha Christer's pack?" Sphinx asks.

Hijack finds a single camera that he can turn on in Alpha Arden's office, watching as he curses and bangs on his computer keyboard trying to get it to come back up.

"Nope, it doesn't look like he's planning to help in the attack," I say.

"That's good for Cyra, right?" Sphinx asks.

"Good for her pack," I say. "Hijack, we need to send the data on Alpha Arden to the Council tonight."

"I agree. I was just pulling it together. Things are moving much faster than we planned, but everything is ready. I'll get it together and send it over to them."

"Connor is pulling warriors together to go to Quirin's pack to help him fight," Sphinx says. "I need to go."

"No!" I say.

"Excuse me?" she says.

"No, Sphinx. Our goal is to keep you safe. Letting you go to a war isn't keeping you safe," I say, not telling her the real reason I don't want her going. Instead, I pull up our chat while Hijack agrees with me.

"This is my family!" she says passionately.

Me: You're not ready. You'll be a detriment to them if you freeze on the battlefield, Wendy. Stay home. Help Madison protect the pack.

When she doesn't respond, I flip on the video, needing to know if she ignored me. She knows the tell now, and she looks at the camera. I can see her jaw is clenched tightly.

I mute our conversation with Hijack and call her. She mutes on her end and answers my call.

"You know I'm right. This is why you're practicing every day. Don't get one of your family members injured because you're being stubborn."

I watch her eyes go unfocused and she huffs before she refocuses on me.

"Fine. Connor basically said the same thing."

"Thank you. You're getting better, Sphinx, but you're not there yet. I know your family is just as important to you as it is to the rest of your family. So do what's best for them."

She nods. "I have to go. I need to go help the pack get ready to send their warriors out for battle."

"Send me a message later, let me know how you're doing."

"I will."

She stares at the camera not hanging up.

"Thanks, Hacker."

"Anytime my little Padawan. Contact me later, I'll update you on what's going on over here."

"Will do."

When she hangs up, she waves at the camera before she gets up and walks out. I finally turn the camera off and return to monitoring everything that is happening all at once.

Chapter 9: Coitus Interruptus

Yorick

I blink as I stare at my mate. There is mischief and excitement in her eyes, but also a small bit of fear.

"You want me to mark you?" I ask, confirming what she just asked me.

"Well, I intend to mark you too, if you're ..."

I don't let her finish before my mouth is on hers, devouring her as I slam her against the wall and shred her clothes.

I feel her claws shredding my clothes as she responds with just as much passion as I am.

Once our clothes are in tatters on the floor, I pick her up by her thighs and carry her to my bed. Since her legs are wrapped tightly around me, I pull the blankets back and crawl onto the bed before lowering myself and settling between her thighs.

"Are you sure, Cyra? There's no turning back once my mark is on you. You'll be mine forever," I say, pulling back to look at her. I search her face for any indication that she's wavering, but I find none.

"Nothing has ever sounded better to me, Yorick, than knowing that I'll be yours forever. Well, except that you'll be mine," she says, making me growl with a possessiveness I'm unused to feeling.

I hold her gaze as I line myself at her already soaked entrance. Then, I slide inside her slowly, watching her gasp as I fill her.

"I know we still have a lot to work through," she moans softly, her breath catching as I slowly pull out and slide back inside her again. "There's a lot we have to figure out," she says, cradling my face in her hands. "But I want everything with you, Yorick. I want to figure out our life, our future, together. I want to become an Alpha you're proud of, I want little Yoricks and Cyras running around calling us mommy and daddy. Maybe not a Kendra or Kaylee, because they're so intense," she says, making me chuckle.

I pull her leg up higher, pushing even deeper inside her, growling as she moans.

"But I want this. Every day. Every damn day or our lives," she says.

"Oh, I want this more than once a day," I growl, nipping at her chin.

"Just one more reason that I love you," she says, lifting her chin and exposing her throat. I accept what she's offering me, leaning down to nip and kiss her throat, sucking on her marking spot until I feel her inner walls fluttering around my cock.

When her moans get louder, I pull off her marking spot and look at her again.

"I love you, Cyra. I love you so fucking much. I'm going to love you every day of our lives for the rest of our lives," I say, increasing the speed of my thrusts as I talk.

"I love you, Yorick, more than anything. Make me yours," she breathes, and I nearly lose control right then.

I growl, my thrusts coming even faster now, the possessive words in my head flowing out of mouth, each punctuated by a thrust, "Mine! Mine! Mine! Mine!"

"Yes! YES, YORICK!" Cyra screams a moment before I feel her inner walls clamp down around my cock. I feel the sting of my canines extending and while she's still coming, I sink my canines into her marking spot.

She screams again, her body jerking as an even more powerful orgasm hits her, her inner walls clamping down so tightly that it feels like they are chocking my cock. I try to hold on, wanting to force her to ride out her orgasm, but the moment her teeth sink into my marking spot, the moment our minds connect and entwine like our bodies, an orgasm stronger than anything I've ever felt before rips through my body.

I roar my release against Cyra's neck as Rina's venom begins pumping into my body, sending waves of pleasure through me, forcing me to ride out the most explosive orgasm I've ever experienced.

I can feel Cyra moaning against my neck, hear it in our shared mind link, as Thad pushes his venom into our mate, greedily filling her with our scent so no one can ever say that she's not ours.

I have no idea how long we stay connected, but our canines are still in the other's necks, and our bodies are still jerking with our continued orgasms when there's an insistent knock at our door.

"Cyra! Yorick! Are you in there?"

Zach.

I ignore him and so does Cyra, just enjoying the feeling of being so connected to each other.

"Come on you guys, if you're in there, you have to get up! I wouldn't bother you in the middle of the night if it wasn't important," he says, banging on the door again.

I hear banging on a door down the hall and wonder if they're at Cyra's door too.

'Yorick?' Cyra asks in the mind link.

"Alpha Cyra! Alpha Yorick! This is Alpha Nevaeh. If you're in there, you need to open this door right now. If you do not, I will use my authority to enter the room. Open the door!"

Then I hear Alpha Michael saying the same thing in the direction of Cyra's room.

We pull our canines out of each other's necks.

"Just a minute," I say, kissing Cyra quickly. "I love you, and we're not done yet."

"Thank the goddess," she says, smirking at me.

I slide out of her and hop out of bed, tossing her one of my shirts as I pull on shorts. As soon as she has my shirt on, I open the door.

"What's going on?" I ask.

"Alpha Yorick, Alpha Cyra, we received notification that an Alpha Stellan is on his way here to attempt to force Alpha Cyra into a mate bond," Alpha Nevaeh says as Cyra walks up beside me.

I yank her to my side, keeping an arm wrapped possessively around her. "Well, that's going to be fucking difficult since my mark is already on her," I snarl.

"Aw shit, is that what we interrupted?" Zach asks.

"Yeah, but it's good to know that piece of shit can't get what's mine. Thad can finish pumping his venom into Cyra later," I say.

"Because she doesn't already smell like you?" Zach asks, raising an eyebrow.

Thad pushes forward. "My scent must linger on her for the rest of her life, Alpha. I will put as much venom as needed to ensure that my scent never leaves her," he growls.

Zach puts his hands up in front of him. "Sorry, Thad. I didn't mean to offend you."

"Congrats, Cyra!" Piper says.

"Thanks."

"Yes, congratulations and I want to celebrate properly. However, now is not the time. We need to talk about how we're going to handle Alpha Stellan's arrival," Alpha Nevaeh says.

"I'll be happy to 'handle it'," I snarl.

"We received the information that he was coming from a source who contacted Alpha Piper," Tracker says. I hadn't even seen her with all the people in the hallway.

Piper turns and looks at her. "You know about Lila?" she asks, then shakes her head. "Of course you do."

"The Council has also been notified because your brother-in-law is planning to attack Alpha Christer's pack later today. We think that's why Stellan is coming for Cyra now," Tracker says.

Cyra looks up at me. "Why would Alpha Quirin attack now? That wasn't the plan."

"Is Christer stupid enough to threaten Quirin's family?" I ask her.

I watch the realization dawn on her face. "Yeah. Yeah, he is."

"That's why. I guarantee it."

"Wait, Lila called you?" Cyra asks Piper.

"Yeah. Remember I called her several days ago to give her the heads up about Stellan? I guess when things started going down earlier, she overheard Stellan and Christer talking. She called to have me warn you that he's on his way."

"I owe her one," Cyra says.

"WE owe her one," I say, kissing the top of Cyra's head. "So, what's the plan?"

When a phone rings, everyone turns to watch Raptor answer.

"Yes, sir?"

He looks at us, then his gaze focuses on Alpha Michael.

"Yes, sir, Steel is here with me," he says, and I watch Alpha Michael stand straighter.

Raptor's gaze tracks back to me and Cyra. "Yes, sir, I understand. I'll let them know, sir."

He hangs up and looks at us. "That was Councilman Edward. He has asked us to detain and remand Alpha Stellan into custody. He's asked that you take him in, Steel, so that I can take my team to Alpha Christer's pack to apprehend Alpha Christer."

"Uh, just so you know, if Christer threatened my sister or Quirin's pups, you'll be lucky if Quirin lets you have him. I've seen what he did to someone who kidnapped my sister. He's vicious in his torture and deadly with his actions," I tell them.

Alpha Michael nods. "We know about Alpha Quirin. I was part of the team that assessed him for entry to the Academy. While he is definitely deadly, we didn't find him to be the kind of person who would follow the leadership of the Council. That's why he was denied admission. The Council is familiar with your brother-in-law, and they don't step in when it comes to matters of pack disagreements or wars for the most part. If Alpha Christer threatened Alpha Quirin's mate or pups, he is within his rights to kill Alpha Christer, and they won't interfere. However, if he leaves him alive, they will remand him into custody."

"What about my father?" Cyra asks.

Raptor turns to her. "There is another elite team going to your pack, Alpha Cyra. Both teams will have two Councilmembers with them to order Alpha Christer and Alpha Arden into custody. After we have Alpha Stellan in custody, you may want to return to your pack, Alpha. They will be in chaos once Alpha Arden is apprehended."

I feel Cyra tense in my arms.

"I'll go with you, Cyra. Remember, you're not alone anymore," I tell her.

She looks up at me and smiles, her eyes full of trust.

"No, I'm not, am I? I'll never be alone again."

I kiss her nose. "No, you won't."

Chapter 10: Confronting Stellan

C yra

The plan was simple. Everyone would be out of sight and we'd wait for Stellan to arrive. We have Lila's warning but can't know for sure that she was telling the truth. However, if she is, we'll need this proof for the Council. It will be better to catch Stellan in the act of trying to force himself on me.

Understandably, Yorick isn't keen on the idea. But as Alpha Nevaeh and Alpha Michael reminded him, he is now connected to my mind. He will know when it's time to rush in.

Tracker and Raptor quickly set up recording devices in my room so that they can see and watch everything that happens. There will be no way for Stellan to get out of this.

'I'm right here,' Yorick says for the hundredth time in my head.

'I want you right here,' I say, sending him an image of us earlier along with the feeling of my mouth attached to his neck and his body inside of mine when we were interrupted.

He groans in the mind link and some of the tension in him shifts like I was hoping it would.

'I can't even say that I'll pick up where we left off once he's gone. We have to go deal with your father.'

'Maybe we should plan to spend a few nights at my pack. We can christen my school-girl bed at home,' I say, making him groan even more.

'I'm pretty sure we'll be spending more than one night in your pack and that innocent bed won't know what hit it,' he growls, just as my phone rings.

I look at the caller ID.

"It's Stellan," I say out loud.

I take a deep breath, grounding myself. Then I answer, making sure my voice sounds like I was just woken up.

"Stellan, it's the middle of the night. What's wrong?"

"Cyra, I'm here at the Academy. I need to talk to you right away. Open your door and let me in."

"What's going on, Stellan?" I ask, walking to the door.

"Just open the door."

I do and see him walking down the hall. He looks intent.

"Stellan, what ...?" I begin before he pushes me back into my room and closes the door.

"Your time is up, Cyra," he says to me.

"What are you talking about?"

"I was hoping to give you a year. Hell, I was hoping to be able to give you back to your fated mate after you gave me an heir, but all that has changed. I need your pack, and I need it now. So, we can do this one of two ways. You can agree and we'll mark and mate now, or you can make it hard, and I'll still take what's mine."

I hear Yorick growl in my head at that.

"You can't just barge in here in the middle of the night and demand that I give myself to you, Stellan," I say to him.

"I can and I am, Cyra. You were only ever a means to an end. You're a pretty one, and that makes it easier. Don't pretend like you haven't been with your mate. I can smell him on you. I'd prefer that you not smell like another man, but this first time I'm not waiting for you to wash off his scent. Get undressed or I'll rip these clothes off you myself," he says.

Thad is snarling in my head. Raptor suggested that I wear one of Yorick's collared shirts to cover my mate mark and Yorick's scent that is now in my bloodstream. This way

Stellan wouldn't immediately realize that he won't be getting what he came for. When you're trying to get someone to incriminate themselves, you need to keep them talking. At least that's what Raptor and Steel said while we were getting ready.

I wrap my arms around my waist. "Fuck you, Stellan! I'm not having sex with you, and I am NOT letting you put your mark on me. Forget it!"

He reaches out and grabs my shirt, fisting it in his hand and yanking me toward him. "Before you leave this room, Cyra, you will be wearing my mark, and your womb will be carrying my pup."

"I'm on birth control, you moron," I growl.

"I took care of that before you left home, Cyra. It's not that hard to pay off the right people to replace your hormone implant with a placebo. You haven't been on birth control in months," he says.

Something tightens inside of me, but I don't have time to think about that right now. Yorick and I haven't used protection the entire time I've been at the Academy because I thought I was on birth control.

I may not have been at the Academy very long, but here, you learn a lot in a short amount of time. I take the heel of my hand and strike the center of Stellan's chest against his diaphragm, pushing him back.

"I said NO, Stellan!" I growl as he wheezes. He looks at me, snarling, then rips the shirt open.

"You fucking bitch!" he says, then leaps at me. Rina pushes forward and extends her claws to slice across his face, but Thad blasts into the room like an explosion and rips Stellan off his feet. Before Stellan can shift, Thad has him by the throat, pinned to the floor.

I pull my shirt together as the others rush in.

"Alpha Thad," Raptor says, taking charge. "If you kill him now, he dies too easily. We have everything we need to put him in prison for the rest of his life. You are within your rights to kill the person who threatened your mate, but do you want him to have a quick, easy death, or would you prefer that he rot in a jail cell for the rest of his life?"

'Cyra, which do you prefer?' my mate asks in the mind link.

"Let him rot, Thad," I say out loud, walking over to where he has Stellan pinned to the floor. Thad is so large I can barely see Stellan underneath him. I run my fingers through his fur, knowing that it will help to calm him.

"If you kill him now, my love, he'll never know that he didn't have a chance to leave his mark on me," I purr at him.

That seems to finally pull Thad out of his killing haze. He releases Stellan and steps back, shifting quickly before Yorick pulls me into his arms, still glaring down at Stellan.

"What the actual fuck?" Stellan growls from the floor, sitting up and wiping blood from his neck.

"We were warned that you were coming, Stellan. As it turns out, I had already decided I wasn't willing to give up my life for you or my father. Earlier this evening, Yorick and I completed our mate bond," I say, pulling the shirt away from my neck to show off my fresh mark, a mark I've barely had time to admire.

Stellan stares up at my neck in fury. "You fucking whore!" he yells.

That's all it takes for Yorick to punch him so hard that it breaks his nose and knocks Stellan unconscious.

"I'm guessing you learned that punch from Alpha Quirin, not your father," Steel says.

"Yeah, I did. There's one thing that my entire family has in common. NO ONE touches or hurts what's ours," he growls, the possessiveness in him so much stronger than I've ever felt before.

I lean into him, letting Rina purr at him to help calm him. His arms tighten around me, but he continues to watch Stellan, like he might suddenly jump up and try to take me away from him.

"Did you get what you needed?" I ask, looking at the others over Yorick's shoulder.

"We did. Stellan won't be able to talk his way out of this. It was obvious he was here to force himself on you with or without your consent. You did well, Alpha Cyra," Raptor says.

"They call her Aphrodite," Tracker says absently as she begins going around my room to collect the listening and monitoring devices.

"I'd say that's an appropriate codename, if you ever decide to work for the Council, young Alpha," Alpha Michael or Steel says, walking past us. He lifts Stellan's weight with one arm and throws him over his shoulder.

Damn. Stellan isn't a small man and Steel lifted him like he weighed nothing.

"How about you? Do you have a nickname?" Steel asks Yorick.

"Shakespeare," he says.

Both Raptor and Steel grunt. "Too close to your real name," Raptor says.

"And not deadly enough if you decide to work for the Council. What do you think?" Steel asks Raptor.

Raptor looks at Yorick. "With a punch like that, I'd say Striker."

"Yeah, I like that. We haven't had a Striker in a while," Steel says, turning to grin at Yorick. "Striker it is."

"I can guess how you got a name like Raptor, but how did you get Steel?" I ask him.

"I took five bullets and still didn't go down," he says proudly.

"Five silver bullets and Steel is short for Man of Steel. Superman was too long, so it got shortened to Steel," Raptor says, obviously proud of his mentor.

"Look pup, don't be telling my story," Steel grumbles good-naturedly.

"No worries, old man. You need something to do now that you're retired," Raptor says, smiling as he slaps the shoulder that isn't carrying Stellan.

Steel growls, but he continues walking.

"Do you need any help, baby?" Raptor asks Tracker.

"This is the last of it," she says. "And I'm coming with you," she says, as if this is an argument that they've been having that got interrupted by Stellan.

He sighs. "Fine. You're right. It's good to have a tech wizard on these ops."

"Glad we finally agree," she says, walking up to him and kissing him. The kiss quickly turns passionate, and I glance at Yorick, but his gaze is far away.

"Hey, what's that look?" I ask him.

He focuses on me, then leans in to kiss me as his hand comes to my stomach.

"We need to get to your father's pack, but after things are settled, you need to get to the pack hospital and get checked," he says seriously.

"Yeah. I know."

That was an unexpected blow and one that I wasn't expecting on top of everything else.

"Let's get going. I want to be there for the pack when dad is taken away," I say, grabbing the bag I packed earlier.

Raptor and Tracker finally pull away from their kiss, thank the goddess, because the scent of her arousal was starting to fill the air in my room.

"We'll be calling my father on our way to Cyra's pack to let him know what's happening. He was planning to be there this weekend, but he'll have to move that up now," Yorick tells Raptor.

"The Council members will know if anything goes wrong at Christer's pack. They should be willing to fill you in, but if not, your father can or I will. There will be a trial for Alpha Stellan and your father, Alpha Cyra. You should expect to be subpoenaed for both," Raptor says.

"Thank you for helping us tonight. It means a lot," I say, stepping out into the hallway. Piper, Zach, Landon, and Chase are standing and waiting for us.

"And thank you all as well," I say to them, reaching out to hug Piper.

"You're welcome but we're coming with you," she says.

"What? Why?" I ask.

"Besides the fact that we're your friends, you don't know what that pack is going to be like once you take over as Alpha. So, Zach, Landon, Chase, and I agreed to be your backup in case you need us. We'll miss a couple days of school, but Alpha Nevaeh already approved it."

"Alpha Nevaeh is also extending her own offer to help tutor you this semester, Alpha Cyra. You have a lot going on, but if you want to finish out this school year, I'll work with you. Personally," Alpha Nevaeh says.

"Thank you so much, Alpha. I was just wondering how I was going to make it all work, especially if ..." I put my hand on my stomach. A part of me is terrified that I might already be carrying Yorick's pup. But another part of me is very, very excited about it.

I feel Thad begin purring in my mind again.

"One day at a time, Alpha Cyra. You have a lot of people here supporting you," Alpha Nevaeh says.

I look around at my small group of friends, and I realize that family comes in all shapes and sizes and these people, my dear friends, are like family to me.

"Yes, I do. I have more people, more family, in my life than I ever knew," I say.

Chapter 11: Quirin's Wrath

Quirin

When I woke up in the morning, I needed to make sure that my mate was safe in my arms. Nothing says your mate is safe like hearing your name screamed from her lips while her body contracts around you as she comes. My mate loves making me lose control when I'm inside her and I did, making her scream until she was hoarse. Her love blasted through me as I emptied myself inside her, sending the darkness back to the depths of my soul.

Connor and Henry arrived early this morning with their warriors in tow. I found out that Stellan had attempted to force his mark on Cyra in order to use Alpha Arden's pack to go against me in this battle. Thankfully, he failed. Not that it would have mattered in the fight, but it would have mattered if he had taken Cyra away from Yorick.

As we make our way to Alpha Christer's pack, I can feel the darkness settling back inside me again. We agreed to drive until we're about ten miles away from the pack. Luna Yara and Kennedy are in my pack ready to take care of any of our warriors that need treatment after the battle. We have multiple vehicles so if anyone is hurt badly, we can get them to my pack hospital quickly.

Since I needed the distraction, I'm driving with Alpha Warren and several of my warriors. We have several vans filled with warriors as do Connor and Henry. I left Beta Kier, Lane, Leo, and Terrance at home to protect the pack, Kennedy, and my pups.

"Are you alright, Quirin? Your aura is becoming heavy and thick," Warren says.

I glance at him. "I will be better when Alpha Christer is dead and everyone understands what happens when someone threatens what's mine," I growl.

"Understood. Will you give me a few moments to speak to the pack, to try to get them to stand down before you kill him? We know there's at least one warrior who doesn't want to fight," he says.

Before I was mated to Kennedy, I wouldn't have cared about destroying Christer's entire pack. Everyone would have died, warriors, omegas, pups, it wouldn't have mattered. But I *am* mated to Kennedy, and she brings a level of humanity to me that I never had in my life before her. My sweet, gentle pups, Quilla and Quinlee remind me every day that while I may be a vicious killer, I have produced pups that are like their mother and should not be held responsible for my violent actions.

With that in mind, I respond to Warren. "Yes, the less blood shed the better. There is only one person who needs to die today and that's Christer. If the others stand down and no one threatens my family, they can live."

"Thank you," he says.

I glance at him. "Thank Kennedy. She's my humanity."

"It's your humanity, Quirin. She just brings it to the forefront," he says. Damn the man for always seeming to know the right things to say.

When we get to our stopping point, I pull up the information the Tech Team gave me on Christer's pack. It has a drawing around the area of the pack lands and marks other areas where there could be access points or barriers to entry.

Warren, Henry, Connor, and I review the area and decide where our warriors will go, spreading out around the pack in case we have to attack. The four of us will remain together, approaching from the front of the pack to face Christer head on.

Once we have a plan, we send most of our warriors out. The four of us, along with a handful of my warriors, get into a couple of vans and drive to the gates of Christer's pack. There is a line of warriors waiting for us and the howl of attack goes up quickly.

We step out of the van and I let Warren take the lead as I look around, trying to sniff out Christer.

Warren gives them the option to step aside, but they refuse. I refocus as the warriors push forward. There aren't a lot of them, but I can hear more coming. I still don't smell Christer. Fucking coward.

I punch a warrior, hearing the crunch of his nose breaking before he hits the ground, out cold. Then I shift and take off running. The others can handle the warriors, I want Christer.

"Shit!" I hear Warren murmur and a few moments later, I hear Arric's paws pounding the grass behind Raif.

As we run, Raif lifts his head and howls the howl of the hunt, letting Christer know that we're here for him. His pack instantly responds and right behind that, our combined packs respond, letting Christer's warriors know that they are surrounded.

When we get closer to the packhouse, I smell him. Raif snarls and pushes harder, slicing through warriors as we go, injuring them, but not killing them. The arrogant asshole is standing at the front of his packhouse with warriors lined up on either side of him when I approach.

I shift quickly, Warren shifting right behind me. I lock eyes with Christer.

"You're mine," I snarl.

"Good luck getting to me," he growls, as I hear Tyrus and Bosche, Henry's and Connor's wolves, rushing up behind us along with the rest of my warriors that I left at the front gate.

Warren steps forward, once again trying to get the warriors to stand down.

"You are surrounded. You are outnumbered. Your Alpha has leveraged your pack with a loan he couldn't afford. Alpha Quirin intended to call the note and take the pack peacefully, but Alpha Christer threatened his mate. This battle is not about you. If you stand down, if you refuse to fight, we will let you live. If not, you will die here today," Warren says as the rest of our wolves come rushing in from all sides.

"How do we know we can trust you?" a warrior asks.

"I wouldn't have bothered trying to talk to you if I didn't mean what I say. We would have just come into your pack and started killing everyone. Your Alpha has put you in this situation, but you do not have to die for him."

"What about our Alpha?" another warrior asks.

"He dies for threatening my mate," I snarl.

I don't look away from Christer, but I can see the warriors all looking at each other, realizing that if they do fight against us, they will die.

"Don't you dare fucking step away," Christer snarls at them, but he's already lost his pack even if he doesn't realize it.

"I hope you're not waiting for your brother to arrive with Alpha Cyra's pack. He was apprehended at the Academy, trying to force himself and his mark on her. He's been taken to jail. There won't be anyone else coming to help you, Christer. Now, it's just you and me. You said you hadn't heard of me? This part of the country doesn't know why I'm considered the most dangerous Alpha on the continent, possibly the planet? You're about to find out," I say, my voice low and vicious.

Almost as one, his warriors step aside. I take a step forward, my claws extending as Christer leaps at me.

I duck out of the way, swiping my claws across his midsection. He snarls and spins, swiping his claws across my arm and shoulder. I slam my claws into his rib cage, hearing the sound of his breathing change as I puncture his lung.

He steps back wheezing, glaring at me. I can feel already Raif healing the wounds on my arm.

"You threatened my mate," I growl, pushing forward again. He spins out of the way, but not before I kick the side of his knee, dislocating it, and sending him to the ground with a howl of pain.

I continue prowling around him, growling and glaring.

"You threatened my mate," I growl, swiping out quickly and removing an ear.

He cries out, pressing a hand to his ear as blood seeps down his face.

"You threatened my mate," I growl again, stomping on his ankle and hearing a satisfying crunch as Christer screams in agony.

I hear others driving up to the packhouse, but I don't look away from my prey. The others will handle whoever is here. The darkness has closed around my peripheral vision and all that's left in this world is me and the man who threatened to take the best thing that has ever happened to me away.

"You threatened my mate," I growl again, raking my claws down his back. He arches in pain, screaming again.

I make another loop around his bleeding, shaking body. "Please," he says, lifting his hand up in surrender.

"You threatened my mate," I snarl, swiping my claws and removing all four of his fingers at once.

"Please," Christer says, pressing his bloody hand against his chest as he looks past me.

"You threatened my twin sister," I hear Conner say, his voice nearly as deadly as mine.

Christer's eyes move to someone else.

"You threatened my daughter," Warren snarls.

Christer's eyes move again.

"You threatened my brother's mate," Henry growls.

"Please," he begs.

"You threatened an Alpha's mate. He is within his rights to kill you," a man says. I don't recognize the voice, but it's much calmer than any of the others.

"You threatened my mate," I growl, stabbing a claw into his eye, just deep enough to destroy the eye, but not kill him.

He screams again, beginning to sob.

"You threatened my mate," I say, taking a chunk out of his hip. He collapses onto the ground, writhing in pain.

I can hear his heartbeat becoming faint. He's bleeding out fast. His breaths are still ragged because I've injured him too many times too quickly for his wolf to heal him.

I stand over him, watching him bleed and sob for mercy, then I look around at the wolves watching in horror.

"Let this be a lesson to anyone who comes after what is mine. Spread the word. Alpha Quirin is my name and no one, NO ONE, threatens what is mine," I snarl before stomping on Christer's face, crushing his skull and ending his life.

"Quirin, you should get home to Kennedy," Warren says. I've only heard him use this tone with me once before, the day I killed Jasper. It's a tone meant to calm a savage, feral beast.

"I'll drive you, Q," Henry says, slowly walking up to me. He is also approaching me as if I might snap and attack him.

"Go see Kennedy. Let her heal you, Quirin," Warren says again. "We'll take care of this."

I look back at Christer's decimated body, then look at Henry.

"Take me home."

Chapter 12: Aftermath

Warren

Everyone stands silently as Quirin walks away with Henry. He's probably the best person to drive Quirin home in his current state. I know I lost my shit when Yara was taken from me. I was ready to burn the world to the ground to find her. But somehow, I don't think I was ever as dark and brutal as Quirin. Goddess help anyone who ever hurts someone that man loves.

I turn back, looking at Christer's previous pack. I realize by the looks on their faces that it's extremely unlikely that anyone will ever dare to touch or even look cross-eyed at a Bishop again. I'm not sure what that means for his myriad of daughters, but as their grandfather, I'm glad to know that just the threat of their father will keep them safe.

"I think I understand now why the Academy denied him," a military man who looks vaguely familiar says as he watches Quirin go.

"Who are you?" I ask him.

"My name is Raptor. This is my team. We were sent here by the Council," he says, gesturing to the two individuals who are obviously not elite warriors. "We were to remand Alpha Christer into custody for his actions of hiding Alpha Arden's embezzlement activities and for using that knowledge to entrap Alpha Cyra in an alliance agreement."

"You were in the courtroom for Alpha Leo's hearing," Connor says, as he walks up reminding me where I know Raptor from. Connor tosses me a pair of shorts, and I pull them on while we talk.

"That's correct," he says. "I'm the leader of the Alpha Squad. Alpha Warren, you should know that another team along with more Council members are on their way to Alpha Arden's pack to take him into custody as well," he says.

"Cyra," I say, reaching for my phone that is back in the van.

"She and your son, Alpha Yorick, were on their way over there when we left."

The two council members step up to us. "Alpha Warren, I am councilwoman Rebecca Kaufmann, and this is

Councilman Jared Jackson. Law dictates that as the Alpha who overthrew the existing Alpha, Alpha Quirin now controls and leads this pack."

"He is aware of that, but believe me, you want him to see my daughter before he addresses the pack members," I say.

"Yes. He's very ... intense," she says.

"Passionate is the word my mate uses for him," I say, smiling as I think of how many times I had to remind Yara that I am just as 'passionate' as Quirin when it comes to wanting her.

"As his father-in-law, how would you like to proceed? The Council can take control of the pack until he returns, or as his family, you can," she says.

I look at Connor. "I need to go help Cyra. Can you stay until Quirin returns? It might be tomorrow."

"I'll call Madison and get things cleaned up here. We'll take the pack temporarily for Alpha Quirin," he says looking behind me at the warriors who are all standing around looking worried.

Before I leave, I feel the need to help Connor settle these pack members. They just lost their Alpha publicly and viciously. I'm sure they are terrified and without a link to an Alpha, they are probably feeling lost.

"Who is Beta here?" I ask.

"I am, Alpha," a man says walking up.

"I'm Alpha Warren, and this is my son, Alpha Connor. We will be taking charge of this pack until Alpha Quirin can return."

"Returns to kill us?" a warrior asks.

"My son-in-law is a vicious man when someone threatens those he loves, that is true. But he's a good Alpha," I say gesturing to his warriors who are still surrounding Christer's warriors. "Ask any of his pack members."

"Alpha Quirin is an excellent Alpha. Luna Kennedy is a kind and loving Luna. Together, they are a powerful team and great leaders. If you're worried about how Alpha Quirin will treat you, imagine that you are his pack member and someone threatens his pack. This," the warrior, Randall, says gesturing to the remains of Alpha Christer, "this is what happens to anyone who threatens our pack."

"Beta, what's your name?" Connor asks.

"I'm Beta Eric, Alpha."

"I'm Alpha Connor. As my father said, he and I will be taking temporary control of this pack. I know you may be feeling a bit uncertain, especially since you don't have a link to your Alpha at the moment. Rest assured we will rectify that as soon as Alpha Quirin returns. Beta Eric, I would appreciate it if you could help me assure the pack that they are safe and help keep them calm until such time as Alpha Quirin returns and takes his official place as your Alpha."

"Will we have to move? This is our home," another warrior says.

Connor looks at me.

"There are a lot of things that need to be decided and none of those things will be decided today. For now, you are safe. Alpha Connor will remain here until Alpha Quirin returns," I tell them.

I turn, looking at Quirin's and Henry's warriors. Since both Alphas are gone, I take charge of their warriors.

"Warriors from Alpha Henry's pack, please return to your pack. Warriors from Alpha Quirin's pack, divide up, half of you stay here to help keep the peace in this pack and the rest return home," I say, turning to Connor.

"Same with my warriors. Divide up, half of you stay here, the other half can return home," he says.

I turn back to Raptor. "How far is Alpha Cyra's pack from here?"

Tracker steps forward. I hadn't realized that she was here earlier. I realize that she smells like Raptor and when I look, I see a relatively new mate mark on her neck.

"Here you go, Alpha Warren," she says, handing me a device with a hi-tech looking map.

"You are here. This is Alpha Quirin's new pack. Alpha Cyra's pack is here, about twenty miles away in that direction," she says, pointing southeast. "This area is the land we talked about that is currently vacant." She's pointing to the areas on the map as she explains where they are to me.

"Thank you," I say, before looking at Connor. "I'm taking one of the vans, but I'm not far if you need me."

"I'll check in later tonight and let you know how things are going," he says.

I look around once more to make sure that everything is as settled as it can be before jogging toward the vans at the entrance of the pack.

I find my phone and call Yorick as I get into the van.

"Where are you?" I ask him.

"We're just pulling into Cyra's pack lands," he says.

"I'm at Christer's pack. I'm headed your way. I'll be there soon."

He's quiet for a moment.

"It looks like the Council is already here, and it's not going well. I need to go," he says before hanging up.

I grab the map and hit the gas. I have no idea what I'm walking into, but I know I need to be there to support Cyra and my son.

Kennedy POV

I've been nervous since my family left. I know my mate is a powerful fighter, but I also know he was barely hanging on when he left me this morning. I hope that he doesn't completely lose control and destroy the entire pack. They are not responsible for what their Alpha did.

My mother has been keeping me busy, having me practice some new lessons I'm learning while she shows Quilla and Quinlee how to stitch an organ inside a body using one of the many dummies we have for practice here. It's a good distraction, but when Quirin's mind connects to mine, I can feel the fury still churning inside him.

"They're back," I say to my mother, jumping up.

'Luna, Alpha Henry is bringing Alpha Quirin to you. He said to stay where you are, Alpha needs you,' the guard at the gate says in the mind link.

'Is he injured?' I ask.

"I'm honestly not sure, Luna. He's covered in blood,' he says. It must be bad if the guard, a previous rogue, sounds worried.

I rush to the doors of the hospital just as Henry pulls up. My eyes lock onto my mate's. He's got that crazed look in his eyes that I've only seen a couple of times in my life.

He gets out of the car, snarling as he pulls me into his arms, his mouth latching onto mine.

I know he's not snarling at me. He's snarling with his desperate need for me, his need to know that I'm alive and safe.

'I'm here. I'm right here. Is any of this blood yours?' I ask in the mind link as I wrap myself around him.

'Don't know,' he growls.

"She'll take care of him, Henry. Thank you for bringing him here. Come on girls, let's let your parents have some time alone," I hear my mother say as Quirin carries me to the showers he had installed in our hospital. Without releasing my mouth, Quirin turns on the shower and when it's warm enough, he moves underneath it.

'I need to be inside you,' he says in my mind. 'But I want the stench of that man off me first.'

I don't have to ask which man or if he's dead. My mate is covered in so much blood that no one could have survived that.

He sets me on my feet and both of us reach blindly for the soap as he continues to devour my mouth. We begin washing the blood off him and when he finally pulls away to wash his hair and face, I quickly look him over, knowing that he won't let any injury keep him from being inside me when he's like this.

I've barely had a chance to glance at his body and ensure any injuries are healed before he lifts me again, pressing me against the wall and thrusting himself inside me. His mouth is on mine, possessively dominating me as he thrusts into me hard and fast. I wrap myself around him, holding on to him, giving myself to him in the way that I know he needs right now.

The first orgasm rips through me, but my mate merely growls, continuing his punishing pace, forcing me to ride out my orgasm and bringing another one right behind it. The force of the second orgasm has me tearing my mouth away from Quirin's as I scream in pleasure.

"Mine!" he snarls, sinking his canines into my mate mark and making me scream again as my body explodes around him.

He begins chanting 'Mine' in the mind link as Raif pushes his venom into my body, keeping me on my incredible high as he possessively floods my body with his scent.

When Echo sinks her canines into Quirin's mate mark, he roars so loudly that I feel pieces of plaster falling from the ceiling as the warm jets of his cum spray my insides.

When he finally pulls his canines out of my neck, I can feel that he's settled again.

"I love you so much, Kennedy," he says, pressing his forehead against mine.

"I love you too, my mate. And let's not forget that you're just as much mine as I am yours," I say, making him chuckle as he kisses me again and the last of his fury fades away.

Chapter 13: Alpha

Cyra

The ride to my father's pack, my pack, is tense. I know my father. I know he won't go down without a fight. But how much fight will he put up? If it comes down to it, will he force me to kill him to take over the pack? Would he rather die than face the consequences of his actions?

Yorick pulls my hand to his mouth. The feel of his warm lips pressing against my skin helps to soothe me. We don't have to talk anymore. He's in my head, following along with my thoughts and concerns. He's a steady, calming presence; something I've never had before and never knew I wanted or needed. But now that we're connected, I know that I never want to be disconnected from his mind again.

'I'll be right there with you,' he says as we get closer to my pack lands. I know he can feel the tension coiling inside me. Piper, Zach, Landon, and Chase are in the back of the SUV. They've been silent during the ride as well, leaving me to my thoughts.

When his phone rings, I'm glad to hear that it's Alpha Warren and that he's on his way to my pack. Yorick's support and having the support of my friends is amazing. But, knowing that I have someone else who is just as strong and supportive as my mate coming to stand behind me makes me feel even steadier. I trust Alpha Warren to not let me fail on my first day as Alpha.

As we pull up to the packhouse, I know I was right about my father.

"I need to go," I hear Yorick say to his father.

My father has called the pack to battle. He is standing in front of the packhouse with what looks like every warrior in the pack standing behind him. Facing off in front of him are two elite fighting teams and two council members. Even from here, I can see the fury on my father's face.

As soon as Yorick stops, I jump out of the car and begin heading toward the mess that my father is about to create.

"You have no right to come here, demanding that I step down as Alpha and come with you!" my father growls.

"As council members for the werewolf packs, we have every right, Alpha Arden. As we have already stipulated, you broke our laws. You are to come with us and face a trial of your peers," the male councilman says.

"I'd like to see you make me," my father snarls.

I step past the elite fighting teams and the council members, standing in front of them and facing my father and the pack head on.

"STAND DOWN!" I say, pushing my Alpha aura over the pack.

I can see the surprise ripple through them, feel it in the pack link. They've never seen me like this. But in the short time that I've been at the Academy, I've changed considerably.

"You are not Alpha here, Cyra. You do not rule this pack," my father growls at me.

"I am not Alpha, *yet*," I say, clarifying to him and everyone here that I intend to take over this pack. "But I will be, effective today. You betrayed me and this pack, Alpha Arden. You embezzled money from one of your companies and when you couldn't cover it up, you used me as leverage to pay off your debts by trying to sell me off in an alliance agreement with Alpha Christer and Alpha Stellan."

"You don't know what you're taking about," he growls.

"I know exactly what I'm talking about. Twenty million dollars, Alpha Arden. Twenty million dollars. Where is that money, hmm? If I had to guess, I'd say you spent it on gambling and whoring around. All those nights you left the pack, not returning until the early hours of the morning smelling like cigarette smoke and cheap perfume, you were spending money that wasn't yours."

"You have no proof of anything you're saying."

"I have all the proof I need. I have everything, the trail of embezzlement, the loan that Alpha Christer took out to gain control of your actions, the recording he made while he threatened you, and the alliance agreement that was created as payment for your crimes and to make Stellan an Alpha of his own pack."

"Well, since I see his mark on your neck, I guess it's a moot point," he sneers.

"This isn't his mark. He was remanded into custody earlier today after attempting to force himself and his mark on me. He is being held awaiting trial. This mark belongs to my fated mate, Alpha Yorick Hill," I say, gesturing behind me to where I know Yorick and my friends are standing.

"You agreed to that alliance agreement," he says, spitting the words out like venom.

"I was seventeen years old, and I was TOLD that I would become Stellan's mate. You never asked me. You didn't even wait until I was old enough to find my fated mate. You just sold me off like I was a commodity. I'll admit, I've lived with blinders on my entire life. I didn't realize that family could and should mean so much more than what it does to you. I didn't know what a real family looked or felt like until I went to the Academy. But I do now. I have a family I created on my own. People who love me and will support me no matter what. I have Yorick and his family who stand behind me and are willing to help me become the Alpha that YOU should have made me into. But you didn't, did you, father? And all because you didn't get your precious male heir. Well, there's nothing in the laws that says a woman can't be Alpha of her pack and as your daughter, I am here to claim what is mine. This pack is mine. You can step down as Alpha quietly ..."

"You DARE to think that I will give this pack to you? You are nothing but a silly girl!" he screams at me.

"Or, I can challenge you for the position of Alpha of this pack," I continue as if he didn't interrupt me.

Since every pack knows what it means for one Alpha to challenge another, they all step back, leaving my father to face me alone.

"You are a stupid girl. Worthless!" he snarls.

"The only worthless one here, is the one who doesn't appreciate the value of the pack and family that he had. You were responsible for caring for this pack and for me. You betrayed all of us."

"I will never give this pack to you," he growls, his lip curling and his claws extending.

"Then I, Alpha Cyra Teymoori, challenge you, Alpha Arden Teymoori, to become Alpha of this pack," I snarl as Rina pushes forward, her own claws extending.

The moment he leaps, I do too, shifting, as he does, into our wolf form. His wolf, Caesar, is slightly larger than Rina, but he's older and my father hasn't kept himself in good shape. Rina and I, on the other hand, have spent hours training every day for months with experienced fighters.

When Caesar leaps at Rina, she dives underneath him, flipping onto her back quickly and raking her claws down his underside. As he crashes to the ground, she flips back over, getting to her feet to face her father. I see the surprise on Caesar's face a moment before Rina leaps at him. He rolls out of the way, but not before she tears a chunk of fur and skin off his back.

He snarls, leaping at us again. This time, Rina leaps at him, facing him head on. Her stronger body slams into his as her teeth sink into his shoulder. I feel Caesar's teeth snap at Rina's neck, but the force of her hit sends him flying backward, yanking his teeth out of her fur. I can feel blood beginning to soak into her fur, but she heals herself quickly.

Since her teeth remain in Caesar's flesh, Rina lands on top of him. I hear the snap of a bone and when I don't feel any pain, I know it's Caesar's.

He howls in pain and Rina releases him, stepping back and snarling at her father, pushing her aura out over him.

'SUBMIT!' she says in the mind link.

'NEVER!' Caesar snarls back.

'I do not want to kill you father, but I will if you force me to," she snarls back.

'You can't kill me, pup,' he snarls back, as he gets to his feet.

He lunges, biting down and sinking his teeth into her flesh. She reaches up with her huge paw and rakes her claws down his side with such force that her claws get stuck on his rib cage. When she yanks her claws away, I hear another snap of bone and Caesar releases his hold on her to howl in pain.

Rina turns, snapping her teeth onto Caesar's back leg, shattering the bone. Caesar collapses to the ground, but Rina isn't done yet. She rakes her claws down Caesar's back, making him arch and howl in pain again.

Then she slowly walks over him, intentionally stepping on his body to show her dominance, before lowering her head to his.

'Submit,' she snarls in the mind link.

'Kill me if you must. I will never submit to you,' he snarls back.

She snarls again, latching onto Caesar's throat.

'Rina, I don't want to kill him,' I say to her. I feel Yorick push into our mind, mentally wrapping his arms around us.

'Drag him to the council members, Rina. Everyone here can see that he's lost. He may not be willing to submit, but there's no doubt that you have defeated him,' Yorick says.

She looks up, focusing on the pack around us, still holding Caesar's throat in her mouth. I realize that Yorick is right. It's clear to the pack that Rina has defeated Caesar, even if he is unwilling to submit to her.

She turns, dragging Caesar by the throat to the council members.

"What is Alpha Cyra's wolf's name?" the female council member asks, not taking her eyes off Rina.

"Rina," Yorick and my friends say together.

"Alpha Rina, it is clear that you are the winner here today. We, Councilman Nicholas and I, Councilwoman Leslie, have witnessed it. You do not have to kill your father. We will take him into custody, and he will stand trial for his crimes."

Rina stands there, the anger and resentment still raging inside her.

'He should pay for his crimes, Rina. He, like Stellan, should be made to suffer the way they've made others suffer,' I tell her.

Finally, I feel her relax and she drops Caesar to the ground, stepping back.

"Thank you, Alpha Rina," Councilwoman Leslie says, gesturing for the elite team on her left to come take my father into custody.

I pull the shift and stand, looking down at my father. "SHIFT!" I command, knowing it will be easier for them to take him in his human form.

Caesar yelps, but he is no longer Alpha of this pack. I am. He may not have accepted me as his Alpha, but I'm still a stronger Alpha than he is.

Once the elite team has him, I turn to the pack.

"Does anyone else want to challenge me for the right to become Alpha of this pack?" I growl.

When no one steps forward, Yorick tosses me his shirt. I see that while I've been fighting with my father, Alpha Warren has arrived.

"I need to address the pack," I say. "I'd like all of you to stand beside me, if you would," I say to Yorick, Warren, and my friends.

"Where else would we stand?" Zach teases.

Yorick comes over and wraps his arms around me. "That was very impressive, my mate. What a strong, powerful Alpha you are," he says, kissing the side of my head.

"Alpha Cyra, I am Javelin, leader of Beta Team. We will be taking your father into custody. Once he has been processed through, I'll call you to let you know it's done."

"Thank you," I say to her.

"We'll be in touch as well, Alpha Cyra. You'll be needed in both Alpha Stellan's and Alpha Arden's trials," Councilman Nicholas says.

"I'll be there," I tell him.

"Alpha Cyra, the pack is yours," Councilwoman Leslie says, before nodding and following the elite fighters to their vans, dragging my father with them.

Once they are gone, I gesture to the others to come stand beside me and I turn to address the pack.

It's time that I officially take my place as Alpha.

Chapter 14: Addressing the Pack

Yorick

Watching my mate battle with her father, I felt so much pride that she's mine. I know it's not standard for a female to take over a pack, but that never mattered to me. I didn't expect to become Alpha of my own pack. That's why I went to the Academy. Now, with Dad training Cyra to be an Alpha, I have no doubt that she can run this pack while I, hopefully, work for the Council.

Although, we still need to figure that out. A lot will depend on whether or not my mate is pregnant. If she is, she's not far along since she was able to shift.

I stand beside my mate when she gestures for us to come over. She takes my hand as my father and our friends surround her.

"My pack, this may seem sudden to you. I know you were not aware that my father was forcing me into an alliance agreement. I know none of you were aware that I met my fated mate when I went to the Academy nor that my father didn't care that I found my mate. He still insisted that I stay true to the alliance agreement, an agreement that I had no say in. It was created when I was seventeen and had no chance of finding my fated mate," she says, turning to smile at me.

"When I met Yorick, I thought I had no options. I believed, as I'd been told, that if I did not go through with the alliance agreement that it would mean war for this pack. I was willing to give up my freedom to protect you from that. However, at the Academy, I made friends who helped me to see that I did have other options, options that included me taking my fated mate as my life partner and stepping in as Alpha of this pack."

I squeeze her hand, and she turns back to the pack.

"So, while this may seem sudden to you, it is not for me. I have been working with my friends and a tech team at the Academy to figure out why my father entered into the alliance agreement to begin with. When the information about his underhanded dealings came to light, I knew it was time to act. Through my new family, Yorick's family, Alpha Christer's pack has been overthrown," she says, causing the pack to gasp.

"Alpha Stellan has been taken into custody, and you all saw that your previous Alpha has also been taken into custody," she continues, ignoring the surprise in the pack. She's so steady, so confident, that my heart swells once again with pride.

"While I fully intend to take over this pack, with Alpha Yorick at my side, you all know that I'm still a student at the Academy. I intend to continue my studies this year while also training to become Alpha of this pack. I'm sure you all know how your previous Alpha felt about a woman running a pack. Since he did not find me worthy, I am not currently confident in my ability to manage this pack in the way that it should be managed," she says, turning to my father.

I realize that she isn't calling Alpha Arden her father, she's calling him 'your previous Alpha' as if she's distancing herself from her father as much as possible. It's a smart tactic.

"Alpha Warren," Cyra says, gesturing for my father to step up on her other side. Piper and Zach step back, allowing him to step forward.

"This is Alpha Warren Hill, Yorick's father. He is a retired Alpha of a very profitable, healthy, and stable pack.

Alpha Warren has offered to become my mentor and teach me how to be the kind of Alpha that I want to be, the kind of Alpha that you, my pack, deserve. As I mentioned, I intend to finish my year at the Academy. I will be at the Academy during the week and here on the weekends, learning from Alpha Warren. While I finish my time at the Academy, Alpha Warren will become the acting Alpha of this pack. He will have full authority over the pack while I am away. I know that this will be a big shift for everyone, but I hope that you will give us some time to show you that you have nothing to worry about. The pack will be safe, we will make it financially stable again, and this will be the kind of pack that you will be proud to be part of," she says.

I know why Cyra is saying these things. When packs change leadership, oftentimes, pack members leave, afraid of what will happen to them and the pack. She is encouraging them to stay, at least long enough to see that this will be the type of pack that they want to be a part of.

"Alpha Warren, would you like to say anything?" she says, turning to my father.

"Thank you, Alpha Cyra," my father says, stepping forward. "What your new Alpha says is true. I know change is difficult. I know you expected to go from Alpha Arden's rule to Alpha Stellan's. I can guarantee you that living with Alpha Cyra as your leader and Alpha will make your lives infinitely better than an Alpha who embezzled and wasted millions of dollars or an Alpha who used that knowledge to manipulate his way into becoming your Alpha. In my dealings with Alpha Cyra, I've found her to be honest and sincere. Both of those qualities are necessary to form a pack that is built on trust. You may have trusted Alpha Arden to run this pack efficiently, but he did not. You may have thought he was strong enough to protect you from outside attacks on this pack, but he was not. Alpha Cyra is. She has proven that by not only gathering the information needed to remove two Alphas from their packs, but by defeating Alpha Arden in a battle of strength for this pack. I am excited to assist Alpha Cyra in becoming an even greater Alpha than she already is. We will become well acquainted over the next year. I know you need to get to know me, but I am a fair and just Alpha. I do not tolerate abuse of any kind, and I will not hesitate to discipline anyone who goes against me or Alpha Cyra. However, if, as Alpha Cyra suggested, you give us time to build that trust, develop an understanding of how we will change this pack for the better, I think you will all be very pleased with the result. I look forward to getting to know all of you better over the next year," he says stepping back.

I'm so thankful to my father for reinforcing what Cyra said. Not that I'm surprised, my father was my first choice to help Cyra because I know he's an excellent Alpha.

Cyra steps forward again. "Our first order of business is for the pack to accept me as your Alpha and Alpha Warren as your acting Alpha," she says, then turns to me, smiling again. "You will also be accepting Alpha Yorick as your co-Alpha. He will be looking into other avenues of employment, working for the Council and bringing money into the pack, but he is my partner, my equal, in all things. He is the reason that I am standing before you today. So, I will not take my place as his Alpha, I will stand at his side as we lead this pack together."

"Cyra," I say softly, overwhelmed by her words. I had no idea she intended to do this. I'd had every intention of being first in line to accept her as my Alpha today.

She puts her finger on my lips. "I know your life will take you away from the pack, but that doesn't mean that we aren't equals, Yorick. I am your mate, and you are as much my Alpha as I am yours," she says.

"I will always stand at your side, Cyra," I tell her, my love for this woman overwhelming me.

"Good," she says, turning back to the pack. "We will have the Alpha ceremonies after lunch, then tonight, we celebrate!"

The cheers from the pack aren't quite as excited as they would normally be, but that's to be expected with so many changes all at once.

I pull my mate to me, kissing her in front of her pack.

'You know I intend to "celebrate" by de-flowering that virgin bed of yours tonight, right?' I ask her in the mind link as I kiss her.

'I expect my new co-Alpha to keep me up all night reminding me why he's the best and only man for me,' she purrs back.

Damn, I can't wait for tonight!

Chapter 15: Disappointment

M^{egan}

When I got back from my morning run, the entire Academy was buzzing about what had happened. Apparently, Stellan came to force his mark on Cyra and take her home with him. That didn't go so well for him.

Yorick went with Cyra to claim her pack from her father who is also in a lot of trouble for stealing money or something like that.

"Alpha Michael carried the unconscious guy out of here over his shoulder like a sack of potatoes," Talek says.

"Where was he taking him?" I ask.

"Jail, I guess. Alpha Nevaeh has cancelled classes for the next two days, so we get a long weekend."

"Why would she cancel classes?" I ask, digging into my breakfast.

"Yorick, Piper, Chase, Zach, and Landon all went with Cyra to reclaim her pack," Katelynn says.

"They *all* went with her?" I ask. That's more than a quarter of our class members. No wonder they cancelled classes.

"Apparently. I guess they didn't know how her pack would respond, and they all went for support," she says.

I look at the group sitting at the table with me. Talek, Katelynn, Helena, and Spencer. He's new to our group since he and Helena started sleeping together. I don't see them following me if I were to go challenge my father to take his pack. And even if they came with me, I don't think any of them, except possibly Talek, would be strong enough to help me keep the pack in line. They're all here at the Academy, so they're strong, but none of these guys will become an elite fighter like I plan to be.

We finish breakfast and since classes are cancelled, I don't really have anything to do. The others go off, probably to have sex, but I linger, wondering if I can find out anything about Stellan and what he might have said about me. I'm a little worried that if Alpha Nevaeh knew that I was feeding him information, she might discipline me. It wasn't like I gave him much. After Katelynn was booted from their group, they were very careful. But Alpha Nevaeh isn't Alpha Leo. She isn't easily manipulated.

However ... I watch as Alpha Michael returns, presumably from wherever he took Stellan. He goes up to Alpha Nevaeh who was obviously waiting for him and they talk for a few moments before he heads inside.

I begin to follow him, wondering if I can get information from him.

He goes to his office, leaving his door partially open. I knock and step inside, closing the door behind me.

"Good morning, Megan. What can I do for you?" he asks.

I tilt my head and step up to him, resting my hands on his chest. "I heard you had a difficult morning, Alpha," I say, using my best seductive purr.

He raises an eyebrow at me. "And?"

"And, I thought maybe you might need to unwind a bit," I say, letting my hands slide down to his stomach.

"And what exactly were you thinking?" he asks.

I raise my shoulder negligently. If I was wearing a negligée, the strap would have fallen off and given him a show, but I'll work with what I have.

"I could give you a massage. I could ... take the edge off. I could give you an outlet to work off all that excess energy," I say, looking up at him through my lashes as I bite my lower lip.

A second later he has me against the wall, his body pressed against mine with my arms pinned over my head. I gasp, not used to a man being quite so aggressive and forceful, but I like it.

He leans in to kiss me, and I lift my head, giving him permission. Just before his lips touch mine, he stops.

"You disappoint me, Megan."

I frown, looking into his eyes. Rather than being full of lust, they're full of disappointment.

I try to pull away from him, but he holds me in place easily.

"I thought you were here to prove to your father that you're NOT the woman he thinks you are. This," he says, gesturing to my body, "is exactly who your father thinks you are. A woman whoring out her body to get what she wants. You're better than this and if you want to become the elite fighter that I think you do, then you need to start treating yourself with respect. And you need to expect that others will treat you with that same respect. You're a beautiful, sexy woman, Megan. But if you don't start acting like you're more than that, then that's all you'll ever be, a manipulative woman who uses her body to get what she wants."

It feels like he's stripped me bare and found me utterly lacking. It hurts more than I thought it would, and I feel tears prick at my eyes.

He steps back, releasing me, as I struggle to breathe.

"Now, why don't you ask me what you were trying to find out," he says.

I shake my head, wrapping my arms around my waist to keep from falling apart in front of this man.

"You were willing to fuck me to get the information you wanted, but you're not willing to have a simple conversation about it?" he asks, leaning against his desk and crossing his arms over his chest.

I feel my cheeks flush with embarrassment. When he puts it like that, it makes me sound so cheap. I guess that's what he thinks of me and for some reason, that hurts so much more than my own father thinking the same thing.

I keep my eyes on the floor. "I wanted to know if Stellan said anything about me."

"First, how do you know who he is, and second, why would he have mentioned you?"

"I knew he was here because of Cyra. He came to campus the second week of school. Yorick punched him, probably would have killed him if his friends hadn't pulled him off. I told Stellan that I would keep tabs on the two of them for him. We've talked a couple of times, but I never really had much information to give him," I say.

"Are you the reason he showed up here this morning?" he asks.

"No. I haven't talked to him in weeks. I haven't had anything to tell him. Cyra and her group don't exactly trust me."

"Can you blame them?"

"I guess not."

He doesn't say anything and eventually, I force myself to look up at him. This time, his eyes are assessing.

"You know, in the elite fighting teams, trust is imperative. I have worked with men and woman who were responsible for keeping me alive on some of the missions I've been on. I had to trust that they would be there for me, and they had to have the same trust in me to have their back. There's no place for manipulation in an elite team. You have a lot of potential, Megan. You could become an elite fighter, if you choose to become the woman I see in you. But if you continue to hold yourself back, if you continue to be the woman your father expects you to be, then that's all you'll ever be, a desperate woman who lets men use her and never gets what she wants out of life. Get your head out of your ass, get some fucking self-esteem, start acting like the Alpha female you are, and start earning the trust of your fellow Academy members. Show me you want this, Megan. Show me that you are willing to become the type of fighter that deserves a spot on an elite fighting team. That takes more than just being a good fighter. You have to be a good, confident, trustworthy person as well. Do you understand?"

"Yes, Alpha," I say quietly.

"For what it's worth, I think you can do it. But that is solely up to you. Dismissed," he says.

I turn and walk out of the office. His words about respect and confidence are so close to what Alpha Cyra said to me the other day, that it rings painfully true.

Rather than go back to my room, I head out to the running path again. Running helps me to think and right now, I need to clear my head. For years, all I've wanted was to prove to my father that he was wrong about me.

Now, I realize I was going about it all wrong. Rather than trying to prove a man like my father was wrong, I should have been trying to prove that a man like Alpha Michael was right.

As my feet pound the pavement, hard and fast to try to outrun the embarrassment and frustration inside me, I realize I've never had a man turn me down before. Getting what I wanted was easy and I assumed I was winning because I got what I wanted. But after hearing Alpha Michael, it makes me feel cheap. I've somehow allowed myself to become the person I never wanted to be.

If I can prove to a man like Alpha Michael that I *am* the person he thinks I am, then it will prove to my father that I'm *not* the person he thinks I am. I've always known that

I could never make my father proud. No matter what I do, it would never be enough.

But now, I'm practically desperate to make Alpha Michael proud of me. I know it won't be easy. Being manipulative has become second nature to me. But I never want to see the disappointment again that I saw in Alpha Michael's eyes when he looked at me today.

He believes in me and now it's time for me to believe in myself and to prove to him and everyone else that I am worthy of a spot on an elite fighting team.

Chapter 16: Pack Response

C yra

After getting our guests settled, I showered and washed my father's blood off my body. I thought Yorick might join me, but instead, he and the others began mingling with the pack.

As I walk downstairs, I realize just how lucky I am to have this group of people here, these people who have become family to me. Every one of them is here to support me and they're doing that by getting to know my pack members.

Yorick turns, smiling as he sees me. I finish making my way down the stairs and walk over to him. There's an excited, nervous energy in the pack. The intensity of it has heightened since I went to shower.

"Hello beautiful," he says, wrapping his arm around my waist.

"Hello Lucy, Hello Charles, Hey Charlie," I say to the pack members that Yorick is talking to. I give a little wave to Charlie who is only three and being held by his mother. He tucks himself up against her, but he's grinning at me.

"Hello Alpha. We were getting to know your mate and learning about his family," Charles says.

I look around seeing that everyone seems to be getting along okay, so I can't quite figure out what the buzzing is in the pack.

"What's going on?" I ask Yorick and the others.

"Word of Alpha Christer's demise and how that came about reached the pack while you were showering," Yorick tells me.

I refocus on my mate. "It was that bad?"

"You don't mess with our family, and you certainly don't threaten one of them. Christer threatened Kennedy, and Quirin made a point of letting everyone know exactly what happens to someone who threatens his mate. He also apparently made sure to give his name and tell the pack that they should spread the word," Yorick says.

I look around the pack again. "That was fast, even by werewolf gossip standards."

"Quirin is scary when he's mad. Think feral animal that escaped from his cage and you're getting close to what he's like when someone threatens his family. Thankfully, Dad got him to agree to give the pack a choice and they didn't fight, so Christer is the only casualty," he says.

"Besides Stellan," I say, still looking around.

"Stellan's lucky to be alive," he snarls.

My eyes snap back to Yorick and I lean into him. "I'm not sure he'll think it's lucky," I tell him.

I refocus on Charles and Lucy. "How are you two feeling about everything?"

They look at each other and I can feel the unease inside them. "That was a lot of information to obtain this morning, Alpha. We're still trying to process it and then to find out that Alpha Christer is also dead, Alpha Stellan is in custody, and you were in the middle of all of that and none of us knew? It's a lot to take in. But I don't think anyone will contest you as Alpha. You clearly defeated Alpha Arden," Charles says.

"They would be foolish to contest my mate. Not only would she defeat them, but where would they go? My brother-in-law now leads the nearest pack and would not allow anyone into the pack who went against Cyra," Yorick says.

"We are sorry for what happened to you, Alpha. We're glad that you found your fated mate and that the two of you are now together," Lucy says.

"Thank you. I'm very happy about it too," I say.

Yorick and I walk around the pack together, helping the pack feel more settled and by lunch time, it feels like everyone is ready to accept Yorick and I as their co-Alphas and Alpha Warren as their interim Alpha.

After lunch, the pack goes outside for the Alpha ceremony. Other than setting up a stage and using the ceremonial knife and chalice, I didn't want to make this into some big event. We're their Alphas now. I don't need a lot of pomp and circumstance for that. And since I have no idea what the pack's financial situation is, I'm not going to do anything that might put the pack at risk right away.

So, Yorick and I stand in front of our pack, with Warren leading the ceremony. We each swear to love, honor, and protect the pack with our lives and then we both let our blood drip into the cup before we sip from our combined blood. Then one by one, each pack member comes up, swearing their loyalty to us.

Once that is done, I switch places with Warren and I lead his ceremony making him interim Alpha of the pack. The pack goes through the same process again, accepting Warren as their interim Alpha.

I noticed that as more pack members accepted us, the pack began to feel stronger. That strength only increased when they pledged themselves to Warren.

'Why does the pack feel stronger?" I ask my father-in-law in the mind link.

'You, Yorick, and I are stronger wolves than your father was. The pack feels that. I couldn't feel it before I stepped into my position, except what I felt through Yorick, but it seemed like the pack members felt the increase in strength when they accepted you both. I'm glad to know that they felt even more strength when I took over as interim Alpha. It will go a long way towards keeping the peace when you're gone during the week.'

'Do you feel like there is any animosity in the pack?' I ask him.

'No. Confusion and uncertainty, yes, but those are normal when a pack has been overthrown. I felt the same in Christer's pack. Of course, Quirin's take over was much more violent than yours.'

By the time we finish the two ceremonies, it's already dinner time. I have the warriors pull out the grills and we throw a bunch of meat on them while the omegas prepare side dishes for us to eat. Someone shows Zach where the speakers are and he gets the music started. The atmosphere feels festive and I can feel the pack beginning to settle.

"We'll need to start work first thing tomorrow, Cyra. We only have a few days before you have to go back to school. As much as possible, we need to dig into the pack's finances so we can make sure that there is nothing we need to handle right away," Alpha Warren says.

"I agree," I say.

"Please tell me I don't have to be a part of that, Cyra. You know I hate the financial stuff," Yorick grumbles.

"Why don't you handle warrior training," I say, instantly making him perk up.

"I would LOVE to. But you're not participating until we get you checked. Speaking of that, I asked the doctor if he had any pregnancy tests in the pack hospital. He said he'd drop off a pee test for you to take in the morning. If it's positive, we can do a blood test afterward."

"And if it's not?" I ask him.

"Then we can talk about next steps. While I love the idea of having pups with you, I'm not sure now is the right time. If it's already happened, we'll make it work. But if not, maybe we wait until we're done with the Academy."

"You can make it work. Yara and I have. When you love someone, you find a way. And it sounds like the Academy is willing to work with you, Cyra. I doubt you'll continue with sparring class if you're pregnant, but the other classes will be available to you," Alpha Warren says.

"And besides, if you aren't pregnant, we can use the rest of the school year to practice," Yorick grins, making his father snort.

"That's my cue to leave," Warren says, walking away to mingle with the pack members.

It has been a really long day for all of us. Yorick and I never went to sleep last night, having been interrupted during our marking and mating. Then the Stellan incident, then challenging my father, then officially taking over as Alphas. So, we end the night early. The pack seems just as tired as we are, so no one grumbles when we turn the music off.

However, once we're back in my room, Yorick's eyes changed.

"I know that look," I say to him.

He growls, prowling toward me. "I know you're tired, I can feel it. I am too. But we never finished our marking and mating, and you did mention something about a virginal bed that needed deflowering."

"Why Alpha Yorick, are you saying you haven't put enough of your scent in my bloodstream?" I ask coyly.

"Is Rina satisfied with how little I smell like you?" he asks, his eyes going black as I pull my dress over my head.

"No, she is not," Rina growls.

"Neither am I," Thad growls in response. I'm not sure if it's Yorick or Thad who rips his shirt off, but the feral need in him that I feel pulsing through our bond wipes away any fatigue that I have left.

I lift my head, exposing my mate mark to him. "Come take what's yours, Alpha," I purr.

My mate, never a man to waste time or opportunity, spends hours flooding my body with Thad's venom and his sperm. Rina, not to be outdone, spends those same hours pushing her venom into our mate, the pleasure forcing both of us to ride out the longest, strongest orgasm of my life.

Hours later when we collapse beside each other exhausted and spent, my bed fully deflowered, I know that if I wasn't pregnant before tonight, I definitely am now.

Chapter 17: Being the Alpha

Yorick

I wake tired and happy the next morning but also feeling different. As I kiss my mate's shoulder and begin rubbing my hand over her hip that is resting against mine, it suddenly dawns on me what's different.

I'm an Alpha now. An Alpha who leads a pack. Yes, I'm leading with Cyra and yes, for me, she's more the Alpha than I am. But mentally, my connection to the pack is so much stronger than it was when I was part of Connor's or Quirin's pack.

In the past, I could feel the pack in my mind, but I had to reach out to find the person I wanted to speak to. Now, it's like all the lines to every pack member are lit up in my head, the connections actively waiting for me.

'I think I understand why our father is having such a difficult time letting go of being an Alpha. Imagine in twenty years this connection going back to the simple connections we had before. This is a bit unexpected, but we'll adjust. I think the adjustment of returning to the quiet, simple pack connections will be much harder,' Thad says.

He's right. Adding the connection to the pack members will take a bit of adjustment, but it's not overwhelming. I now have a better understanding of why some Alphas look and feel more confident. The pack's power is the Alpha's power. I was a strong Alpha before, so was Cyra. Our mating made both of us stronger. But adding the pack's power to mine makes me even stronger.

I think about Connor and Henry and their confidence and strength. Connor was always confident and from what I remember of Henry, so was he. But when Connor took over as Alpha, something changed in him. It was subtle, but there was a new confidence in him. I thought it was my imagination, but he seemed to stand taller than before, prouder. I assumed it was because he had become the Alpha, and it is, but not for the reasons I originally thought. He felt the strength of my father's pack that was passed to him. And now, I feel the strength of Cyra's pack, shared with me.

Quirin is a little different. He built his pack from the ground up. All of them are previous rogues and fighters. It makes sense that they would be drawn to an Alpha who is also a fighter, and it also makes it more clear to me why he's so dangerous. His pack's ferocity has made Quirin even more ferocious.

I reach out to feel the pack's connections, brushing over them in a way that is similar to how I brush across Cyra's mind now that we're mentally connected. I can feel the areas of deficit in the pack as well as their strengths. They are powerful, but they could be more so. It makes me excited to lead warrior training. The stronger the pack, the stronger Cyra and I become. If I strengthen the pack by increasing their fighting skill, we will automatically become stronger.

I'm so excited, I nearly leap out of bed, ready to start the day.

'Got it all figured out?' Cyra asks in the mind link.

I lift my head and smile as she turns to look at me.

"How long have you been awake?" I ask.

"Long enough to feel you working through the logistics of being an Alpha who leads a pack."

"You feel it too, right?" I ask her, wrapping my arms around her more tightly.

"I do. I wasn't expecting the change, but Rina is adjusting easily."

"So is Thad," I say, lifting my head to look at the clock. When I see the time, I sigh.

"What?" she asks.

"I was hoping I had time to make love to my mate again before warrior training, but I don't," I say, making her giggle.

"You spent hours inside me last night," she purrs.

"I intend to do that every night. I'll just have to get this pack stronger faster so I have more stamina and can get up early enough to start my day the same way I intend to end it, inside my mate."

"How about ... we shower together after warrior training?" she asks.

"Deal! Now let's get up. You have a test to take, and I have warrior training to lead for the first time in my life," I say, excited but also a little nervous.

"You'll be great at it," she says, kissing me deeply enough that my body, already hungry for her, begins throbbing with need.

I growl. "Up, before I skip warrior training altogether."

She laughs as she gets up and I watch the fantastic view of my mate's backside, as she saunters to the bathroom, watching me over her shoulder.

I growl again, flopping onto my back, before leaping out of bed to get ready. I pull on my clothes and go into the bathroom to brush my teeth. Cyra is washing her hands, and the pee stick is sitting on the counter.

"How long do we have to wait?" I ask.

She looks at the box. "A couple of minutes."

I look at the stick.

"What are we looking for?"

"One line, not pregnant. Two lines, pregnant."

I begin brushing my teeth, closing my eyes to force myself not to stare at the stick. When I hear Cyra begin brushing, I pull her against me, holding her while we wait.

When I open my eyes again, she's watching me in the mirror.

"Ready?" she asks.

I spit the toothpaste out of my mouth, feeling excited again. I'm almost positive that Cyra is pregnant.

"Ready," I say, wiping my mouth.

She lifts the stick then frowns. I feel the disappointment inside her before she pushes it down and looks at me in the mirror.

"It's negative," she says.

Now it's my turn to frown.

"Really?" I ask, feeling my own disappointment. I know the timing isn't perfect, but the thought of Cyra carrying my pup was exciting.

She hands me the stick and grabs the box. "One stripe, not pregnant."

I look at the stick. Definitely only one stripe. I pull her to me again, kissing the top of her head.

"This isn't a bad thing, Cyra. We can talk to the doctor today and see what he thinks about why you're not pregnant. But this gives us a chance to get you on birth control so that we control when you get pregnant. This way, you can continue with sparring training at the Academy and finish out your already over-filled scheduled without adding a pregnancy and newborn into the mix," I tell her.

"Yeah, you're right," she says, still feeling disappointed. She smiles at me in the mirror. "I just really liked the idea of carrying a little Yorick in my belly."

I growl possessively and pull her in front of me, laying my hands across her stomach. "One day soon, we will make that a reality. But for now, let's go kick some warrior ass."

She laughs and hurriedly dresses before we walk downstairs for warrior training.

Before we get to the training field, we run into my father.

"Good morning. First, do you mind if a co-lead warrior training today?" he asks.

"No, of course not. You'll be leading it during the week, so it's probably good for the pack to get used to your style and the differences between mine and yours," I say, knowing my style has more of Quirin's flair added in.

"Agreed. And second, I talked to Quirin this morning. He's heading back to his new pack today. He's bringing Kennedy and Yara. He's going to bring Yara here so she can meet the pack, but he also wants to talk to the two of you."

"About what?" Cyra asks.

"About taking over Christer's old pack."

"Taking over his pack?" Cyra asks, stopping to look at my father, then at me.

"Yes. It's too far away for him to manage both packs. I know you have concerns about the money you feel you owe him, but he's not worried about that. You and I are going to dig into your pack's finances so we can see where things are financially and if you have the ability to set up a payment plan with Quirin. But for him, the distance makes this pack unmanageable. We talked about the vacant land between the packs. He's already been looking into the cost of that, or he heard from the Tech Team about it, I'm not sure. Either way, he has a proposal for the two of you and when he drops Yara off today, he wants to talk to the two of you about it."

I can feel Cyra's nerves and her hesitation. I pull her hand to my lips and kiss it.

"Let's see what he has to say. Quirin is just as intelligent about finances as he is about fighting. If he has a proposal, I'm guessing it will be a good one."

Cyra nods.

"Oh, and if mom's coming today, let's wait and ask her why she thinks you're not pregnant. I'm sure your doctor here is good, but mom's the best," I say.

"Sounds like a plan," she says.

"Now," my father says, rubbing his hands together excitedly. "Let's go whip this pack into shape."

Chapter 18: Quirin and Kennedy

Cyra

Warrior training was fun. Besides being in the best shape of my life because of the Academy, I also know a lot of the skills that Yorick is teaching our warriors. However, it was nice to also see Warren's more pure form of fighting, the parts that, according to Yorick, he's mixed up with Quirin's style of fighting.

The warriors felt the difference immediately. Having Piper, Zach, Landon, and Chase here made a difference as well. My father, while always ensuring that the pack's warriors were trained, wasn't as intelligent a fighter as Warren and Yorick are. When the warriors began grumbling at the intense pace the two men were keeping, they quickly

showed them why their fighting knowledge was inade-
quate by defeating them in one-to-one combat.

Since I defeated my father yesterday in front of the pack,
I wasn't tested as much as Warren and Yorick, but after
warrior training, I felt the pack settle even more. They not
only feel the strength coming from myself, Yorick, and
Warren, they've witnessed it and personally felt it on the
sparring field.

As we begin walking back to the packhouse, I hear Warren growl before taking off at a fast jog.

I look at Yorick who looks ahead of us, smiling, as the
other warriors pause to see what Warren's growling at. A
moment later, Luna Yara steps outside the back of the
packhouse and is immediately wrapped in her mate's embrace, his mouth devouring hers like he needs her air to
breathe.

"After talking to Dad this morning, I told the gate patrols to let them in when they arrived," Yorick says, taking
my hand.

"Is that what you're going to be like when you have a job
and are away from me for any length of time?" I ask him.

"I'll probably be worse at first. Dad's had years to get
used to being away from Mom while they go back and
forth between the packs."

"I don't think he's adjusted during that time," I say,
hearing Luna Yara's wolf purring loudly as we pass. Nei-

ther of them seems to care that they're in the middle of an unfamiliar pack. Arric, Alpha Warren's wolf, continues to growl possessively as Warren dominates his mate's mouth.

Yorick pulls me to a stop, turning me to look at him.

"The men in this family love their mates with everything in them," he says, stroking his fingers over my cheeks. "I will hate every moment that I'm away from you and I will make sure that you know just how happy I am when we're back together again."

He glances back at his father who has now lifted Luna Yara up and is walking toward the stairs. "Which is what I'd guess my father is planning to do."

I hear Luna Yara giggle. "Warren!"

"What?" he growls, but instead of stopping or letting her answer, he takes her mouth again and begins climbing up the stairs to his bedroom.

"I guess we're meeting alone this morning," Quirin says, smirking at Warren and Luna Yara.

"Kennedy!" Yorick says, pulling his sister into a hug.

"Hello, Alpha Quirin. Welcome to our pack," I say to him.

"Just Quirin, Cyra. We're family now. I haven't always known what that means, but I do now."

A hush falls over the pack, and I realize they just heard who our visitors are. Quirin, the Alpha who brutally killed Alpha Christer and his mate, the reason for the brutality.

"Everyone," I say loudly, getting their attention. "We have visitors this morning."

I wrap my arm around Luna Kennedy, hugging her since I haven't had a chance yet. "This is Luna Kennedy, Yorick's older sister and mate to Alpha Quirin."

All eyes turn to Alpha Quirin. He doesn't seem particularly perturbed by their uneasy glances. If anything, he looks pleased that word of who he is and what he did has spread.

"I know everyone has heard by now that Alpha Quirin defeated Alpha Christer in a battle yesterday and has taken over that pack. I'm sure you all also heard that Alpha Quirin was particularly vicious in his defeat of Alpha Christer because he made the mistake of threatening his mate. I met Alpha Quirin previously, and while yes, he is powerful and can be vicious, he is also kind and generous," I say, seeing Quirin turn to look at me with a raised eyebrow.

Kennedy pulls away from me to wrap her arms around her mate's waist, smiling up at him. Instantly the look on his face softens as he wraps his arms around her.

"I imagine that we will be seeing more of Alpha Quirin, Luna Kennedy, and their pups in the future as they are now part of our family," I say, turning to look at Quirin. "I do hope that being a part of family means that we can create an alliance together, Quirin."

"It's one of the things that I want to speak with the two of you about today. I'm guessing Connor and Henry will be doing the same soon," he says and I nod, turning back to the pack.

"This pack has nothing to fear from Alpha Quirin. We are family, we will be allies. Anyone who goes against Yorick and I, goes against Alpha Quirin and his pack. Anyone who goes against Alpha Quirin, goes against us. Things are going to change in this pack. They've needed to for a while. Yorick and I have spoken to many of you about this already. I know change can be difficult and uncomfortable, but I know you can already feel the difference. You feel the calm that our leadership is providing and the strength that my father was lacking. That strength will only increase as we solidify our alliances with other strong packs. Please take some time today to at least introduce yourselves to Alpha Quirin and Luna Kennedy," I tell them.

I wait until the pack goes back to getting breakfast, then I turn to Quirin and Kennedy.

"You're just in time for breakfast. Have you eaten?"

"No, and I worked up quite an appetite last night," Quirin growls softly, looking at his mate. I guess being with your mate takes a lot more energy than defeating an Alpha.

'You tell me. Were you more tired after defeating your father or after I'd had my way with you last night,' Yorick asks in the mind link.

'That's different. We were finishing our marking and mating,' I say.

'Did you not see that Kennedy's mate mark has a fresh bite mark in it?' he says.

I turn, looking at her as we make our way to the breakfast buffet. He's right, she does.

'Okay, point taken,' I say.

"So, Alpha Quirin, I'm Alpha Zach. I go to the Academy with Yorick. I was wondering if, while you're here, I might be able to test my skill against yours."

"You want to spar with me?" Quirin asks him.

"We all do," Piper says. "I'm Alpha Piper."

"Alpha Chase."

"I'm just Landon," Landon says, making Quirin smile.

"Just Landon still managed to get into the Academy. Don't think I'll underestimate you," Quirin says, making Landon smile. "I'm not sure how long we'll be here today, but I'm happy to spend some time testing your skills. I was hoping to see what Yorick is learning anyway," he says.

"Maybe you can spar with them while Cyra and I speak to Mom," Yorick says as we find a table. I notice that Quirin settles his mate first before sitting beside her, then pulling her closer before digging into his food.

"Is everything okay?" Kennedy asks.

I realize that without conscious effort, Yorick is doing the exact same thing that Quirin did for Kennedy. He's getting me settled before sitting beside me. I send a wave of love through the bond.

His head snaps to me. "What?" he asks softly.

"I love you."

He growls softly before kissing me then turning to his sister.

Before he answers, he looks back at me. "Do you mind if I tell her? She's been studying to become a doctor for years. She's still in school but she's amazing, just like Mom."

"She's beyond amazing. She's the most brilliant woman I've ever met," Quirin coos at her.

"I wouldn't go that far," she says, blushing slightly. "Mom is pretty amazing."

"Equally brilliant, then," he says, kissing her nose before turning back to our friends and talking about the Academy.

I look at Kennedy. "It's just, Stellan told us that he replaced my birth control with a placebo. We thought, since we hadn't been careful, that I might be pregnant. I took the test this morning and it was negative," I tell her.

She nods. "Pee test?"

"Yes."

"They're not the most reliable. False negatives happen. What kind of birth control were you on?"

"Hormone implants," I say and her eyes narrow.

"When did you have them replaced?"

"Right before I left for the Academy. It was a little early, but I wanted to make sure I was covered."

She nods thoughtfully as she chews her food.

"Hormone implants are a slow release that work over time. How long did you have the implant before you replaced it?"

"About a year," I say.

"Werewolf metabolisms do burn through them faster than the human metabolism but I'm guessing the hormones in the implant hadn't completely absorbed. It's possible that there were some still in your body and since it's a slow, long-term process, it doesn't just stop right away. You could have had hormones in your body even after the placebo was injected. It's a simple blood test. If Mom isn't available, I can do it for you. We'll test your hormone levels, and we can test for a pregnancy at the same time."

She looks up and points to my neck. "When did you mark and mate? That looks very fresh," she asks.

"Two nights ago. We were interrupted with the whole Stellan shitshow," Yorick tells her. "So, we completed what we started last night."

She narrows her eyes again. "Marking and mating nights are intense. If you're going to get pregnant, even if you are on some sort of birth control, that would be the time. The blood test will confirm it, but even if you are negative, I'd say, and I'm guessing Mom will agree, that you need to test again in a week and possibly a week after that. She won't put you on birth control until she's positive you're not pregnant, so you will have to be careful unless you're actively trying for a pup."

I look at Yorick. He shrugs. "Let's see what the blood-work says."

"What I would ask," Kennedy says, leaning forward, "is how did Stellan replace your implants with placebos? Because if he was able to get to your doctor, you need to know. That sort of underhanded behavior can't be allowed. It's against the code for doctors and if he was involved, Mom can have his medical license taken away."

I look at Yorick. "I didn't even think about how Stellan got to the implants. We do need to speak with Dr. Walker. Your sister is right. If he undermined me, he can't be allowed to stay in the pack."

"Agreed. Since I'm guessing Mom and Dad will be gone for a while, let's meet with Quirin and Kennedy first, and when Mom re-emerges, we can all go to the pack hospital together and have a little chat with Dr. Walker," Yorick says.

Chapter 19: Quirin's Proposal

Cyra

After breakfast, I notice a couple of my more daring pack members come over to introduce themselves to Quirin and Kennedy. Kennedy draws them in quickly, the pack latching on to the love and kindness that she exudes.

Surprisingly, after the initial nervousness of meeting Quirin, our pack members seem to relax around him. He oozes confidence which makes a pack feel safe and since he's not being aggressive in any way, more pack members start coming over, at least to say hello.

"We're going to go warm up and wait for Alpha Quirin to come show us some new moves," Zach says, practically bouncing on his feet. "Plus, I need to come up with a good code name for him. Slasher, maybe," he says, making all of us roll our eyes.

"I'm pretty sure I've made my own name sufficient to put the fear of the Moon Goddess into anyone who thinks of crossing me," Quirin says as we head to the office.

"Well, yeah, there's that. Hmmm, maybe we need to find someone who *gets* the codename Quirin," he says to the others as we walk away, making Quirin chuckle.

When we're in the office, I have us sit around the table.

"Warren and I haven't had a chance to go through our pack's finances yet, Alpha. But I would definitely be interested in your proposal. Once I have a better understanding of our finances, I'll be able to review your suggestion and let you know if it's possible," I tell him.

"It's possible. I've made sure it is," he says, pulling some paperwork out of his back pocket.

"First, congratulations. This is our gift to you as the incoming Alphas of this pack. It's not done yet, but it should be by the end of today or tomorrow," he says, sliding a piece of paper over to us.

I lean forward to read as Kennedy smiles up at her mate. He wraps an arm around her and kisses the top of her head as he watches us.

"This is the intent to purchase the land between our pack and your new one," I say, looking up at him.

"That's correct. That is our gift to you, mine and Kennedy's," he says, his body jerking slightly and his features softening. I would guess that his mate just sent a wave of love to him through the bond.

"This is too much, Quirin. You've already done so much for us," Yorick says, echoing my own thoughts.

"The twenty million was a loan. This is a gift," he says.

"I don't even know if we can pay you back for the twenty million, Quirin. I have no idea what my father's finances look like. I don't know if we can accept this," I say.

"It's a gift, and I'm not taking it back. As for the other part, don't argue with me until I'm done explaining my proposal," he says, gently but firmly.

I look at Yorick. I can feel his same resistance to accepting such a generous gift when we're already so indebted to Quirin.

"What's your proposal?" Yorick asks.

He holds up a finger. "Before we get to that, I'd like to take care of that pesky alliance business, as if our families wouldn't be allied. But for the sake of other packs knowing, I'd like to make it official. I've also brought a second copy with Connor's information so you can sign one with him before he returns home. You'll have to make time to meet up with Henry to sign one with him," he says.

I quickly walk to the desk and grab a couple of pens. "This I don't have to think about," I say, moving to the last page of the two copies of the agreement and signing it quickly. Quirin and Kennedy have already signed them.

I slide it to Yorick, and he quickly signs both documents. We return one of them to Quirin, who folds it and puts it in his pocket before looking at us.

"In the future, you should read all documents *before* you sign them," he says, turning the copy in front of us to the second page and pointing to the spot that says that we accept our gift of the land between our packs.

My mouth drops open, and I look back up at him. He's smirking and he shrugs negligently. "It was Kennedy's idea. She knew you'd argue," he says, pulling his mate into a hug again.

"I see Quirin is rubbing off on you, Ken," Yorick grumbles to her.

"This is an important time for you, for both of you. It's a big deal. I know you never planned to lead a pack, Yorrie, but this gives you all sorts of options. Mom's going to be here, taking this as her primary residence, for a year. If you wanted to build a new teaching hospital here, under her direction, you could. That could help fund your pack. None of the rest of us had to start from scratch like the two of you are. Well, Quirin did, but even he had his father's investments to help him out. It's very possible that your father has nearly bankrupted this pack and if that's the case, you'll need options for income. My brilliant mate has some great ideas, but this is too important for either of you to let your pride get in the way," she says, looking from Yorick to me.

"Okay, maybe we should talk about your proposal," I say.

"Good, because this is exciting," he says. His grin is so wide it's practically splitting his face.

"And in no way was this my idea. Like you, Yorrie, I hate the financial stuff," Kennedy says.

"And you? Do you hate it too?" Quirin asks me.

"I love it, I just don't understand it all yet," I say.

"You and I are going to get along great," he says, leaning forward and walking us through his proposal.

"The money you borrowed from me is just under twenty million dollars. That number is shown here. This line is blank until you and Warren get a handle on your pack's finances. Once you know how much you can repay me each month, that amount will go in here. And once that number is available, these other numbers will be filled in, but for now, we'll talk in general numbers."

Yorick is watching, but I already know the look on his face. Now that we're mated, I can feel it in the bond, too. It's the miserable feeling of having to look at and understand these numbers.

I smile and reach out to put my arm around Yorick's shoulders. "Don't worry, lover. I've got this."

"Thank the goddess," he says, sitting back.

Quirin chuckles but continues. "When you pay me each month, I'm going to invest that money in one of my accounts. I have multiple investments that I know are profitable. I monitor them constantly and if, at any time, the investment I have your money in is no longer profitable, I'll move the funds to an investment that is. I'll make sure you know that I've done it, but I'll be monitoring the money and the investments on my end. I will send you the statements quarterly when they arrive."

That's great since I'm not savvy about investments at all.

"Eventually, I'd like to learn about those investments, how you monitor them, how you determine if they're good investments, all of that, if you're willing to teach me," I say.

"Absolutely," he says, before turning back to the sheet. "Each quarter, you'll get a dividend statement. Half of that money will go to me, to repay your loan, and the other half will be reinvested into the account."

"Creating compounding interest?" I ask, starting to get excited.

"Exactly," he says, grinning at me.

"Each month, you'll continue to pay the loan, each quarter you'll pay an additional chunk of the loan out of your dividends, and the rest will go back into the account."

My mind begins spinning with the possibilities. I have no idea how much money we can afford to pay him each month, but if the investments are profitable, that compounding interest will earn more and more each time we reinvest it.

"Cyra?" Yorick asks, leaning forward.

"This could work, Yorick," I say, watching Quirin.

"Of course it will work. I won't let you fail. As I said, if one investment begins to falter, I'll move the money. Over time, you may want to spread your investments out. But, and this is the good part," he says, pushing another paper in front of me. "I did some quick math."

I lean forward excitedly again.

"I used easy numbers, knowing you don't know how much you can repay each month. It doesn't matter to me if it's a thousand dollars or ten thousand dollars. Obviously the more you can afford, the faster you can pay off the debt. I went with a split of five thousand a month. Based on the current return of investment in the plan where I intend to put your money, if you provided five thousand dollars a month, your first quarter's dividend would be this. Fifty percent of that comes back to me, and the rest reinvests," he says, showing me the numbers.

"The second quarter would be here," he says, pointing to a number and making Yorick whistle. "Is that really how fast it would accumulate?"

"Current market value, five thousand dollars a month, and the entire fifty percent of your dividend reinvested, yes," he says, looking at me excitedly.

"At the end of year one, you could have paid me back, two hundred and fifty thousand dollars," he says, flipping the page.

"Whoa!" Yorick says, but I'm focused on Quirin. This could really work!

"At the end of year two, that doubles, so you will have paid me five hundred thousand dollars at the end of year two and seven hundred and fifty thousand dollars in total. That doubles again in year three, and ..."

"How many years before it's paid off?" I ask excitedly.

"Eight. But there's more. If you continue with the investment, and you know markets shift, so again, these are easy numbers, and we still don't know what you can afford, but if you continue to reinvest your dividends at the end of that eight years, all one hundred percent of your dividends, you could have twenty million dollars of your own money before you pass this pack to your Alpha heir," he says, sitting back with a smug look on his face.

"Holy Mother Moon Goddess!" Yorick says beside me.

"I told you he was brilliant," Kennedy says proudly.

I look at Yorick and then back at Quirin.

"Where do we sign?"

"Here. But, and this time I'll make sure you understand it, this agreement is also the purchase of Alpha Christer's old pack. So, not only are you paying me back, but you're also buying his pack lands which will connect nicely to your newly gifted lands and this pack," he says. "It's too far away for me to manage it, but it bumps up right against your new territory."

Chapter 20: Plan

Yorick

I'm still in shock at Quirin's proposal. I knew we could trust him. I never would have gone to him in the first place if I hadn't. But I had no idea he'd come up with an idea that not only helped us pay off our debt to him but also helped us make our own pack wealthy.

In addition, he's basically doubling our pack size and nearly tripling our pack lands which will instantly add more income and credit to our financial situation.

"I don't know what to say," I tell him, hugging him as we stand.

"You're Kennedy's brother. That makes you my brother. You're family, Yorick."

"Thank you, my brother," I say, hugging him more tightly before releasing him.

When I step back, Cyra and Kennedy are still hugging and murmuring to each other. I look back at Quirin. "Are you working with Connor and Henry to invest also?"

"Of course I am. Henry has been invested for a while," he says smirking. "Although he didn't always know it. On his thirtieth birthday, I gave him the information on the investment I started for him when my pack started prospering. It was a nice little sum of money."

For Quirin, 'a nice little sum' is probably more than some people make in a lifetime.

"Is that why he threatened to punch you during his party that year?" I ask him, making Quirin laugh.

"Yeah. He's such a bastard. It's perfectly fine for him to do nice things for me, but he hates it when I do nice things for him. He says it freaks him out."

"I'm guessing it was a bit more than 'nice'," I say.

He just shrugs and shifts the subject. "I offered to work with Connor after we signed our alliance agreement, and he took me up on it. His pack is also doing very well."

"That explains the upgrades he's been doing to the packhouse and how he paid the Tech Team to improve his security."

"Exactly," he says, holding out an arm for Kennedy when our mates finally pull apart. She slides into his embrace as if she was born to be there. Curious, I open my arm and Cyra does the same.

Yep, she was born to be right here in my arms.

"Ready to go see if Mom and Dad have emerged yet?" Kennedy asks.

"Yes. If not, I'd still like to head over to the pack hospital. The sooner we speak to Dr. Walker, the better I'll feel," I say.

Quirin kisses the top of Kennedy's head. "Let me know if you need me. I have to go kick some Academy cadets' asses," he says grinning.

"Don't have too much fun," Kennedy says, scowling.

Rather than heed her warning, Quirin's grin widens. "Why not? I have two of the best doctors in the world at my disposal today. If I hurt them, I'll send them over."

Kennedy just shakes her head as we walk into the main area of the packhouse.

There we find my mother, charming the pack members like she always does. Her hair isn't quite as put together as it was before my father got his hands in it, and her cheeks definitely have a pink glow to them, but she's here and I'm thankful. I want her impressions not only of Cyra's lack of pregnancy but also of Dr. Walker.

"Hey mom," I say, walking up.

She says goodbye to the pack members, asking one of the young mothers to bring her pup to the pack hospital later today to be seen, then she turns to us.

"Good morning," she says, going first to Cyra and pulling her into an embrace.

"Good morning, Luna," Cyra says, smiling and closing her eyes as my mother hugs her. I can feel the need, the desire from Cyra to feel a mother's arms wrapped around her. It's something she never had growing up, and my mother gives the best hugs I've ever had. Well, besides my mate's.

My mother holds my mate longer than a normal hug, recognizing as she always does, what someone else needs and giving it to them.

"Thank you, Luna," Cyra says, finally pulling away.

"I'm always available for a hug, Cyra," she says, turning to me and opening her arms. "See?"

I chuckle as I pull my mother into a hug. Mine is faster and then she turns to Kennedy.

"You already hugged me this morning," Kennedy says.

"So? Give your mother another hug," she says. Kennedy shakes her head but hugs her again.

"Why does Quirin look so excited? He's got that look on his face, the one that makes me think someone is about to learn a lesson they didn't know they were going to get," my father says, looking in the direction that Quirin went.

"Our friends said they wanted to spar with him," Cyra tells him.

Dad's head snaps back to us and he smiles. "This I've got to see," he says, kissing mom quickly before jogging after Quirin.

"So, what can I do for the three of you?" my mother asks astutely, turning back to us after watching my father jog off.

"Can we walk and talk? We're headed to the pack hospital," I tell her.

"Perfect. I'd planned on going over there first thing this morning anyway. I need to make sure this hospital is prepared to run smoothly since I'll be spending a lot of time here," she says.

I'm not at all surprised.

On our way to the hospital, we fill my mother in on what happened, and Kennedy tells her what she was thinking. We stop before walking inside the hospital, wanting a plan before confronting Dr. Walker.

"First, Kennedy is exactly right about the hormones. They're not just there one day and gone the next. So, it's very possible that you still had some in your system when you went to the Academy, even if you had a placebo put in. We'll do the blood test for your hormone levels and for a possible pregnancy. How do you want to proceed with Dr. Walker? This is your pack. Do you want to confront him as Alphas and let me handle the medical side if he tries to use jargon to get out of it, or do you want me to confront him?" she asks.

I look at Cyra. "I think we should do it. Stellan told us what he did. He'd have a harder time lying to us, plus we can give our Alpha command if we think he's lying."

"I agree," she says.

With that, we walk into the hospital.

"Alphas! I was hoping to see you this morning. I thought you might want to come confirm some results?" Dr. Walker asks, smiling as we walk in.

"Is there someplace we can speak privately, doctor?" I ask sharply. The smile falls from his face.

"Yes. Yes, of course, follow me. Is something wrong?" he asks.

"We're about to find out," Cyra says.

"I'll wait out here," Kennedy says.

"Feel free to look around, Ken," I tell her.

"YAY!" she says excitedly. I will never understand my mother's and sister's fascination with medicine.

Dr. Walker leads us to a small office that has a round table which just fits the four of us.

"What's this about?" he asks.

Chapter 21:
Confrontation

Yorick

    I can feel that Cyra wants to take the lead, so I sit back.

"When Alpha Stellan came to the Academy to force his mark on me, he made a comment about putting a pup in me at the same time," she begins and Dr. Walker snorts.

"Well, that would have been impossible. You are on birth control. I thought he knew that."

"He said he replaced it with a placebo," she says.

"Impossible, I did the injections. How could he have ... son of a bitch," he snarls, standing up. I'm up and standing between him and my mother and mate in an instant.

He jolts, looking at me, then looking behind me at Cyra. "You think I did it?" he asks.

"Did you?" I growl.

He scrubs his face with his hands. "We've had an influx of unwanted pregnancies in the pack lately. I've been trying to figure out why it keeps happening. With younger mothers, it isn't as big of a deal, but with the older she-wolves, the ones who have already had their pups, it has put them at higher risk. I have several she-wolves right now that are borderline high risk because of their age. I would have to confirm, but I believe all of them were on the hormone implants.'"

I turn and look at my mother. This is getting into her territory.

"How long has this been happening?" she asks.

He turns and looks around the office, finding what he was looking for. "There are four of them, all of them have turned up pregnant in the last three to four weeks," he says, grabbing some files and handing them to my mother. "I am a *doctor*! I would never go against my Hippocratic Oath," he growls.

"That's good to hear," my mother says, quickly looking through the files. "All four of these women were on hormone implants," she says, looking up at me. "Can you get Kennedy for me?"

I reach out in the mind link. In the past, connecting to my family link was easier than other links. Now, as an Alpha of my own pack, I find that it's not as easy as it was before. She's a leader in a separate pack. I still have the connection to her, but my connections to my pack are now stronger than my family connections.

'Kennedy, can you come to the office?'

'Be right there,' she says.

"Who is the manufacturer of these implants?" my mother asks as she goes through the files.

While she and Dr. Walker are talking, I open the door for Kennedy.

"What's up?" Kennedy asks.

"Kennedy, this is Dr. Walker. Dr. Walker, my daughter Kennedy. She's a medical student. Ken, can you go with Dr. Walker to get the shipment of hormone implants that he's been using and test them to see if they are placebos?"

"I take it you weren't aware of the placebo issue, doctor?" she asks him.

"I was not," he growls. "But it explains a lot."

"Did Stellan have access to the pack hospital?" my mother asks.

"No. He would have no reason to be here, and I don't allow just anyone to wander around my hospital," he says.

"That's good to know. You and I will get along well, doctor," my mother says, smiling up at him.

"I've heard a lot about you, Dr. Hill. It would be my honor to work with you while your mate is here helping to manage our pack," he says.

"Please, call me Yara," she says, instantly charming the doctor.

"Then you must call me, Kevin," he says, before walking out with Kennedy.

"So, how could he have exchanged these implants for placebos, mom?" I ask.

She shrugs, still looking through the files. "The distributor, the delivery person, there are numerous ways he could have switched out the implants. We'll have to report this to the Council. They'll want to know why we're seeing a spike in high-risk pregnancies, but it's good that I'll be here. We all know the rule in my hospital," she says, smiling as she sets the paperwork down and stands.

"What rule is that?" Cyra asks as she stands.

"No one dies in my hospital," Mom says. "Now, let's go get your bloodwork done. With this many unwanted pregnancies in the pack, we need to be sure."

We follow my mother to a medical room where she begins looking around. "Let me go find what I need. You two get comfortable. I'll be right back," she says, stepping out again.

"No matter what happens, no matter if you are or aren't pregnant, we face the future together," I say to my mate.

She smiles and leans into me. "I'm not going to lie, I'm feeling a bit overwhelmed by everything that is happening all at once. But if my choices are to have you and be overwhelmed by life, or to not have you and feel settled, I choose you, all day, every day."

"And I will always stand by your side, working with you to overcome whatever obstacles come our way," I say, leaning in to kiss her.

I've just started deepening the kiss when the door opens and my mother walks in with Dr. Walker and Kennedy.

"What tests did you want me to run on these mother?" Kennedy asks.

"Have a seat on the table, Cyra," my mother says before answering Kennedy that she wants to test the level of hormones in the remaining boxes of implants.

My mother comes over and begins preparing Cyra's arm to draw blood.

"Luna Kennedy, perhaps I should run the tests. I know your mother said you're a medical student, but you're awfully young for this sort of test," Dr. Walker says, making me smile.

"I graduated high school with a double major in college, Dr. Walker. I'm currently in my third year of graduate school," Kennedy tells him.

"But you're so young," he says, frowning at her.

She shrugs. "I grew up in my mother's hospital."

"She'd be done with school already if her mate wasn't so passionate," my mother murmurs.

I look up at Kennedy who smiles at me. She holds her hand up to Dr. Walker to stay silent and I send Cyra a mind link to stay quiet as well. Sometimes, you learn more from my mother's mumblings than you do from the words she intentionally speaks.

"Yorick is his father's son, so it's much more likely that Cyra is pregnant with twins than not pregnant at all," she mumbles, making Cyra's eyes go wide.

"Of course, if he's as passionate as Quirin, poor Cyra could be pregnant with quads. Well, Kennedy figured it out and still went to school. I'm sure Cyra could figure it out too. And of course, she has the most amazing man in the world helping her to succeed. Goddess, I love that man."

"Who is the most amazing man in the world, Mom?" Kennedy asks, grinning.

Our mother looks up. "Oh, did I say that out loud? I was just thinking of your father."

"We'll have to agree to disagree about who the most amazing man in the world is," Kennedy says, making my mother smile as she pulls the needle from Cyra's arm.

"Yes, we will," my mate says, her eyes glimmering with possessiveness as she looks at me.

"Let me process this blood and I'll be right back," my mother says, but I don't look away from my mate.

I hear the others leave and when the door closes, Cyra speaks.

"Quads?"

"Hopefully not. I still have too much fun teasing Quirin about having glitter in his hair."

"Twins?" she asks.

"Much more manageable and with my parents around, definitely manageable," I growl, pulling her to me and taking her mouth in a dominant, possessive kiss.

'If the number of pups is directly related to my mate's passion, we'll be lucky to only have quads,' Rina purrs in our mind, making Thad growl possessively and deepen the kiss even more.

Chapter 22: Sparring with Quirin

Piper

I'm not sure I like the excited, almost maniacal grin on Alpha Quirin's face when he walks out rubbing his hands together.

"Alright! Let's see what they're teaching you Academy brats these days," he says. "Kennedy says I'm not supposed to put you in the hospital, but since she AND Luna Yara are here, I feel confident that any damage I do can be undone."

Word spreads quickly that we wanted to spar with Alpha Quirin and since everyone heard about what happened to Alpha Christer yesterday, most, if not all, of the pack warriors not currently on patrol, are here to watch.

"So, how do you want to do this? Do you want me to take on all four of you at once?" he asks.

I frown.

"No. Then we wouldn't be able to tell how we do individually against you," Zach says and the rest of us agree.

"Okay, who's first?" he asks.

"You choose," Chase says.

He looks the four of us over quickly then points to me. "Piper."

Of course he picked me. I thought that maybe he'd be different than other Alphas and treat me as an equal, but I guess not. As usual, my mouth starts to run before I can stop it.

"Picking the easiest target first, Alpha?" I snap, stepping forward. I'll show him 'easy'.

He stills, tilting his head at me. "I'm very fast, even by Alpha standards, but I'm not as fast as most she-wolves. In my experience, she-wolves who know how to fight well use their smaller stature, their speed, and their agility, which is almost always better than a male warrior's, to their advantage. I chose you first because I see you as my biggest competitor in this group."

"Oh," I say, startled at his words.

"Oh," he says, giving me a look that says I shouldn't underestimate him again. Then he settles into a stance that isn't exactly offensive, but it isn't defensive either. "Don't prove me wrong."

While I'm still trying to figure out if he's taking offense or defense, he leaps at me. I duck quickly out of the way, instinct kicking in as I punch out, connecting with his hip.

"I see I was right," he says, the excitement of the fight back in his eyes.

"Get him, Hellfire!" Zach says.

"Hellfire?" Alpha Quirin asks me.

"I have a sharp tongue and a bit of a temper," I say, dodging a punch to the face.

"I see," he says, dodging my punch.

After that, it takes all my training and focus to spar with him. He doesn't fight like most Alphas.

After I tag him again, he steps back.

"How is it that an Alpha female from an existing pack knows how to fight like a rogue?" he asks.

"My family took in a rogue girl when I was younger. No one else in the pack would spar with her, so I did. She taught me her fighting skill, and I taught her mine," I say, thinking of one of my very few friends. Well, Vivienne would say we aren't friends because rogues don't have friends. Even though she joined our pack, she's always considered herself a rogue.

"My pack of rogues would like you. My daughters would too. You should come visit my pack sometime. If you're going to become an elite warrior, it would be good for you to learn how to fight a bit dirtier than you do. My warriors could teach you that."

"Thanks. Next time I see Vivienne, I'll see if I can't get her to come with me," I say.

"Tell her my pack is made up almost entirely of previous rogues. They're a different breed of fighter, but we've all become a very tight-knit family because of Kennedy."

I can see the pride in his eyes and on his face when he talks about his mate. Damn, I really hope that I have someone that looks at me like that someday.

"How old were you when Luna Kennedy turned eighteen?"

"Thirty-one. You're way too young to give up on the idea of finding your fated mate, if that's where your thoughts are going," he says as we begin sparring again.

It was, but I don't say that.

"Nice!" he says as I get in another hit. I'm landing hits, but I also realize that while he said he wouldn't mind putting us in the hospital, he's pulling his punches. He's making sure they hurt. He's making sure that I walk away with enough pain to learn from the lesson, but he could have already taken me down and he hasn't. He's using this as a teaching opportunity.

Alpha Quirin has more control in his fighting technique than most. I realize that someone with this much control who wanted to make someone suffer for threatening his mate, would be lethal. It gives me a much better idea of how much torture Alpha Christer experienced yesterday.

I've let myself get distracted with that train of thought, and because of it, Alpha Quirin grabs me, pinning my back to his chest with one arm. In this position, he has a free hand that is able to punch me in the head, the ribs, or the hip easily.

Before he can do that, I drop my weight, throwing my arms up and sliding down his body and out of his hold. I spin quickly, swinging a leg out and knocking Alpha Quirin off his feet. I let the force of the spin keep me in motion as I rise back up to a standing position.

I turn just in time to watch Alpha Quirin do some sort of incredible acrobatic stunt where, rather than landing on his back as I intended, he arches his back, lands on his hands, then using his strength and the force of the fall, he flips himself over and back to his feet, squaring off with me just as I get to mine.

"What the fuck? How did you do that?" I ask, stepping back.

Alpha Quirin grins at me. "Practice. And I knew you'd be tough competition. I like you. You remind me of me, only nicer. That invitation to visit my pack still stands. My warriors would love you."

"You just want her to face Kendra and Kaylee. Don't do it, Piper. It's a trap!" Alpha Warren says. I didn't even realize that he'd come out to watch us as well.

"Who are Kendra and Kaylee?"

"The deadliest almost three-year-olds you'll ever met," Quirin says, obviously very proud of his daughters.

"Imagine twins that look sweet like my daughter but act like their father. I'm not sure you could get any more deadly than that. Trust me," Warren says.

"They're not even three," Chase says.

"The last warrior who said that ended up on the ground at their feet," Quirin says, his chest expanding with pride.

"Damn," Zach murmurs.

"Alright, who's next? Just Landon, you're up."

I laugh at Alpha Quirin's name for Landon, but step back, or limp back to stand with Zach.

He throws an arm around my shoulders. "You did great, Hellfire."

"He's really good," I say as we watch Quirin square off against Landon.

"I knew you'd be a smart fighter. And a dirty fighter, too. You'd have to be to get a position at the Academy ahead of Alphas," Quirin says, dancing around Landon who also gets his share of hits in.

By the time we're done, we're all limping except Alpha Quirin.

"Well, that was fun!" he says, making us chuckle.

"Thank you for not sending anyone to the pack hospital," Luna Kennedy says, smiling at her mate. His entire demeanor changes as he strides purposefully toward his mate, taking her mouth in a very dominant, possessive kiss.

"I like it when my mate is happy with me," he growls against her mouth before continuing their kiss.

Damn. I want that. I want a man who looks at me the way Alpha Quirin looks at Luna Kennedy, the way Alpha Warren looks at Luna Yara, the way that Yorick looks at Cyra.

I want it so much it hurts.

Chapter 23: News and Announcement

Yorick

"Yorick, sweetheart, can you please disengage from Cyra so we can finish our conversation. Then the two of you can continue," my mother's voice says from somewhere behind me.

I've gotten totally lost in kissing my mate. I forgot we were still in the pack hospital.

I reluctantly pull away from my mate, who is quickly turning a bright shade of pink.

"Sorry, Luna," she murmurs.

"Never apologize for loving your mate, especially when that mate is my son. I am well aware of the 'passion' of the

Hill men," mom says, making me chuckle and Cyra blush an even deeper shade of pink.

"I have your results. First, your hormone levels are back to normal, meaning you were definitely given a placebo. I'm guessing the hormones from your previous implant lasted just long enough for me to confirm your negative pregnancy test," she says.

I feel the same wave of disappointment in Cyra that I'm feeling. I was excited to start a family with my mate, even if it would be difficult for the next year.

"Now, your test result was negative, but the two of you have only recently completed your mate bond and that is what we need to discuss. I know Kennedy told you that I might not be willing to put you on birth control and she's right. With your hormone levels normal and your recent marking and mating, it is very likely that you are now pregnant, just not far enough along for it to show on a test. If I understand the agreement you have with Warren, the two of you will be coming here every weekend, correct?"

"Yes," I say.

She nods. "I'll check you next weekend and if you're still negative, we'll go one more week. If at that time you still show a negative blood test, then I'll put you on birth control if that's what you want. For now, if you aren't actively trying to get pregnant, you need to make sure you use condoms," she says, looking at me with a question on her face.

"Yeah, I have them," I say. "Dad made sure we all did."

"Good. Of course, it's up to the two of you if you want to use them, but I won't feel completely comfortable putting you on birth control for two more weeks."

"Okay, thanks Mom."

"Of course. I'm going to walk back to the packhouse with you," she says, as we walk out of the room.

"I need to let your father know that Kennedy and Dr. Walker found that none of the implants that came in that particular shipment had the hormones required to prevent pregnancy. I'll need to contact the Council, and you can expect an investigation. I'm not sure if they will contact one of you or your father since things are a little different in this pack right now. I've had Dr. Walker set aside the shipment that was tampered with, the results of Kennedy's tests, and he's also collecting the information on who ordered this shipment, when it was ordered, which company they ordered through, and which delivery company was used. The Council will want all that information when they arrive to complete their investigation. I also asked Dr. Walker about the possibility of a nurse being involved, but he didn't feel that was likely. He feels that whoever did this was outside of the pack. But you should be aware that the Council will interview all medical professionals and anyone else who handled the shipment from the moment it entered the pack lands."

"Thanks Mom," I say as we walk into the packhouse.

"Did you talk to Quirin? He seemed very excited about the proposal he came up with for the two of you," she asks, just as I hear my sister giggling and complaining to a growling Quirin who probably looks a lot like I did a few minutes ago when my mother interrupted my kiss with Cyra.

I look at my mate and wink at her.

"He's created a very generous offer for us, Luna. It's just amazing what he's done for us," Cyra says as my mother watches Kennedy and Quirin with a happy smile on her face.

"He always was such a sweet and generous young man," she murmurs.

Quirin pulls away from Kennedy suddenly, frowning at my mother who has no idea she just said that out loud. Of course, NO ONE other than my mother and Kennedy would ever say that Quirin is *sweet*.

"Luna, you've always had blinders on when it comes to me," Quirin says, setting Kennedy back on her feet.

My mother walks over and cups his cheek. The soft look he gives her is reserved for a very select few in Quirin's life, my mother, Kennedy, Luna Farrah, and Quirin's pups. Even I don't warrant that level of softness in him.

"Perhaps I'm one of the few who sees you clearly," my mother says.

"I definitely agree with that," Kennedy says, smiling up at her mate.

It's obvious my mother's praise makes Quirin uncomfortable, but she lifts her cheek to him so he can kiss it, then she goes to my father.

I watch my friends limping in behind Quirin.

"Well, at least he didn't put you in the pack hospital," I say, laughing at them.

Quirin grins at them, then turns to look at us. "We need to talk to your father and tell him what we've agreed to. Then we need to go to your new pack. They need an Alpha and Connor needs to get home. I would suggest having an Alpha ceremony immediately after we arrive there," he says, as my father walks up.

"So, you are taking over the new pack?" he asks us.

I can see that the pack members around us shifting, watching, and listening to the interaction.

I look at Cyra who shrugs. "It's apparently a done deal," she says.

I nod and clap my hands. "Attention everyone! I know a lot has happened in the last twenty-four hours, but there is more to come. Some of you just overheard my father asking about Alpha Christer's old pack. Earlier today, Cyra and I signed an alliance agreement with Alpha Quirin. He has generously gifted us the vacant land between this pack and Alpha Christer's pack," I say, stopping as the gasps and murmurs begin.

I hold up my hands for silence. "Alpha Quirin has also agreed that, as part of our repayment for the loan we used to help get Cyra out of the alliance bond that her father created with Alpha Stellan, we will be taking over Christer's old pack. We will be working with them and you to figure out the best way to patrol our new pack lands. We will begin staking out the areas this weekend and starting patrols once that is complete. We will also need to have a gathering to incorporate the two packs into one. All of this is happening quickly, so I don't have answers yet about how we will combine the two packs, but as we make those decisions, we will make sure all of you are aware of what's happening. This is a good thing. It's good for our pack and strengthens us overall, but it will take adjustment and patience from everyone. If you have any questions or concerns, please see Cyra, my father, or me. We will be happy to discuss them with you."

I can feel the shock, like a mini wave, through the pack link. The pack is so startled, they really don't know what to say at this point.

"Cyra and I need to go address the other pack and officially take our place as their Alphas. We will be back this evening and we can begin planning a gathering in our new plot of land in between the two packs for everyone to start getting to know each other," I say, then look at Cyra, seeing if she has anything to add.

"We told you things would be changing, but even we didn't know that it would be changing this quickly. As Yorick said, this is a good thing. Change can be difficult, but we will work through this together. We will be stronger together. We will be unified, together."

We look around, getting a feel for the pack's response to our statements. Overall, the pack feels positive, just very surprised at this turn of events.

"She's such a natural leader. She'll make a lovely Alpha," I hear my mother murmur.

I look over and see my father grinning as he wraps his arm around her shoulders and pulls her into a hug.

Once the pack goes back to what they were doing, my father looks at us.

"I'm not comfortable leaving Yara here unprotected. I don't know this pack well enough, but I also know that she wants to start working in the hospital here. Do you have any ideas?"

"Yo, Pipes!" Cyra calls out to Piper.

"Yeah?"

"Are you up for some guard duty today?"

"Who am I guarding?" she asks, walking over.

"My mother-in-law."

"Ahh, the lovely Luna Yara. I'd love to," she says, smiling at my mother.

"What are we, chopped liver?" Zach asks, walking over.

"I'd be thrilled if all four of you would look after my mate while we're gone," Dad says.

"I'm sure that's not necessary," Mom says.

"Don't worry, Luna Murmur, we've got you," Zach says.

"Luna Murmur?" Mom asks, frowning.

"Zach's big on nicknames, Luna. Just ignore him," Piper says.

"Yeah, we all do," Chase says, grinning at my mother.

"I was talking out loud again, wasn't I?" she asks my father.

"Always, my love," he says, grinning and kissing her lightly on the lips.

She sighs. "I'm going to the pack hospital. I have some things I need to do there."

"We're with you, Luna. See you later," Landon says to us.

"Yeah, have fun taking over the world," Zach says, grinning.

"You're such an idiot," Piper says as they walk off.

"I like your friends," Quirin says. That's high praise from him.

"Yeah, they're pretty awesome."

"Are we ready?" Dad asks.

"Let's do this."

Chapter 24: The New Pack

Cyra

Since Quirin and Kennedy are planning to head home after they make their announcement, we drive two cars to Christer's old pack. I guess it's our pack now, or it will be by the time we return to our 'other' pack tonight.

"How are you feeling about everything Cyra?" Warren asks me. He and Yorick are sitting in the front while I chose to sit in the back. I'm behind Warren, so when I look up, I meet his eyes in the rearview mirror.

Yorick turns to look at me, reaching out to put a hand on my knee.

"There's just so much to do," I say. "It was already a lot, but now, with another pack, adding pack lands, increasing patrols ..." I stop, getting overwhelmed with everything that still needs to be done.

"It will all get done. We didn't have time to sit down today to go over the finances, but we still have two more days before you return to the Academy, and you aren't the only Alpha in your pack. Yorick can work on patrols along with your father's Beta and Gamma, if you trust them. Yara can help us plan the gathering of the two packs. While we're in Christer's pack, we'll look through his old office and talk to his Beta and Gamma. Connor can let us know his impressions of them, but I think he was already impressed with Beta Eric."

When we arrive, I can feel the tension in the pack. I realize immediately that it has nothing to do with Yorick and I, and everything to do with Quirin.

"Hey!" Connor says, walking out to greet us. I notice that while everyone is stealing glances at Kennedy, no one is looking directly at her as if they're afraid that Quirin might take offense.

"How are my future allies?" he says, hugging his father, then his brother, then me.

"Quirin gave us the paperwork to sign the agreement with you before you leave today," Yorick tells him.

"Q's awesome like that," Connor says, hugging Quirin and then his twin.

"You've been hanging out with Henry again," Quirin grumbles.

"He's the closest one to me. Plus, you've been busy taking over the world or some shit," Connor says, easily joking with Quirin.

"Yeah and that 'some shit' is about to be done. I want to get home to my pups."

"Good, your hair is looking a bit dull without any glitter in it," Connor says, grinning widely as Quirin growls at him.

Kennedy just smiles and leans into her mate. He kisses her quickly before stepping forward.

"Attention everyone!" he says, his voice booming out around the pack. Everyone goes quiet and the tension gets heavier.

"As you all know, I defeated your Alpha yesterday. That would make me your Alpha, except for one thing. Alpha Cyra and Alpha Yorick are the ones who were impacted by the loan your previous Alpha took out and I bought. They will be taking over the loan from me and this pack is included as part of that loan, meaning, they now own this pack," Quirin says.

Everyone turns to look at Yorick and I.

"For those of you who haven't heard, Alpha Cyra defeated her father in a battle for her pack yesterday and she made her mate, Alpha Yorick, a co-Alpha of that pack."

He turns to look at us. "I'm assuming it will be the same here?"

"Absolutely," I say without hesitation.

"So, I will not be holding your Alpha ceremony today. Alpha Cyra and Alpha Yorick will be doing that. They will explain to you why Alpha Warren is here and his role in your lives over the next year." He turns to look at us. "I'll leave you to it."

We say our goodbyes to them as Quirin obviously meant what he said about not sticking around.

When we turn back, I step forward, feeling the tension recede. It's not gone completely, but without the fear of Quirin, it's greatly reduced.

"For those of you who don't know me, I'm Alpha Cyra. As Alpha Quirin said, I defeated my father in a battle to overtake his pack yesterday. This," I say, gesturing to Yorick who comes to stand beside me, "is Alpha Yorick, my mate. We are both currently attending the Warrior Academy and Yorick intends to take a position with one of the elite warrior teams that work for the Council. So, while he will be co-Alpha, there will be times when he is working away from the pack. Once I complete my year at the Academy, I will become a full-time Alpha managing what will become our one, unified pack."

I can already tell that some of the warriors here are not sure about following a female Alpha. They'll get over it, or they'll find themselves a new home.

"This is Alpha Warren. He is a retired Alpha of his own pack and Yorick's father. I believe you all saw him yesterday before Alpha Quirin challenged Alpha Christer. He has agreed to manage our pack while Yorick and I finish the Academy. The three of us will be working closely together over the next year, with Yorick and I coming home on the weekends to focus on the pack, using our week at the Academy to focus on our studies."

"Excuse me, Alpha. Why not just quit the Academy and take over?" someone asks.

"An excellent question, and most Alphas would probably do that. However, my father never intended for me to take over his pack. I was never trained to be an Alpha who leads a pack. Between Alpha Warren and the Academy, I intend to learn everything I need to know about being the kind of Alpha this pack deserves. I can see that some of you are hesitant to accept a female as your Alpha. I will tell you now, I am done being undermined. If you don't think you can be led by a female, you have one hour to pack your things and leave. If you have concerns about my ability to lead, rest assured that's why Alpha Warren is here. I know that I'm capable, so is Yorick. But as a second son, he also never intended to take over a pack. What we're lacking is knowledge. Over the next year, we will both be getting a crash course on managing a pack. We have an excellent teacher in Alpha Warren, and as you may have heard when we arrived, we have already signed an alliance agreement with Alpha Quirin and will be creating that same agreement with Alpha Connor before he leaves today. As we told our pack yesterday before they accepted us as their Alphas and interim Alpha, a lot is going to change and it's changing very rapidly. Change can be difficult, but that doesn't mean it's a bad thing. Any questions?"

"Alpha, how are you going to combine our packs? There's a huge piece of land between this pack and your pack," someone says

"Oh, right. I'm glad you asked. Alpha Quirin and Luna Kennedy gifted us the vacant land between our packs," I say and once again, everyone gasps. "It was very generous of them, I agree. But it will allow us the opportunity to expand our borders and create a unified pack land. Tomorrow night, we'll be having a pack gathering for everyone so the packs can meet and we can start integrating together. However, today, as I mentioned, you have one hour to decide if you want to stay or leave. I know that doesn't give you a lot of time to decide, but we have a lot to do. Everyone, meet back here in one hour's time to accept Yorick and I as your Alphas and Alpha Warren as your interim Alpha."

I watch for a moment as everyone begins milling around and talking to themselves.

"I guess we'll see in an hour how many remain," Yorick says, also watching the pack.

"Quirin's such an asshole. How am I supposed to compete with him giving you a swath of land?" Connor grumbles walking over.

Warren laughs and slaps his son on the back. "I think that was the point. Quirin likes to shut down his competition before there is any."

"Come on, I'll give you a quick tour and we can sign that alliance agreement. Also, I'd like to introduce you to Beta Eric. I think he'll be a great help to you during this transition. Gamma Hugo I'm not so sure about," he says as we begin walking toward the packhouse.

The rest of the day goes by in a blur of accepting nearly everyone from Christer's old pack. Each person who accepted us added even more strength to our already strong pack. The afternoon was spent meeting pack members and getting to know them, having a quickly pulled together celebration, and planning this pack's part in tomorrow's event.

It was nearly midnight when Yorick, Warren, and I climbed into the van to head back to the other side of our pack lands.

"It will be faster to get here in wolf form," Warren says as we drive back.

"Agreed," Yorick says, turning to look at me. I feel the same fatigue in him that I feel in myself.

"How are you doing?" he asks.

"Better than I thought," I say, and I mean it. Connor was right about Beta Eric. I can already tell that he's going to be a great help in integrating our packs into one. "How about you?"

"The same. It went better than I thought it would, but maybe that's because they were all excited about not having to accept Quirin as their Alpha."

When we return to the packhouse, Luna Yara is waiting for us.

"I spoke to the Council today. They are sending a team to begin investigating the placebo implants tomorrow," she says, as Warren pulls her into his arms.

"We were supposed to go over the finances tomorrow," I say, looking at Warren.

"And we will. Yorick can handle the Council, I'm sure," he says, looking at his son.

"Remember, Cyra, you're not alone anymore. I'd rather spend the day with the Council than in a room pouring over numbers. Divide and conquer, my mate," he says, pulling me into a hug.

I lean against him, letting his love and support embrace me. I feel so lucky to have this man in my life.

Chapter 25: C-Squad

Yorick

With the addition of a second pack, I feel even stronger than I did before. The buzzing in my mind, the connection to our pack members is also stronger. I hope that feeling of connection will continue to improve and strengthen as our pack gets stronger. I'll be interested to see how I feel tomorrow after our gathering tonight.

Because I have more strength, I enjoyed my mate before we fell asleep last night and then woke her up again this morning to have her again. It's the best possible way to start and end my day.

After another fun morning of warrior training, we sat down for breakfast. We talked about tonight and decided to send Beta Lewis and Gamma Elliot from this pack, and Gamma Hugo from the other pack to find a space and start preparing for tonight's event. Cyra and I agreed that while we'd like Beta Eric to also be a part of that, we need him to be in the other pack making sure the pack members there don't have any problems with all the changes happening.

We had just finished finalizing those plans, when I got an alert from the gate guard that the Council and a group of enforcers had arrived.

"Why would the Council send enforcers? We notified them. It's not like we're being secretive," I say, standing to go greet them.

"I don't know, but we're going to find out," Cyra says, standing beside me.

We walk to the front of the packhouse with my parents following closely behind.

"Oh, before I forget, Yana, Yvonne, and Wade are coming this weekend. Since we'll now be splitting our time between three packs, they wanted to decide on their rooms here. If you have any suggestions for which rooms you'd like them to have, please let us know before they arrive," my mother says.

"Any rooms are fine," Cyra says at the same time that I say, "As far away from our room as possible."

My mate grins at me. "They won't be here all the time."

"You have no idea how loud it gets with them."

"Hopefully, your father and I can afford to build a house here like we have on the other pack lands, if that's okay with the two of you," she says.

"I think that's a wonderful idea. Dad, you should tell Connor that his gift to us could be sending warriors to help build your house. That would make him feel better about whatever gift he feels he needs to give us."

"That's a good idea. I'll let him know," he says, just as four black, windowless vans pull up to the front of the packhouse.

Councilwoman Leslie gets out of one of the vans and nods at us. "Alpha Yorick, Alpha Cyra, I didn't expect to see you both again so soon," she says. Councilman Edward also steps out of the van.

"I'm surprised that you've brought such a large group with you today. Are you worried we won't cooperate with you?" I ask, stepping down the stairs to greet them.

"On the contrary, this is the Gamma Team. As you know, we have three elite fighting teams. This one is the team we use for 'domestic disturbances'. They are the quick in-and-out team, if you will. While Alpha and Beta Teams can go under cover, or deep into the shady under-worlds of our existence, this team handles things such as this. With all of us here, we'll be sure to finish up today and be out of your hair. Oh, and I've brought the paperwork that you'll need to file indicating that you have officially taken over these two packs," Councilwoman Leslie says. Cyra takes the paperwork from her.

"Good morning, Alphas. My name is Saber. I'm the leader of the Gamma Team or as we like to call ourselves, the C-Squad."

"It's nice to meet you," I say, shaking her hand. Cyra does as well.

"You're both at the Academy, correct?" she asks.

"That's correct."

"I assume now that the two of you have taken over this and the next pack that you won't be continuing after this year?" she asks.

I look at Cyra, who smiles. "I won't be, but Yorick is still very interested in a place on one of the elite squads."

Saber turns her attention back to me. "Is that so?"

"Yes. While I'm happy to take my place here as Cyra's co-Alpha, my calling is to become an elite warrior, like all of you, and serve the Council."

"You should consider the C-Squad then. I'm Nix," another woman says walking up.

"Why is that?" I ask, shaking her hand.

"As Councilwoman Leslie said, we handle more of the domestic disputes. It's very rare that I don't get to go home to my pups at night. Many of us have rotated off and on this squad because it allows us the ability to continue having families and being a part of their lives. Lace is leaving

Alpha Team to have a baby, but I expect in the next year, she'll reach out to see about joining this squad," Saber says.

"Yep, and I'm going out at the end of this year to have a baby, but I plan to return once my little nugget is weaned," Nix says.

"So, we'll have an opening at the end of the school year," Saber says, holding my gaze.

I growl low. "I want it."

She smiles. "Good. Why don't you show us around today, meet the squad and get to know everyone. If I'm not mistaken, Raptor and Steel already gave you a codename."

I realize that she knew before she arrived that she was interested in me joining her group. She's already been doing research on me.

"That's correct. I'm Striker."

"You already have a codename? Nice!" another warrior says, walking up and holding out his hand. "I'm Viper. Don't screw up this year. The team already likes what we've heard about you."

"I don't intend to," I say, getting excited about the possibility of joining this squad. It would be perfect. I could be at home every night, spending time with Cyra, our pups, and the pack.

"Why don't you show us to your pack hospital, Alpha Yorick. You can join us in our investigation and get a feel for how this squad works," Councilman Edward says.

"It would be my honor," I say, then hear my father clear his throat.

"Oh, sorry, I'm so excited to meet all of you. Let me introduce you to my mother, Luna Yara Hill. She's the one who helped us realize the problem with the placebo implants."

"Dr. Yara, it is an honor to meet such a prestigious and esteemed doctor in our community," Councilman Edward says, his tone turning from amused to awed in a second.

"You're so kind. It's nice to meet you as well. Have all of you had breakfast?" she asks.

When everyone nods that they have, I gesture toward the pack hospital. "If you'll follow me ..."

"Yorick, let me know if you need anything," Cyra says, stepping up to stand beside my father while my mother continues to charm the council members.

Once I've introduced the team to Dr. Walker and he and my mother explain what they found, the C-Squad divides up, interviewing different members of the pack and beginning to dig into the makers of the implant, the distributors, and the delivery people.

Saber lets me sit with her while she researches, calling Tracker to ask her to find the trails she's looking for.

She hands me the data for the company that makes the implant, telling me to research what I can and let her know what I find. I excitedly begin digging, but find no connections to anyone at the company or Stellan.

Saber has just told me that she hasn't found anything with the distributors when she gets a call.

"Give me some good news, Tracker."

"I tracked your delivery truck. Thankfully, all trucks with that company have GPS tracking devices on them, so it was fairly simple. On that day, this particular driver went out of his way, just a few miles," she says.

Saber looks at me and I can see the gleam of excitement in her eyes. She's been on the hunt and now she's caught the scent of her prey. I feel the excitement too.

"A few miles in which direction?" she asks.

"Towards the pack previously run by Alpha Christer, now led by Alphas Yorick and Cyra."

"Send it to me," Saber growls.

"Already in your inbox."

"You're the best, Tracker!" Saber says.

"So Raptor tells me," she says, making Saber laugh before hanging up.

She pulls up the email, showing me the file. "We've got him," she growls.

A moment later, she gets an email from Hacker. It's all there. The driver, Marcus Steward, was friends with Alpha Stellan in school. There's a record of a phone call from Stellan to Marcus two weeks before Cyra went to the Academy.

"Son of a bitch," I say. "We've got him."

"Yeah, we do. And now we can add to the growing number of offenses that Stellan will face at trial."

She gets an email from Tracker with a live feed on where Marcus Steward is.

"Time to pick him up," she says, closing her laptop. "We'll send you a final report and Alpha Cyra is already on the docket to attend both trials. But on a side note, what do you think of the work we do here in C-Squad?"

"I love it. I *want* that spot," I say seriously.

"Good. We work well together. I'll talk to Steel and let him know C-Squad is interested in you."

"Thank you!" I say, shaking her hand.

We walk out of the room we've been working in, Saber approaches the council members who have been watching the interviews and talking to my mother about her future teaching plans.

"Well?" Councilman Edward asks.

"We have our target. Tracker has him in her sights. Time to execute," she tells him.

"That's what I like to hear. We'll meet you back at the council chambers once you have your target in custody."

"C-Squad! We're moving out. Target has been identified," Saber announces loudly.

"You'll have our report by tomorrow, sir," she says to Councilman Edwards before turning to me. "It was a pleasure working with you today, Striker."

The implication of her using my codename, rather than my Alpha title, is not lost on me. She sees me as one of the team.

"I hope we can work together again soon, Saber."

"Count on it," she says, watching her team file out. They all say goodbye to me as they pass, then I follow the Council members back to their van.

'They're leaving, Cyra,' I say to my mate in the mind link.

'Don't let them leave before I get this paperwork to them. Your father and I filled out all the forms today,' she says.

As we approach the packhouse and I wave to C-Squad who is already pulling out, Cyra and Dad walk out of the packhouse.

"Councilman Edward, here is the paperwork you need. Alpha Warren and I filed it electronically, but here is a copy for your records," she says, handing the paperwork to him.

He takes the papers, then looks from Cyra to me. "You two make quite the team. I look forward to seeing more of you in the future, and hopefully to having you as part of the Council's elite warriors," he says.

"Yes, sir. I won't let you down," I tell him.

"No, I don't think you will. I think the only one who might be disappointed is Raptor. I think he had his eye on you as well."

"C-Squad is a better fit for me, sir."

"I agree."

"We'll see you soon. Dr. Yara, it was a pleasure speaking with you today. I do hope you'll come speak at the Academy like we discussed."

"I would be happy to, Councilman," my mother says.

I pull Cyra in my arms as we wave goodbye to the Council members.

"You've been very excited all day. I guess it went well?" Cyra asks me.

"Cyra, it's perfect! It's so perfect. I could do that job and come home at night to you and our pups. And it was *fun*! I had so much fun today!" I say excitedly. "How was your day?" I ask her as we turn to head inside.

"Oh, my day was so fun too!" she says sarcastically. "Your father and I poured over financial statements all day."

"And how are our finances?"

"There's good news and bad news. The good news is, my father seems to have only used the money he embezzled to gamble and party his life away. The bad news is, Christer was bankrupting that pack to keep my father in line and force the alliance bond."

"Something about that still doesn't make sense," I say.

"Yeah, I agree. Your father and I haven't figured it out yet, but we made some headway today. Now, however, it's time for us to get ready for our party tonight."

I nod as we make our way upstairs. If I'm going to have this life, I'll need to learn to switch gears like I am now, from Striker to Alpha and back again. It may take some getting used to, but it will be so worth it in the end.

Chapter 26: Pack Gathering

Cyra

Even though I know the area isn't cleared out the way we would like, when Beta Lewis and Gamma Elliot returned to our pack later that afternoon, covered in dirt, sweat, and grass, they assured me that the area had been sufficiently cleared. Neither of them seemed particularly pleased with Gamma Hugo, which I found interesting. I'll have to talk to Warren about our plan to assess him and his position.

Because Yorick didn't have a chance to get the patrol schedules set up, I sent a group of warriors with the omegas from our pack and coordinated with Beta Eric on the other side to send warriors with his omegas to set up the food.

Eric said he has some ideas to make the area look festive, which is good, since we don't have electricity out there yet.

I arrived early, intending to help with the final set up and make sure that everything was in order. However, when we arrived, Beta Eric was already there. He had the warriors start a large bonfire in the center of the space that had been cleared earlier and he had tiki torches lit around the area.

He had obviously orchestrated the grills to be set aside so the smoke didn't choke our pack members and warriors from both packs were bringing in tree stumps along with a large number of folding chairs for people to sit.

"Alphas!" he says, jogging over when we arrive. We brought some electric lights that the warriors found for us along with some folding chairs and tables to put the food on.

"Eric, this is amazing," I tell him, looking around as Yorick begins pulling chairs out of the back of the truck.

"Well, I had a lot of help, but I know how important this is. I wanted to make sure our packs have a chance to mingle and enjoy themselves tonight."

He takes a group of chairs from Yorick and calls over some warriors to help.

"What do you need us to do?" I ask him, just as our friends pull up with two more trucks loaded with supplies.

"Now that we have more tables, we can get everything set up properly. I've got some warriors out getting wood for the fire so we can keep it going all night."

"The food smells delicious," Zach says walking over.

"It looks like we have quite a variety, and each pack made different sides, so there's going to be a lot of different food to choose from," Eric says, holding out his hand. "I'm Beta Eric."

We go around and do introductions. "So, any chance that our side gets to test its strength against so many Academy cadets while you're all here?" he asks.

I look at Yorick. We hadn't even considered warrior training for the other side. He hops down out of the truck bed.

"We'll come to your side tomorrow and do warrior training there, so you can get the full Academy experience as well," he says, grinning at Eric. "But you're right, we need a more centralized location for warrior training."

He looks around the space then at me. "We can talk to Dad, but maybe we could finish clearing this space over the week and begin using it as a centralized training ground."

"I love that idea."

"What idea is that?" Warren asks, walking up. He and Yara just arrived with coolers full of drinks.

As the pack members from each side begin to arrive, Yorick and I spread out, saying hello, making sure the packs are integrating together. I notice Yara and Dr. Walker talking to the doctor from the other side. I like the idea of having a centralized pack hospital as well and if we can get Luna Yara to teach sometimes while she's here, that could be another revenue source for the pack. Warren and I talked about it today and how successful both Connor's and Quirin's hospitals have become with Yara and now Kennedy providing educational courses to young medical students.

"Cyra!" I turn, seeing Piper walking over with a female from the pack on the other side. I can't remember her name. Yesterday was a blur with everything happening so fast. Taking on so many pack members in two days made my head spin and names were the first thing that flew out of my mind.

I notice the woman looks nervous as they approach. "Cyra, this is Lila. She's the one who warned us about Stellan."

"Lila," I say, my eyes going wide. With all the chaos, I hadn't even remembered that she was the one who called Piper. "I cannot thank you enough for what you did."

She breathes out a sigh of relief.

"I told you she wasn't angry," Piper says, putting her arm around the woman's shoulders.

"I'm so sorry I didn't say anything sooner, Alpha. Stellan told me you were the reason for the alliance agreement and that you wouldn't let him out of it. It wasn't until after I spoke to Alpha Piper..."

"Just Piper," Piper says, grinning at Lila.

"Anyway, after she told me that you'd found your fated mate and you didn't want this agreement, I started asking questions. Some of the blinders that I had for Stellan finally fell away and when I heard him and Alpha Christer that night, I knew I had to do something. I was so hurt to find out that he'd been lying to me all that time, using me ..."

She stops, her voice getting choked up.

I reach out and take her hands in mine.

"You'll have to go to his trial, you know?" I ask gently.

"I know. I already received my summons."

"Have you rejected him yet?" I ask.

"I didn't have a chance," she says, her lips trembling.

"I'll speak to the Council, see if we can have you reject Stellan in court where they can force him to accept it. That way, you'll be free of him, if that's what you want," I say, not sure if she wants to remain bonded to Stellan even after what he's done.

"I definitely don't want him. Do you think they can force him to do that?"

"They're the Council. I'm sure they can," I tell her.

Because she looks like she needs it, I pull her into a hug. "I am indebted to you, Lila, for helping me. I know that must have been hard for you, but I really appreciate you giving us that warning. It allowed us to prepare a trap for Stellan and that's ultimately what got him arrested."

She nods against my chest before stepping back. "I'm just glad he didn't get to you or get his hands on your money."

I frown, glancing at Piper who is also frowning at her.

"What money?" I ask her.

She shrugs. "I don't know. Stellan just said something to Christer about forcing you into the mate bond so he could get the money and pay off the loan."

"Thanks, Lila. If you ever need anything at all, let me know. And I'll be in court with you. You won't be alone."

"Thank you, Alpha," she says, before walking off to get some food.

"What the fuck is she talking about, Cyra? What money?"

"I have no idea, but I'm going to let Warren know. Pay off the debt? Pipes, are you kidding me?"

"You didn't see anything close to that amount when you and Alpha Warren went through the finances today?"

"Twenty million dollars? You'd have heard me howling from the rooftop in excitement. There was nothing even close to that. Geez, I was excited we weren't bankrupt."

"Well, you'll have to dig deeper and if that doesn't work, we thankfully know some really amazing tech people who can probably find it for you."

She gently punches me in the shoulder. "Damn, two packs, a mate who adores you, AND you're independently wealthy? How do I sign up for that gig?" she asks, making me laugh.

"Apparently, it comes when you least expect it, or don't expect it at all. And we still don't know if I'm wealthy. We just know Stellan and Christer thought I was." I turn to her. "And let's not forget another important point."

"There's another one?" she asks, drolly. "As if that wasn't enough?"

"Yep. I have the best friend any girl could ever ask for."

"Dammit, don't be trying to make me cry during your party. That's just rude," she says, hugging me tightly.

I laugh, holding on to her just as tightly.

"You really are amazing, Piper. Your mate, when you find him, will undoubtedly be just as amazing as you are."

"Well, maybe I'm not meant to find him for a while. I'm thinking about trying out for Alpha Squad. I know Zach has a really good chance of getting on the squad, but I don't have a family to keep me from doing some of those deep undercover jobs and I'm guessing they need women as much as men for that work."

"Raptor would be lucky to have you," I tell her.

"Let's hope he agrees. But I still have to beat out Nick-name."

I snort. "If it's based on nicknames, you're hands down the winner, Hellfire."

I spend the rest of the evening talking to pack members and watching the two packs get to know each other. It's late when Yorick calls for everyone's attention, letting them know that this week, while we're back at the Academy, Warren will begin setting up patrols that include the land between our packs and also joint warrior training.

"Cyra and I are excited to return in a week and see what everyone has accomplished. We're proud of all of you. We both greatly appreciate everyone coming together and getting to know each other. While we are still currently separated by space, we are one pack, and we will become more unified over time. Thank you again for being here and making tonight a success. Stay as long as you like but know that I'll be coming to the other side for warrior training tomorrow and bringing my friends," Yorick says, grinning widely. There's a little bit of grumbling, but mostly excitement about that from the other side.

"Good night, everyone," I say.

Yorick and I return to the packhouse, and he ends the night in our favorite way with our bodies, our hearts, and our minds wrapped around each other.

Chapter 27: Friends

Yorick

On Sunday morning, I left Cyra to train the warriors on our side of the pack with my father, and I took our friends to the new side of the pack.

"You're really going to have to do something about the literal divide in your pack lands," Zach says on the drive over.

"Yeah. The only thing I can think of is to build a centralized packhouse, which we can't do until Cyra has our financial situation in hand."

"It's a good thing the two of you like hard work. You're about to have a year of it," Chase says.

"Yeah, but you have us too," Piper says.

"Thank goodness for that," I say.

Warrior training went really well. The pack responded positively to my form of training, and they enjoyed sparring against my friends. Since all of them but Landon are Alphas, and he's an incredible warrior, they're all very good at instructing others on how to fight. The feeling in the pack when we were done was relaxed and excited.

Afterward, I met with Beta Eric and Gamma Hugo to go over patrol schedules. While we were doing that, I got my first real dose of Gamma Hugo. He's lazy, that's the only way to put it.

"That's a really big area to patrol. Our patrols will be running miles if you expect them to cover both packs," he says.

"First of all, we're one pack. Second, if the shifts are the same length of time, then the amount of miles they run will be the same, they just won't be looping around the same area over and over. And rather than two sets of patrols, we're going to have four, two from each side of our ONE pack," I say, stressing that we are one now.

"I mean, I guess it will work," he says, shrugging.

"What doesn't make sense about that, Gamma?" Beta Eric asks him.

"It just seems like as a much larger space and our patrols will have to work harder. Maybe we should shorten the patrol times."

"Why would we do that? The space is larger, yes. But if they've been patrolling as they should, there won't be any additional running involved. If anything, having more space to run will give their wolves an opportunity to stretch their legs more. According to Thad, he and every other wolf he's ever met would be thrilled to have that opportunity to run. If your patrols need stamina training, start working on that. We're not decreasing the shift time, but we are increasing the area that they'll be patrolling."

When we finish creating the patrol assignments, I stay behind with Eric.

"How is he as a Gamma?" I ask him once Hugo is gone.

"He was friends with Christer and Stellan."

"Do you have any problem with me demoting him?" I ask him.

"No, although me being here on my own with a pack that is still feeling a little disconnected could be difficult if he starts causing problems," he says.

"I'll talk to my father. If Hugo doesn't improve over the next week, he's out. If he keeps complaining or starts causing disruption or discontent in the pack, he's not only going to be demoted, he'll be out of the pack," I tell him.

"Do you want me to keep you or Alpha Warren informed?" he asks.

"Both of us, but obviously my father is closer. Cyra and I are leaving tonight and won't be back until Friday night. So, call my father first, then me if there are any problems."

"Will do."

"I'll send you the patrol schedules from the other side so you know who to expect on patrol. I'm also going to split the patrols so the groups are intermixed. I think that will help build some cohesiveness and have the different sides start mingling and getting to know each other. It will also tell us if the patrols on this side have gotten lazy along with Gamma Hugo."

"Send it over when you have it and I'll make sure Hugo implements it."

"Thank you."

When we're done, I get the others and we go back to the other side of the pack. Zach is right, we need a centralized location. We'll never be able to act like one pack while we're separated like this.

"Hey! How did it go?" Cyra asks, walking up when we return.

"Great! And I got the patrol schedules set up on that side. I'm going to meet with Beta Lewis and Gamma Elliot over here to do the same before we leave."

"Perfect. The purchase of the land came through this morning. We sent the final specifications for our land to the Council. I also sent it over to Beta Eric. What did you think of Gamma Hugo?"

"Lazy and probably not long for his ranked position. I need to talk to Dad about that before we leave. I was going to demote him today, but Eric made a good point about things not being stable and that would leave only him to manage things over there."

"So, next weekend we're spending the weekend on that side?" she asks.

"Yes, and we need to figure out how we can combine these two packs. Anything new on the financial front?"

"No. Warren and I looked through everything and didn't see anything about any money tucked away or invested somewhere. Warren suggested talking to Hacker when we get back. I'll need to see what it would cost us, but if there really is money hidden away somewhere, it would be worth the cost to find it."

"Maybe he'll give us a discount if we tell him it's a good learning opportunity for Sphinx," I say grinning.

Cyra laughs. "I'm not above throwing your sister's name in if it means getting a discount. I'm also going to talk to them about cyber security in our pack. I know they said Connor's pack wasn't secure before and I want to make sure ours is."

"Hmmm," I say, thoughtfully.

"What? I know that look. You're cooking up a plan," Cyra says, narrowing her eyes at me.

"Well, what if we invite Hacker out here next weekend to physically look over the two packs and work to connect them to the same security system? Since Mom and Dad are here, and Yana, Yvonne, and Wade were already planning to visit this week ..." I say, watching my mate's smile grow.

"Then Wendy should come too, decide what room she wants and if Hacker just so happens to be here ..."

"Another great learning opportunity," I say, grinning as I pull my mate against me.

"I love that we think alike," she says.

"I love that you're mine," I growl.

"I love that we have friends who are Alphas and have lots of land in case I need to get away from the Academy," Zach says, interrupting our moment.

"I love that we have friends that we can rely on for anything. I can't thank all of you enough for being here this weekend. It's meant a lot to both of us," Cyra tells him as the others walk up.

"I keep telling you, Cyra, that's what friends are for," Piper says.

"Hey, can we get in on this," Chase asks, walking up and putting his arms around me and Cyra.

"We definitely can," Zach says, wrapping his arms around us from the other side.

"GROUP HUG!" Landon says, somehow joining the hug.

"Y'all are all a bunch of idiots," Piper says, walking up and wrapping her arms around all of us too.

"Yeah, but we're your idiots," Zach says, making all of us laugh.

We stand like that for a moment, just being together.

"I love you guys," I tell them.

"Hey, hey, hey! Don't go getting all flirtatious with us in front of Aphrodite. I'm no match for the Goddess of Love," Zach says playfully before stepping back.

I use the rest of the afternoon to set up patrols on this side. I let both Beta Lewis and Gamma Elliot know that they are to work with Beta Eric and Gamma Hugo.

Lewis grunts at that.

"Problem?"

"We'll make it work, but that guy's lazy. Not Beta Eric, the Gamma," Lewis says.

"Agreed. But why do you say that?" I ask.

Now Elliot snorts. "He barely lifted a finger when we were clearing that land. Sat around working his jaw muscles about that not being a Gamma's job, as if we weren't both ranked members out there helping too."

"Let my dad know if you have any more problems with him. I'm going to give him some rope, see if hangs himself," I say.

"He will. From what I gather, he's had a free ride until now, just skating by letting Beta Eric do all the hard work. I don't see him wanting to change that," Lewis says.

"Then he'll find himself demoted and running those extensive patrols he thinks pack members can't run," I say.

"Honestly, my wolf was excited about it. I was going to run the perimeter just to give him the opportunity to stretch his legs and make sure there aren't any unknown problems in the perimeter. We did see what looked like bear tracks and maybe a mountain lion's tracks when we were clearing yesterday. I want to make sure we don't have a den anywhere on that vacant land that might cause an unexpected attack," Lewis says.

"Good thinking. Take a couple of warriors with you, just in case, and let my father know what you find. Cyra and I will be heading back to the Academy after dinner."

When it's time to leave, I say goodbye to my parents, asking mom to invite Wendy to come this week as well.

"Tell her I'm going to try and get Hacker out here next weekend to look over our security systems."

"Do you think that's a good idea, Yorick? Wendy is underage and your father is very protective of his family," my mom asks.

"Mom, if Hacker tries to sneak a kiss and Wendy doesn't want it, I expect *her* to put him on his ass. And if she does want it, then he's not worth his codename if he can't work around Dad," I say, knowing full well that I'll be threatening Hacker if he does anything to hurt my sister.

"I'll be going to the other pack tomorrow. Dr. Benson wants to show me around his pack hospital, and I'd like to meet the pack and see if any pups need a medical assessment."

"Thanks, Mom," I say, hugging her.

"And next weekend, we'll do another test and see what we find," she says, hugging Cyra.

My mom then goes around and hugs each of our friends while we say goodbye to my father.

As we head to our car, Chase turns to look back and wave at my parents.

"Dude, your mom has to be the sexiest MILF alive. If it weren't for your dad ..."

"I'd still kill you for talking about my mom like that," I growl.

"Dude, sorry but she's hot, she's smart, and she's loving. She's the total package."

"And you're going to be unconscious if you don't stop talking about my mother like she's a conquest," I say, glaring at him.

"Seriously, dude, Hellfire is the one with no filter. Don't make Striker show you how he got his name," Zach says, shaking his head at Chase.

"I'm not wrong," Chase insists.

"But you keep that shit to yourself, especially in front of her son, you moron!" Landon says, smacking him upside the head.

"Ow!"

"Just trying to knock some sense into you."

"As I said before, you're all a bunch of idiots," Piper says as we get into the car.

I wave at my parents one more time before pulling out and heading back to the Academy so Cyra and I can start our new, very busy, life together.

Chapter 28: Apologies and Requests

Cyra

Going back to the Academy was a little surreal. After the craziness of the last four days, the Academy seems calm.

Yorick and I talked last night about combining our rooms. It's not like we're ever going to sleep apart. We plan to speak to Alpha Nevaeh about it today. The spare room isn't needed for someone else. There aren't any more admissions coming this year to the Academy, but this way, we can let them know that it's available if they need it.

The first surprise came at breakfast Monday morning. Our group was sitting around chatting about the weekend and the week to come when Megan showed up at our table.

I sigh, ready for a fight.

"I just wanted to say congratulations to both of you," she says to me and Yorick.

I look at her, waiting for the rest. There isn't any more.

"What's the catch, Megan?" I finally ask.

"No catch. I was wrong to go after your mate, even if I didn't know you were fated, you were still together. I apologize for that," she says.

"I'm sorry, what? You don't expect us to believe that you're here apologizing for your actions, do you, Megan?" Piper asks her.

"No, I don't. But someone reminded me recently that I don't have to be the person others think I am. I have the power to be the person I choose to be. I was wrong, and good Alphas acknowledge and apologize when they're wrong. I'll see you in class. Congratulations again," she says, walking off.

I stare after her.

"What is she up to?" Yorick murmurs.

"I have no idea," I say. I watch her walk past the table with her cronies, not even acknowledging their presence.

"Maybe it's an invasion of the body snatchers," Zach whispers.

"You're such an idiot," Piper says, laughing.

We've just about finished eating when I see Hacker enter the dining hall.

"Hey, I'm going to go talk to Hacker," I tell Yorick.

"I'll throw our trays away and come join you," he says.

"Hacker," I call out. He turns, waving. He looks tired, like he was up most of the night.

"Hey, I wanted to ask you about a couple of things," I say as he gets a tray and plate and begins piling food on it.

"There's a possibility that I have money hidden away somewhere, money that my father put away. Stellan and Christer alluded to it, but Alpha Warren and I looked over the weekend and didn't find any trace of it," I tell him.

"It'll cost you. This is personal, not for the Council," he says, not looking up.

"I'm aware. Let me know how much."

"How much money do you think is hidden?" he asks, still focusing on his plate of food.

"Stellan alluded that it would pay off the loan," I say, making his hand stop partway to his plate. He turns to look at me.

"The twenty-million-dollar loan?"

"That's the one."

"And you didn't find a single trace of it?" he asks, nodding to Yorick when he walks up.

"Nothing that would make us believe that there is any money, much less that much money, hidden away somewhere."

"How would Christer and Stellan have known about it?" he asks, resuming his food collection. How does one man eat so much?

"My father, I guess. It's the only thing that makes sense. We never heard anything on that recording that Christer had that made me think there was money hidden anywhere," I say.

"Unless Stellan and Christer knew where to look," he murmurs thoughtfully. "I'm intrigued. I'll take it. It will still cost you, but since this is sort of related to the Council issue and I may have to eventually report it to them, it'll cost less. If it turns out that it's related to charges for either man, the Council will foot the bill entirely," he says. "I'll draw up the paperwork, and you can come sign it tonight after class."

"We thought maybe this would be a good learning opportunity for Sphinx," Yorick says, making Hacker look up at him.

"Sphinx is getting a lot of learning opportunities lately, but yeah. This would be a good one. You said there were two things?" he asks, finally moving to pay for his food. His tray now has three plates full of food.

"Is all that for you?" Yorick asks.

"I missed dinner last night," he says.

"The second is, and I'm not sure you heard that Yorick and I took over two packs this past weekend ..." I begin.

"I heard. Congratulations. I also heard they're looking at you for the C-Squad. Nice."

"Thanks," Yorick says.

"Well, after hearing about how weak Alpha Connor's security is, I'd like to have our security assessed and combined. We, Yorick and I, thought that you might want to join us this weekend so you can physically see the pack-houses and decide the best way to combine the security defenses and improve them," I say.

"Sphinx is supposed to be coming to our pack to set up a room for when she's there with my parents. It could be another learning opportunity for her," Yorick says.

"Are you trying to hook me up with your sister, Striker?" Hacker asks.

"No, not at all. And I will warn you that I will come for you if you hurt her. And I won't be the only one. But I know she's extremely excited about coming to the Academy next year. She is on early acceptance and under the Tech Team's supervision, so I thought this might be a good opportunity for the two of you to work together on a project," he says.

He looks at us for a long moment. "I won't know how much it will cost you until I see what we're working with. Depending on Sphinx's ability to assist, I can reduce that cost, if she's willing to work for free."

"We'll pay the full amount. I don't want to take advantage of my sister," Yorick says.

"When are you going back?" he asks.

"Friday after class," I tell him.

"Until Sunday night?" he asks.

"Yes."

"Okay, I'll clear my schedule."

"Thanks, Hacker."

We say goodbye as Yorick takes my hand, and we head outside for Sparring class.

Hacker POV

A chance to spend the weekend with Wendy? Hell fucking yeah I'm in. I'd do this for free if I didn't think it would clue Striker in that I'm interested in his sister. I might have been a bit too excited that he was using her as bait to get me to agree.

Little does he know just how good his bait is.

As soon as I get back to my room, I pull up the chat. I didn't tell Yorick and Cyra that I missed dinner last night because I was talking Wendy through a meltdown. She's hit a wall with her warrior training. She's struggling to push past it. Since I still haven't told the others on the Tech Team about it, I'm making it my personal mission to get her through it. If I have an entire weekend with her, I'm sure there will be an opportunity for the two of us to get away from the others. I have some ideas on how to push her in her training and help her get past this mental block she has.

Me: I hear you're going to your brother's pack this weekend.

Sphinx: How did you know? Apparently, I need to pick out a room until we have a house built on Yorrie's pack lands.

Me: Apparently, they need some help with their security and guess who's coming to visit as well?

Sphinx: You?? Really?? Do I get to assist?

Me: I'd be offended if my young Padawan didn't assist me.

Sphinx: Ohhh, I could use this as my gift to them for becoming Alphas!

Me: That's between you and your brother. But I want you to plan to spend time sparring with me.

I can almost hear her sigh.

Sphinx: Do I have to?

Me: Yes, you do. This is important. Your brother and father haven't been able to push you past this. Even Quirin hasn't been able to get you past this. Give me a chance to try.

Sphinx: Maybe you're wrong. Maybe I *am* broken.

And this was our discussion last night. She's frustrated that she can't move past the attack. She still freezes on the sparring field when the fighting becomes too intense.

I flick on the camera and dial her number.

She answers the phone as the camera comes on, and I can see her lips pressed tightly together. Since this is important to me, I flip my camera on so she can see me too.

"Say it to my face," I growl at her.

She looks down but stays quiet.

"This weekend. You and me. I'm pushing you past this."

"How?"

"If I tell you how, you'll just find a way to block me and make it harder for me. This way, you can mentally prepare to be pushed hard, but not how to get around my intervention."

She looks back up at the camera. "Do you really think you can fix me?"

I lean forward, letting her see my irritation.

"Fixing you implies that you're broken, Wendy. You are NOT broken. You're traumatized and your family is using kid gloves with you. I'm about to put you in a big girl boxing ring and make you fight your way out of it," I tell her.

"Do you think it will work?" she whispers.

"I'm not going to let you stop until it does," I say.

"Thanks, Jude," she says.

"Don't thank me yet. I'm sure you'll be cursing my name this weekend."

"No pain, no gain, right?" she asks.

"That's the spirit," I say, watching as she smiles. Finally. She didn't smile at all last night.

This opportunity couldn't have come at a better time. I was already trying to figure out how I was going to get to her so I could push her through this mental block before she comes to the Academy next year.

"So, I'll see you this weekend?" she asks.

"Yes, but before that, your brother and Alpha Cyra gave me a new project. Want to help?"

"Yeah, what is it?" she asks excitedly.

"Apparently, we're going on a treasure hunt."

Chapter 29: Steel and Hacker

Yorick

"Alpha Yorick, please see me after class," Alpha Michael says as Cyra and I walk out to Sparring class.

"Yes, sir," I say, looking at Cyra and wondering what this is about.

Having Alpha Michael as one of our instructors has really pushed our Sparring class to new heights. He is teaching us some very technical holds, captures, and escapes, all of which are exciting because they are new and difficult.

I get paired with Zach today, but Cyra gets paired with Megan. Since I know she's up to something with her morning apology that no one believed, I'm distracted, wanting to make sure she doesn't take any cheap shots with Cyra.

However, unlike before, Megan seems focused on the skill we've been taught, not trying to take Cyra out.

"Alpha Yorick, how about you focus on your own sparring match and let your mate focus on hers," Alpha Michael says, catching me.

"Yes, sir," I say, refocusing on Zach.

He and I have always been very evenly matched but since this is a new skill for both of us, we struggle to achieve the goal but help each other and talk through where we think the other went wrong.

When class is over, I'm feeling good about what I achieved today, and I pull Cyra in for a quick kiss making sure she's okay.

'It was actually a great sparring session,' she says in the mind link.

I frown. 'Maybe Zach was right. Maybe someone did snatch her body and it's not Megan at all anymore.'

Cyra laughs then catches up to our friends as I walk over to Alpha Michael.

"You wanted to see me, Sir?"

He stands in the way that Raptor and his team were standing during Alpha Leo's court session, like he's at parade rest as he looks me over, assessing me.

"I hear Saber wants you on her team," he says.

"Yes, sir. She was in our pack over the weekend because of problems we encountered. I was very excited to be able to work with her and the C-Squad and learn more about the work they do."

"Did you know that Raptor also has his eye on you, Striker?" he asks.

"I might have heard that rumor, sir. But honestly, with Cyra and I taking over two packs and needing to combine them into one, C-Squad is a better fit for me."

He nods. "You do realize that C-Squad isn't a weak squad, right? Just because the work they do isn't as intense as the work that Alpha and Beta squads do, that doesn't mean that you don't still have to maintain a higher level of fighting knowledge. There's a reason we don't allow pregnant she-wolves on any squad. The possibility of a fight is always there. It's less in C-Squad, but it's still a possibility when you're arresting people who disagree with being caught."

"I understand, sir."

"Good, because distractions, like focusing on your mate and not practicing the skills I'm giving you, are going to be the cause of you not making it onto a squad."

I press my lips together tightly. "No offense, Alpha, but Megan has been a problem since the beginning of the school year. I was worried she'd hurt my mate."

"First, your mate is at the Academy on her own achievements. She's perfectly capable of holding her own in a sparring match. As an Alpha of her own pack, she doesn't need you or anyone else fighting her battles for her. All you're doing is undermining her when you do that. Second, Megan isn't going to be a problem any longer."

I'm not sure what he means about Megan. It makes me wonder if Alpha Michael hasn't put her on notice. But the part about standing up for Cyra I'll have to think about. I don't want to undermine her, especially in front of our pack. But I do want to protect her when needed.

"Yes, sir."

"I'll be the one assessing you for C-Squad. Just so you know, Nix wasn't originally on the list of openings we had for the squads this year. There will now be an opening on each squad at the end of the year. Since you aren't interested in the other two squads, I'm only assessing you for one. If I don't feel you're the best candidate for C-Squad, you won't be making any squad."

"Understood, sir. But, if for some reason you feel I'm not making the cut, could you pull me aside, like today and tell me what I need to do to get better?"

"I can do that. But for the most part, just keep doing what you're doing and focus on you more and your mate less in class."

"Yes, sir."

The rest of the week goes by in a blur. Cyra and I took classes all day, then would spend an hour on the phone with Dad every night hearing about what he's been doing and the decisions he's making for the pack. By Tuesday, he demoted Gamma Hugo and brought him over to his side of the pack lands. On Wednesday, he sent Gamma Elliot over to assist Beta Eric with unrest on the other side. On Thursday, he started group warrior training in the center of the pack. By Friday, I was exhausted, but ready to get back to our pack and continue working to bring our pack together.

Before we left the Academy on Friday, Alpha Nevaeh approached us.

"These are the summons for the two of you to attend Alpha Stellan's court date next Tuesday. Your father's is scheduled for Thursday," she says, giving us the summons for both court dates.

"I know you both have a lot going on, but your studies here are also very important. If you need any tutoring at night during the week, I will make myself available to assist you."

"Thank you, Alpha."

Since Hacker is joining us this weekend, he's riding with us. I've just finished packing our things when I see him walking out of the Academy loaded down with boxes, and bags.

I jog over to take some of it out of his hands. "What's all this?" I ask.

"The stuff I need to test your security system, lines to lay to connect them, and all the equipment I'll need to do what you've asked me to do," he says, as if it's obvious. I guess it is if you're a techy.

As I put one of the boxes into the trunk, I realize it's filled with laptops. I guess it takes a lot of laptops to work on security.

"Some of those I'll be leaving with you," he says, seeing me staring at the box.

After we're packed, we get in the SUV, with Cyra beside me in the front and Hacker sitting behind me.

"Any luck finding the money?" Cyra asks him, turning in her seat to look at Hacker. Because I can, I pull her hand to my mouth for a kiss, taking a deep breath of her scent. My scent still lingers on her since I took the little bit of free time we had before leaving to make my mate moan and scream for me.

She glances at me, her eyes darkening and I know I'll get to take my time with her later tonight.

"Alpha, do you know who Soraya Castor is?" Hacker asks.

She frowns. "Yes, that was my mother."

"What do you know about your mother and her family?" he asks.

I glance in the rearview mirror at Hacker. His eyes are intense.

"Not much. My father didn't talk about her really. She died when I was young and when I was old enough to ask, I was told there were no living relatives."

"Your mother came from an extremely wealthy pack. She, like you, was the daughter of an Alpha. It is true that her parents are deceased. But her brother, your uncle, Alpha Ramin and his son, Alpha Arman, are alive and well."

"How wealthy?" I ask.

"Not Alpha Quirin wealthy, very few are that wealthy, but wealthy enough that your mother had a will and named you as her benefactor. Technically, it was you and any children that she had, but since you were her only child, you are the sole heir to her fortune."

"Fortune?"

"Yes and your mother was smart enough, or perhaps her father was smart enough, to keep the money and the will in their family's hands. I've been in touch with your uncle. He's ... interesting. However, he was quite surprised when I reached out. There is apparently a lot of bad blood between your father and your mother's family. He didn't go into detail, but I got the distinct impression that it was about money."

I look at Cyra. "Your parents weren't fated mates, were they?"

"No. That's why my father had no problem signing my life away for an alliance bond," she says.

"So, the arrangement between your parents was probably for money on his side," I say.

"Most likely," she says, looking back at Hacker.

"I didn't dig into that as it wasn't part of our agreement, but I can if you'd like me to," he tells her.

"Not yet." I can feel Cyra getting overwhelmed again. "Hey. One day at a time, remember?"

"I have family I didn't even know about. A cousin and an uncle ..." she begins.

"And we'll reach out to them. We can do that this weekend. We'll make contact with them. Let them know that you didn't know about them until now."

"I would definitely recommend that you reach out to them. You have quite a hefty inheritance waiting for you. There were two stipulations on you receiving that money. The first was that you would receive half of your inheritance when you were mated. The other half you'll receive when you have your first child," Hacker says.

I look at Cyra. "And that explains Stellan's need to get you marked and mated."

"Yes, and that information will be sent to the Council for his trial. It should seal the deal on his conviction. And it also means the Council will pay for the work I've done on this," Hacker says.

"How much money are we talking about?" Cyra asks him.

I look in the rearview mirror.

"Fifty million dollars."

I jerk the wheel so hard I nearly caused an accident.

Chapter 30: Security System

Hacker

Besides nearly getting killed when I told Striker and Cyra that the money her mother left her is a ridiculously large amount, I feel on edge when we pull into their pack lands. I haven't seen Wendy since Alpha Leo's court date, not face to face. Since that time, it feels like she and I have gotten closer. I know Hijack is interested in her as well, but I feel a possessiveness towards her that I'm unused to feeling about anyone.

When we get out of the car, I'm a bit disappointed that she isn't waiting for us. I was hoping that maybe she was as desperate to see me as I am to see her. If I'm reading this wrong, I need to dial myself WAY back. I won't do anything to jeopardize the Tech Team and if my attention is unwanted, I won't push it.

We've just opened the truck to start unpacking when I hear feet rushing toward us. I turn and there she is, all beautiful long brown wavy hair and dark green eyes.

She stops, staring at me, her cheeks going pink.

"Dad waited to tell me you were here until you had already pulled up," she says. I don't bother fighting the grin. I'm happy that she's excited to see me.

"Did you tell them what we found?" she asks excitedly, rushing to hug her brother.

"I did. Your brother nearly ran the car off the road," I say, watching as she looks up at her brother, laughing at him.

Damn, I can't see that sparkle in her eyes through the camera. I planned on giving her one of the laptops that I brought, since it's got added security on it, but now I'm really glad I am. The camera on it is MUCH better than the one on her current computer.

She goes over to hug Cyra as the rest of the family walks out to greet us.

"Good evening, Alpha Warren, Luna Yara," I say, greeting them.

"Mom, Dad, you remember Hacker, right?" Wendy says, coming to stand beside me.

"How could I forget the man who has helped my son and daughter-in-law with so much," Luna Yara says, walking over and pulling me into a hug. My eyes go wide, and I look at Alpha Warren to make sure he's not going to punch me.

"Mom's a hugger," Yorick and Wendy say together.

Yara pulls back and looks at me. "You've done so much for our family, you feel like family already."

"Thank you, Luna." She reminds me of my own mother, loving and kind, and no one ever feels like a stranger in her home.

"You haven't met my youngest children yet, have you?" she asks.

"No, ma'am."

"Such a respectful young man," she says so softly I'm not sure I was meant to hear it.

"Mom mumbles to herself a lot. You get used to it," Wendy says quietly.

"This is my daughter, Yana," she says, introducing me to a female version of Alpha Warren. Unlike Wendy who looks like her mother, Yana takes after her father, although her eyes are lighter like her mother's where Wendy's are darker with brown flecks in them like her father.

"Hey, Wendy's told us *all* about you," Yana says in an obvious tease to Wendy. From the corner of my eye, I can see Wendy's lips press tightly together as she glares at her sister.

"Only the good things, I hope," I say, teasing her right back. I come from a large family too, so brothers and sisters teasing each other mercilessly is very familiar to me.

"According to Wendy, there's nothing bad about you. I'm Yvonne," the youngest daughter says. This one looks more like Wendy and their mother.

"Yvonne!" Wendy groans, making me chuckle.

"I'm Wade, Yvonne's twin," he says, stepping up to me and shaking my hand. He may be the youngest son, but the look he gives me is no less protective of his sister than Yorick's.

"I'm Hacker."

"Is that your real name?" Yvonne asks me.

"No, it's a codename. In our line of work, it's better if people don't know your real name. It makes it harder for them to find you."

Both Yana and Yvonne turn to Wendy. "Do *you* know his real name?"

She looks at me like she's not sure how to answer. "Uh ..."

"Sphinx is part of our Tech Team. She may not be at the Academy yet, but she's already been accepted. As a junior member of the team, she's given access to confidential information that others aren't," I say, making Wendy stand a little taller and smile proudly.

"So, what's this I hear about my son nearly running off the road on the way here?" Alpha Warren asks.

"Dad, Hacker and I found the money!" Wendy says excitedly.

He blinks at her, staring before responding. "And you didn't think that was important information for your father to have?" he asks, his voice stern and disapproving.

"It's appropriate to tell the requestor the results of our investigation before telling anyone else who may have access to that information," I say, once again jumping in to defend her.

"Already so protective of my daughter. What a nice young man," Luna Yara says softly, cutting the tension in the air. I look at Wendy again, not sure if that was intentional or not.

"Mumble," she mouths to me.

How very curious. The woman is intriguing, but she'd be terrible with classified information.

I see Alpha Warren noticeably relax as he pulls his mate into his arms and kisses the top of her head. "Shall we head inside? Apparently, I have some information that I need to hear, and I think you're going to have a busy weekend, Hacker."

"I'm prepared, sir."

"Is all of this for this weekend?" Wendy asks, turning back to the car.

"Most of it. Three of the laptops are staying here. One for each packhouse and one for you," I tell her, making her smile at me again.

Damn, my new favorite hobby is making this woman smile at me.

"Can I help?" Yana asks.

"I need to see what I'm working with first, but there's plenty of work to go around," I tell her. Wendy looks a little disappointed, but she doesn't realize yet that I mean what I'm saying. I could have used Hijack this weekend, but I wasn't willing to share my time with Wendy.

"How about you show Hacker to his room, Wendy. Then you can take him on a tour of the two packhouses before dinner. After that, Hacker, you can decide if you want to get started tonight or tomorrow."

"Thank you, Luna."

Wendy, Yana, Yvonne, and Wade all grab boxes and help me carry them up to the room where I'll be staying. They put me on the Beta floor which is good. I might struggle if I was sleeping in a room next to Wendy. Being in the same packhouse with her, spending the weekend with her is already going to test my ability to remain professional. Unless, of course, she acts like she wants more. If she does,

I'll happily show her that a Hacker's kiss isn't something that she'll ever forget.

I pull the two laptops that I intend to leave here out of the box and turn to Wendy. "Okay, I want to see everything so I can get the lay of the land, literally, but for now, why don't you show me where the security equipment is."

"And, I'm out. If you need any more help with lifting, let me know. But I'm more like Yorick, I'd rather spar than sit in front of a computer any day," Wade says.

"Yeah, me too," Yvonne says. "See you at dinner."

"See you then."

"I'd like to stay, if that's okay?" Yana asks. I can tell Wendy would rather she didn't, but I do need the extra hands. And since nothing that I'm doing is illegal, it's perfectly fine if Yana helps.

"Like I said, I could use the help. Although sometimes our work is really boring, but it has to get done to make sure everything is set up properly," I say.

"Okay, let's start with the security system," Wendy says.

She leads me back downstairs and I take the opportunity to get to know Yana. If she's interested in technology, she could end up on our team when she's older.

"How old are you, Yana?"

"Fifteen, almost sixteen," she says excitedly.

"And are you interested in tech like Wendy is?" I ask her.

"It seems really interesting. Wendy is *always* at her computer these days," she says.

"Sphinx is a sponge with information, absorbing it as fast as we give it to her," I say proudly. I'm rewarded with another huge smile.

She knocks on a closed door and when I hear Striker tell her to come in, I realize this must be the Alpha's office.

"Hey, Hacker wants to see the security system in here. Is it okay if we come in?" she asks.

"That's why he's here. Do you need us to leave?" Striker asks.

"No. You won't bother me as long as we won't bother you."

"Yana?" Alpha Warren asks.

"He said I could watch, Dad. I asked," she says defensively.

"If you have another techy in the making, I'm happy to encourage her excitement," I say, grinning at Alpha Warren.

He frowns at his daughter. "You're interested in technology? Since when?"

"Since Wendy started talking about it non-stop."

"I don't tell them anything confidential," she rushes to tell me.

"I know," I say, and I do. We've tagged her phone to alert us with keywords or phrases so we can monitor if she slips up. So far, she's been perfect.

She frowns at me, obviously wondering how I know. I lift my phone up and wave it.

I watch understanding dawn on her face. "I want to know more later," she says softly.

"Okay."

When she opens the panel to show the security system, I see right away that there's a problem.

"Uh, yeah, this isn't a security system," I say.

"What do you mean?" Striker asks. He and Cyra come over to look. "We have monitors that watch the borders."

"Yep, you do and that's all they do. You have a monitoring system, not a security system. If someone breached your borders, you wouldn't know it until your patrols alerted you or they reached your packhouse. This though ..." I say, looking at what is most definitely a security system. "This is a security system."

"For what?" Cyra asks.

"Wendy, can you go get the small toolkit in my room? It's in one of the boxes. It will have the equipment I showed you that measures power and where it comes from. You know the one?"

"Yep, I'll be right back."

"I'm guessing this is the security system for your internet protection, but we'll know for sure in a few minutes," I say, answering Cyra's question.

When Wendy returns, I hook up the device to the wires and set it to track the destination. A moment later, the computer on the desk pings.

"Bingo. It's the internet protection. We knew your father had it, that's why Hijack had to hack into his computer. He was smart enough to know that he needed to hide information from others."

"That is *fire*!" Yana says, excitedly.

"I'm more than just a pretty face," I say, making her giggle.

Since Wendy obviously doesn't like me giving her sister attention, I put her to work testing the other lines just to make sure I'm right about them going nowhere. While she does that, I set up the computer that I will leave in this packhouse.

"Okay, Yana, you're up," I say once the computer is ready and Wendy is done confirming that the other lines have no security protocol.

"What do you need?" she asks excitedly.

"I need you to watch these lines as they connect. Periodically, the system will ask you if you want to continue. Always say yes. As the security system starts activating, these lines will go from red to green. If any of them turn yellow, we'll have to fix them. I'm going to take Wendy to the other packhouse and get this started over there. When I come back, I'll need to know how many are yellow and how many stayed red."

"You got it!"

I smile at her, then grab my tools and the other computer.

"Let's go straight to the other packhouse. We can do the pack tour tomorrow. If that security system is as bad as this one, it's going to take a while to get things started and we can let the system drone through it overnight," I say to Wendy.

We walk outside to an SUV similar to the one we drove in to get here. Wendy hops in the driver's seat and I get into the passenger seat. Once she turns on the car, I turn to her.

"Finally, I get you all to myself," I purr.

I hear her soft gasp as her cheeks begin to turn a lovely shade of pink.

Chapter 31: Alpha Ramin

Cyra

After Hacker and Wendy leave to go to the other pack to set up the security system, since we apparently don't have one at all, Yorick and I sit back down with Warren.

"That was smart to get him out here so quickly," he says, still frowning at his daughter who is happily watching the screen in front of her and periodically clicking keys and quietly cheering to herself.

"Let it go, Dad. Just because they didn't end up working in a hospital like Kennedy, it doesn't mean that my sisters aren't more like mom than you. They're just finding a different mental path to follow."

"I guess so," he says, still frowning. He shakes his head and refocuses on us. "So, tell me about this money."

We lay it out for him, just like Hacker told us.

He whistles low and sits back in his chair. "I can understand why you nearly ran off the road. What are you going to do?"

"Well, I have family that I didn't even know about until today. I want to call them. I don't even know where their pack is. I'd like to make contact and see if I can meet the and maybe develop a relationship with them. I mean the money is great, but we already had a plan with Quirin, so that's icing on the cake. What I'd really like is to get to know my mother's family and hopefully learn more about her. I have no idea how old my cousin is, but I'd think he'd have to be close to my age. Geez, I don't even know if my Uncle Ramin is older or younger than my mother was. But they're family and thanks to all of you, I know how important that is."

I reach out and take Yorick's hand, squeezing it. He pulls my hand to his lips, kissing my knuckles while holding my gaze and sending waves of love through our bond.

Damn I love this man.

"Let me look up the contact information for Alpha Ramin," Warren says.

"Hacker gave it to us. He talked to him earlier this week."

We hear Yana squeal behind us and softly clap her hands. I grin looking at her.

"Sorry, they're going green. This is so exciting!"

I look back to see Warren frowning at his daughter.

"Why don't we go find another room to call my uncle," I suggest to Yorick, just as Luna Yara knocks and enters the room.

I watch Warren turn to look at her, the frown replaced by a loving smile. When I look at Luna Yara, I realize she must be feeling her mate's disgruntlement at not knowing about his daughter's new interest.

As Yorick and I stand, she comes to sit in her mate's lap, wrapping her arms around his neck.

"You can't know everything, my love," she says as we walk out.

I hear him grumble something I can't hear as we step out of the room.

"Are you nervous?" Yorick asks. I know he can feel my nerves. I have no idea what to expect from my uncle. Does he even know about me?

"I didn't know my mother at all, so I have no idea what to expect from my uncle. He could be like your father, or he could be like mine, or somewhere in between."

"No matter what he's like, we're fine. I love you. You're mine. We have a beautiful life ahead of us and if they want to be a part of that life, great. If they don't, their loss," he says.

I pull my mate into a hug, loving how supportive he is of me every minute of the day. I take a deep breath of his scent, letting his strong arms give me strength.

He kisses my neck as I pull away, but takes my hand in his, keeping a physical and mental connection to me as we sit at the desk in Beta Lewis' office.

"After this call, do you want to head over to the other side and get settled for the night? I'd like to talk to Beta Eric before we go to bed, make sure all is well and check in with Hacker and Wendy too," I say.

"Sounds good. I'm with you, Cyra. Always," he says.

Did I mention how much I love this man?

I take a deep breath and dial the number Hacker gave me, putting it on speakerphone.

"Alpha Ramin," a deep voice answers.

"Alpha Ramin, my name is Cyra Teymoori. Do you know who I am?"

I hear a chair creak, like my uncle is sitting back in his seat.

"Well, that didn't take long, did it?"

I frown. "I'm sorry? What didn't take long?"

"You're calling about the money, right? You had your private investigator search for the money. He found it a couple of days ago and here you are, calling to get it."

I feel Yorick tense beside me.

"I didn't know anything about you, my cousin, or any money until today."

"Wow, less than a day and you're already calling to get it. Your father raised you well," he growls.

"What is that supposed to mean?"

"Your father is a money-grubbing asshole, and I see he raised you to be the same." His tone is practically a snarl.

"You don't know me at all," I say softly.

"Right. Well, there are stipulations on that money. You can't access it until you're marked and mated."

"My mate and I marked each other a week ago," I say, feeling disappointment wash over me. I was so hoping that he'd be like Yorick's family and not mine.

He laughs, but there's no humor in it.

"One week. Wow, I see Arden really did train you well," he says contemptuously.

Yorick begins growling beside me, but I've had enough. This asshole of a man doesn't even know me. He's decided that I'm just like my father without even getting to know me which makes him no better than my father in my book.

"I will have you know that my father is in jail for embezzling money, money that he tried to repay by selling me off in an alliance bond with a neighboring pack. He did it when I was seventeen and didn't care about me finding my fated mate."

"So, you need the money to pay off his debts. Sounds about right," he says, obviously not caring that my father used me to pay off his debts.

I'm about to speak, but my mate beats me to it.

"Alpha Ramin, my name is Alpha Yorick. Are you familiar with the name Alpha Quirin?"

"Everyone is familiar with Alpha Quirin. If they didn't know the name before, they certainly do after his recent, violent takeover of another Alpha's pack. I don't see how that has anything to do with this," he says.

"Alpha Quirin is my brother-in-law, mated to my sister. He used his own money to pay off that debt and get my mate out of that alliance bond. He has also come up with a plan for us to pay him back for that loan within eight years. So, we don't need your fucking money, and you can go to hell," he snarls, ending the call.

I stare at the phone while Yorick pants angrily beside me.

"Well, that didn't go like I hoped it would," I say softly. I guess my entire family is a bunch of assholes. Alpha Ramin probably paid my father so he could get rid of my mother.

Yorick stands and pulls me into a hug. "This changes nothing. I know it's disappointing, but we already had a plan to repay the money. We already had a plan to live a beautiful life together. That doesn't change."

I nod. "I guess I hadn't realized just how much I wanted to have at least some family that was decent."

"You do. You have a great family. They just aren't blood relatives."

I let him hold me, breathing in his scent and breathing out my disappointment until I feel ready to face our next challenge.

"Alright, let's get to the other side. We have work to do," I say.

He leans back, not releasing me from the hug. He cups my cheek and leans in to kiss me, gently, lovingly, taking his time and reminding me that I'm not alone.

Chapter 32: Alpha Arman

C yra

When we finally leave the office, I feel stronger. So, when Warren asks us how it went, I don't break down. Instead, I lift my chin and tell him that my mother's brother is exactly like my father, and we won't be creating any type of relationship with my mother's family.

Warren looks at me a moment, then pulls me into a hug.

"I'm sorry. I know that must be very disappointing for you."

"It is. But I'm not going to let it ruin my life. They haven't been a part of my life up until now, so really, nothing changes."

"You're heading over to the other side?"

"Yes. Anything we need to know?" I ask him.

"Things feel more settled over there now. Demoting Hugo caused a bit of a stir, but I think the pack realized very quickly that he wasn't doing anything. Having Gamma Elliot over there has shown them how much they were missing by having a lazy Gamma. Oh, and Yana wants you to let Wendy and Hacker know that they have some yellow lines over here."

"Will do."

When we get to the other side, we check in with Wendy and Hacker, letting them know that some lines on the other side are yellow.

"We have that over here too," Hacker says distractedly. From what I can tell, he and Wendy work very well together. He's saying things that make no sense to me, but she seems to understand what he's saying and does whatever he's asking.

We leave them to it, then go to meet with Beta Eric. He's great. He is very organized and with Gamma Elliot's assistance, he's been able to stabilize the pack.

We have dinner with the pack and since Hacker and Wendy are still working over here, I have food sent to the Alpha office where the security system is. Yorick and I spend the evening with the pack members, getting to know them better and nurturing the relationships with them that we need in order to create a loyal and happy pack.

It's late when we finally get to bed. Tonight, Yorick takes his time, as if he's showing me again that no matter what, our life with be beautiful together. As always, time with my mate heals all wounds; emotional, mental, and physical.

In the morning, we join the pack for joint sparring training. Here I get my first look at what Warren is doing to bring the packs together. Partners are set up so that they spar with someone from the other side, and I realize that Warren has been assigning partners so that every day, they spar with someone new. It's obvious that this is building relationships within our joined pack very quickly.

When warrior training is over, people linger, talking to each other, but eventually, they head back to their respective packhouses for breakfast.

Yorick and I let Warren know that we'll be by later to start going over pack business, then we return to the side we're staying on.

"Let's do breakfast in the central area tomorrow," I say to Yorick. "It seems like everyone wants to continue talking and being together, but they are hungry and eventually that's what draws them away. What do you think?"

"I think that's a fantastic idea," he says.

When we return, I let the omegas over here know what I want to do, and rather than meeting with the omegas on the other side, I have the Lead Omega here contact the Lead Omega on the other side to plan a joint meal. Our omegas need to become unified as well as our warriors.

We've just about finished with breakfast when Yorick and I get a mind link from Warren.

'Alpha Ramin and Alpha Arman just arrived at the guard gate on this side. They are requesting to see you, Cyra.'

'What do they want?' I ask as Yorick growls.

'I don't know. Do you want me to send them away?'

I look at Yorick. "Let's go see what they want."

"I'm with you," he says, but he's still growling at their audacity.

'Tell them they will have to wait until we get to them. I don't want them on our pack lands.'

'Will do. Do you want me to send warriors?'

'Did they bring any with them?' Yorick asks.

'Only a handful. It doesn't seem like this is an attack of any sort. But that doesn't mean they don't have warriors hiding outside the pack lands.'

'Send some warriors to keep them contained. We'll run so we can get there faster,' I say.

Yorick and I say goodbye to Eric and Elliot, then step outside before stripping and shifting.

'If they think that they can come here and intimidate us, they will find out just how wrong they are,' Rina growls, ready for a fight.

When we get close, I stop and shift, unwilling to approach my uncle and cousin naked. I get dressed, then reach out my hand to Yorick. We approach the guard gate hand-in-hand.

A man in his early twenties is leaning against an SUV similar to the ones we have in our pack. When he sees us, he pushes off the car and knocks on the window. The door opens and a man who looks like an older version of the first steps out.

"Luna Cyra, I'm ..."

"It's Alpha Cyra," I snap, cutting him off. "My mate and I are co-Alphas of our pack."

I watch the surprise flicker across his face before being replaced with admiration. He glances at Yorick, then back at me.

"Alpha Cyra, I am your cousin, Alpha Arman. This is my father, Alpha Ramin. I understand the two of you had a ... discordant conversation yesterday."

"Discordant? Yeah, I guess you could call it that."

"My father and I are not in agreement with how he handled your call yesterday. We've come to apologize and make amends."

"Really," I say, turning my focus to Alpha Ramin. "Let me guess. You heard we're related to Alpha Quirin and suddenly you're concerned that your actions may have caused us rally our family to decimate your son's pack. Is that why you're here?" I snarl.

Alpha Arman opens his mouth, but I hold up my hand silencing him as my eyes remain on Alpha Ramin.

"Well, I am nothing like my father. So you can take your Merry Menagerie and get the fuck off my pack lands."

He steps forward, but Yorick's warning growl makes him stop.

"Alpha Cyra, I really did come to make amends," Alpha Ramin says.

"It doesn't feel good when people make assumptions about your intentions without listening to you, does it, Alpha?" I snap.

"No, it doesn't," he says, watching me. A slow smile spreads across his face. "You not only look like your mother, you have her fire too."

"I wouldn't know. I never had a chance to get to know my mother."

"Alpha Cyra, please. My father and yours have a lot of bad blood between them. That tainted his conversation with you yesterday, but we really are here to make amends. And whether or not you accept this olive branch, the inheritance is yours."

"I don't want your money," I growl.

"It's not our money. It's yours by birthright. Please Alpha, just give us a chance," Alpha Arman says.

I look at Yorick.

'It's up to you, Cyra. They're your family,' he says in the mind link.

'Rina? Thad?' I ask our wolves.

'Our cousin is sincere,' she says.

'I'm not sure I trust the uncle, but as my mate said, the cousin seems genuine,' Thad says.

I look back at the two men. "The packhouse is that way. We'll let Alpha Warren, Yorick's father, know that you're coming, and we'll meet you there."

"May we walk with you while our warriors pull the cars up to the packhouse?" Alpha Arman asks.

I look between the two men, then nod.

Alpha Arman extends his hand. "Alpha Cyra, it's nice to finally meet you. I've heard about you over the years."

I shake his hand. "Alpha Arman, it's nice to meet you. I had no idea you existed until yesterday. My father told me I had no family."

"Hopefully we can begin to rectify your lack of knowledge about our family while we're here. I'm sure you have some, but my father and I brought some pictures of your mother."

"I only have one picture of my mother. It's of her holding me on the day I was born," I tell him as we begin
walking.

I see the men exchange glances and Alpha Ramin's lips
press into a tight line.

"Then I'm glad that we brought the pictures with us,"
Arman says.

As we walk, Yorick deliberately switches sides with me,
putting himself between me and my uncle and cousin. It's
a very clear message. While we may be allowing them onto
our pack lands, we don't trust them.

Chapter 33:
Breakthrough

Hacker

I spent a very enjoyable evening with Wendy last night. We worked hard and she's an amazing assistant. She never once complained, and she seemed to enjoy working with me as much as I enjoyed working with her.

I tested the waters a bit while we were working, just to see if she is open to something developing between us. Every chance I got, I'd touch her. It might have been a casual touch of my hand against hers, putting my hand on her back as I moved around her, or leaning closer to her when she was showing me something. But every time, every single time I touched her or got close to her, her heartbeat would increase, and her breath would hitch.

By the time I called it quits for the night, her cheeks had a permanent pink hue, and her sweet scent of caramel apples was driving me insane.

Hijack called last night, wanting to get together this weekend to go over a project we're working on together. Since I know he can find me anyway and probably already has, I told him that I was in Cyra's and Striker's pack working on their security system.

He was quiet for a beat. "Isn't Sphinx in Striker's pack this weekend?"

"Yes. She's helping me assess the security, or lack of security as it turns out," I say.

"I see. I'm surprised you didn't ask for my help. It seems like a big project."

"I have Sphinx, and her little sister Yana is a techy in the making. We should keep our eye on her."

"Mmhmm. Well, let me know if you need anything."

"Will do."

I hung up knowing I wouldn't call him even if I do need help. This opportunity to spend face-to-face alone time with Wendy is priceless.

I wanted to spar with Wendy this morning, but as expected, her father pulled her aside to spar with her. I'm not surprised. Her family is very protective of her. They're very protective of each other. I respect that. If anything or anyone came after my family, I'd destroy them.

But while I respect his intentions, I think his methods are keeping his daughter from making progress. They're afraid of hurting her, so they don't push her. I'm not afraid of hurting her. She's stronger than she realizes and that's where she needs to push past her own fear. She needs to regain the confidence she lost in herself when she nearly died.

Over breakfast, I tell Wendy and Yana about my plans for the day. "I need to see the pack lands, all of them, so we can decide where to lay cable. We need to connect the two packs' security systems and that's the way to do it."

Just before we finish eating, Alpha Warren growls out loud. Everyone goes quiet and we wait until his eyes refocus.

"Dad?" Wendy asks.

"Cyra's uncle and cousin are here."

I wasn't privy to what happened, I just know the conversation between them yesterday wasn't good.

We wait while he informs Cyra and Striker that they're here.

"Are you sending them away?" Wade asks.

"No, Cyra wants to meet with them and see what they want," he says.

"Do you want to stay and make sure everything is okay?" I ask Wendy and Yana.

"I do. I want to meet the asshat who thought it was okay to be a total douchebag to my sister-in-law," Yana says. She was here when the call occurred, so she heard more about what happened than Wendy and I did.

"I'll take you around," Wendy says. I can feel her body vibrating with excitement that it will just be the two of us again. I'd already planned to make that happen. The training field is in between the packs and it's a perfect place for me to get her to spar without anyone else watching. Now, I won't need to keep Yana busy elsewhere.

"I'll catch up to the two of you later," she says.

"Yep, have fun intimidating the asshat," I say, chuckling as Wendy and I walk out.

We do a tour of the packhouse, and I point out where we can connect the cables. I may be interested in spending time with Wendy, but this is a job, and I take that seriously. I have a reputation to maintain and my job with the Council is dependent on me continuing to deliver what I promise and remaining truthful and ethical in my work.

As we begin walking toward the second packhouse, I see SUVs driving up to the packhouse.

"I guess Striker and Cyra are allowing them onto their pack lands," I say.

"That's a bit surprising based on what I heard yesterday," Wendy says.

I make notes on my tablet about where on the property I want to lay the cable as we walk. But when we get to the training field, I stop, setting it aside.

"Okay, time for some sparring."

"Really Jude? Do we have to?" she asks me. I love that she uses my real name when we're like this. She's careful about using my codename in front of others, but alone, she uses my birthname.

"Yes really, Wendy, we have to."

She huffs, but I ignore her. More than anyone outside of her family, I know how much she struggles with this.

I get into a defensive stance. "Show me what you've got, Sphinx."

She sighs again, then takes an offensive stance and comes at me. I can tell she's testing me, seeing how strong I am, but she doesn't have to worry. I may be a tech guy, but the Academy still trains us to be in the field so that on the occasion we do have to go out, we can defend ourselves and we don't become a liability to the squads.

I let her adjust to my fighting strength and when she really starts coming at me, I start pushing back. This is where she freezes on the sparring field. It's that first or second hit that puts her back into that trauma mode.

I tag her once, spinning around, ready for her to stop. She impresses me by coming right back for me. This time, I tag her a little bit harder and that's when she steps back.

"I can't," she says.

"Yes, you can," I tell her.

She shakes her head, and I can see the memories coming back, the fear filling her eyes.

"You're going to get hurt if you don't fight back, Wendy," I say to her.

"I can't," she whispers.

"Yes, you can. Get ready," I growl. This is where her family backs off. This is where I'm going to push her forward.

She doesn't move. I go at her anyway, pulling my punch so I don't hurt her too badly, but hitting hard enough to make it impactful.

"Ow! That hurt!" she growls.

"Then you'd better fight back," I say, getting back into an offensive position.

"You don't understand!" she yells.

I come at her again, tagging her a little harder this time.

"What don't I understand?" I ask. I can see she's getting angry. Good, anger burns off fear.

"You don't know what it was like!"

"You're right, I don't. What I do know is that if you make it to the Academy and you go out on a job with one of the squads, you're a liability, and I can't allow that on my team," I say, swinging my leg at her head.

I have enough control that my foot connects but doesn't push through. I stand with my leg against her face until she pushes it away.

"Stop it!" she snarls.

"Make me," I growl back. This time I don't get into a stance, I just swing my leg out and knock her off her feet. She lands hard, but she's up again in an instant.

"I said stop it!" she snarls, leaping at me.

She comes hard and fast, the adrenaline of the pain of my hits and her fall coupled with the emotional hurt that I'm pushing her, is making her strong and very fast. It takes all my training to block and parry with her. She still gets in her shots, some that will sting for a couple of hours, but in the end, I finally get her pinned to the ground, her arms over her head, my body covering hers.

Both of us are panting with the effort of our sparring.

"THAT'S the Sphinx I was looking for. I knew you had it in you. You just needed someone to push you," I say. Her eyes are still blazing with her anger, her chest is pressing against mine as both of us gasp for air.

As I watch her, something shifts in the air around us. The angry fire in her eyes is replaced with the fire of desire.

Chapter 34: Surprise Guest

Hacker

Slowly, very slowly so she can tell me to stop at any time, I lean forward before pressing my lips to hers. I realize instantly that she's inexperienced, so I gently guide her, slowly showing her how to kiss me back. When I slide my tongue across her lips, she gasps and I slide my tongue into her mouth. I growl against her lips as I get my first taste of her caramel apple scent.

I release her arms and her hands slide into my hair. I slide one hand into her silky brown hair and the other up her side, taking my time as I tease her tongue with mine. She moans softly against my mouth and I growl again, feeling even more possessive of my little Sphinx than I did before.

I take my time, exploring her mouth and her taste while letting her get used to my kiss.

When I finally pull away, her eyes are glassy, and her lips are puffy.

"Did you like that?" I ask softly.

She nods. "That was my first kiss," she whispers, as if it's a secret.

I run my thumb over her bottom lip. "I hope it was everything you'd dreamed it would be," I say.

She smiles shyly. "It was."

I growl again. "Let's see if your second kiss is everything you dreamed it would be," I say, lowering my lips back to hers. This time, I'm a bit more demanding, a bit more possessive in the kiss. When she begins whimpering, her hips pressing up against me, I know that she's enjoying the kiss as much as I am.

This time when I lift my head, I smile at my beautiful Sphinx. "You taste so sweet," I murmur, kissing her chin.

"Do I get a third kiss?" she asks. She smiles mischievously, but her voice is still timid.

"Do you want one?" I ask her.

She nods again.

"You're going to have to earn it," I tell her.

She frowns. "How?"

I hop up, putting my hands out to take hers. "Fight me. Pin me. And take what you want," I say as I help her up.

"You want me to fight you in order to kiss you?" she asks slowly as if my request makes no sense.

"That's exactly what I want," I say, stepping away from her. "How badly do you want another kiss?"

She debates long enough that I think I might have pushed her a bit too hard, but then she takes an offensive stance.

"That's my girl," I growl proudly.

She comes at me hard again, and I test her by sending punches hard enough to sting. When she starts to get in her head, I don't back down.

"Stay with me, Sphinx. You can do this. Eye on the prize," I say, licking my lips. Her eyes track to my mouth, and the fear is replaced with determination. Before long, she has me pinned underneath her, her body straddling mine, my arms pinned over my head. I might have let her win, but honestly, this is a win-win for me.

As she leans over me, I grin up at her.

"Are you going to take your prize, my little Sphinx?"

She lowers herself to me and tentatively presses her lips to mine. I let her take the lead. Eventually, she releases my hands and slides her hands down my arms and into my hair.

I slide my hands up her thighs and her hips, stilling them when she begins grinding against me.

"Look, my little temptress, I only have so much restraint. I liked you before I got a taste of your sweetness. But now, I'm practically desperate for more. We should be careful. I wouldn't want your first time to feel rushed. If we ever get to a point where we take things further, it will be when we have time and there is no risk of getting caught because if that day ever arrives, I will ruin you for any other man," I vow.

She bites her lower lips, making me growl.

"Stop. Tempting. Me." I sit up, so she's seated in my lap.

"We need to get moving. I don't want your father and brother sending the calvary after us because we took too long to get to the next pack."

"I could show them that you helped me get past my issues," she says.

I take her face in my hands and press another kiss to her lips. "I'm glad I was able to, but you'll have to keep practicing. Moving past what you went through isn't a one and done."

I reach up and pull some pieces of grass and twigs out of her hair.

"Your hair is like silk," I murmur, running my fingers through it.

"So is yours," she says, starting to pull pieces of the earth out of my hair too.

"I like the way it feels when you're running your fingers through it," I say.

"Like this?" she asks, sliding her hands into my hair and making my body shiver at her touch.

"Just like that. And you? Do you like it when I run my fingers through your hair?" I ask, sliding my hand through her silky locks.

"It feels really good," she breathes.

I allow myself a couple more minutes to enjoy just being with her. Then I kiss her once more before putting her on her feet.

"Come on, let's go," I say, taking her hand.

I steal several more kisses as we walk, not dropping our clasped hands. When we get to the other packhouse, she pauses.

"I'm not sure it's a good idea that my family finds out about what happened today," she says.

"I understand, but if things between us progress, I won't be okay keeping it a secret, Wendy," I tell her.

"Okay. But for now, can we?"

"For now, yes," I say, dropping her hand.

She shows me around and I make notes of where we need to lay the cable. Since it's close to lunch time, we stay and eat lunch on this side of the pack.

As we're eating, Wendy's eyes go unfocused and when she refocuses on me, she smiles.

"Dad was wondering where we were."

"Good thing we're in a good spot," I say grinning.

After lunch, we make our way back to the other side. I take several opportunities to pull her under a tree or just into my arms and kiss her again. We walk hand in hand until we get close to the packhouse again, and then we separate.

"Maybe tomorrow we can practice sparring again?" she asks, biting that delicious lip and making me groan.

"I definitely think we should," I say, laughing as we walk out of the forest line.

I smell him before I see him, my head whipping around.

"Hijack, what are you doing here?" I ask. This was supposed to be *my* weekend with Wendy.

"I figured you could use an extra hand. Yana and I were just about to come looking for you," he says, watching Wendy closely. I stifle the growl that tries to erupt from my wolf, Saggio. I already know Hijack is interested in Wendy. If he knows I am too, that I'm staking a claim on her, it will just encourage the Alpha in him to compete.

"We were just coming to get the cable and start laying it out. Do Striker and Cyra know you're here?"

"Alpha Warren knows I'm here."

"So, Yana, does this mean that everything got sorted out with Alpha Cyra and her family?" I ask her.

She shrugs. "I don't know. They've been locked in a meeting room all day. If I'd have known that, I'd have come with you. Can I still help?"

"The hard work is about to begin," I say, handing the tablet to Hijack to let him see where I intend to lay the cable.

"Did you get everything running in the two packhouses?" he asks, handing it back.

"The other one, yes. This one no. For all his protection of his internet, Alpha Arden had absolutely nothing in the way of security for his pack. I'm having to reconnect the lines, sometimes in multiple areas," I tell him.

"Do you want to see? I can show you. That's what I was working on yesterday," Yana says excitedly.

"Are you good with me working on this end?" Hijack asks me.

"Sure. It will have to be done before we connect the two packs anyway," I say.

"I can set it up to connect on this side while I work on reconnecting the lines," he says.

"That would be great."

"Can I watch? I promise I won't get in the way," Yana asks excitedly.

Hijack looks at her. "Hacker said you were interested in technology."

"I am."

He smiles at her. "Come on, then. Show me where everything is housed."

We follow them inside, since I need to get the cables out of my room.

"We'll see you at dinner," I say, as we veer off toward the stairs.

Wendy follows me to my room. As soon as she's inside, I close the door and press her against the wall.

"I'm glad I don't have to share you yet," I growl, before taking her mouth in our most possessive kiss yet.

Chapter 35: Soraya

Cyra

When we arrived back at the packhouse, Warren was waiting for us. He wasn't the only one. Yana stood on one side of her father with Wade and Yvonne standing on the other. It felt like the Hill family showed up to prove a point. 'She doesn't need you, she has us.'

I feel warmth spread through my chest at their silent pronouncement of love and acceptance of me. They're right. I don't need anyone else when I have them.

Warren comes down the steps, he nods at Arman, but his gaze remains fixed on Ramin. He's making a point that no one hurts his family and Ramin hurt me.

"I'm Alpha Warren Hill, Cyra's father-in-law."

Not Yorick's father. MY father-in-law.

"Alpha Warren, I'm Alpha Ramin," my uncle says.

"Yes. So, I gathered."

There's a tense moment of silence as Warren continues to stare my uncle down in some sort of Alpha display of aggression.

"Alpha Warren, I am Alpha Arman, Alpha Cyra's cousin. As we mentioned to Alpha Cyra, my father and I are here to make amends and to speak to Alpha Cyra."

"Apparently one of you has some good sense, then," Warren says. It's an obvious insult to Alpha Ramin and a threat. He won't tolerate him hurting me again.

My uncle growls at the threat, but Warren just continues to stare him down. Arman, however, gives his father a warning growl of his own, quieting my uncle.

"My father was wrong in how he treated my cousin. As I mentioned to Alpha Cyra, my father and hers have a lot of bad blood. But we are here to make amends."

Finally, Warren looks at Arman. "Cyra is my family, and I take family very seriously. You would be wise to tread lightly."

"Understood."

He turns to look at me. "Where did you want to meet?" he asks.

I've seen Warren do this with his family, go from an angry discussion with one person, then turning his warmth onto one of his family members, flipping like a light switch. It's what he does with me now and my love for my father-in-law and the entire Hill family grows even stronger. It's a wonderful and powerful feeling being engulfed in a family's love. It's something I've never had before, but now I'd never want to live without it.

"I thought we'd meet in the conference room," I say.

He nods. "This way," he says, turning to walk inside. Without any discussion on their part, the Hill children surround me. Yorick is already between me and my cousin, but Wade takes point in front of me with Yana on my left and Yvonne falling in behind me.

The physical show of protection by their entire family does not go unnoticed by my uncle and cousin.

We're quiet as we walk inside, the pack watching as we basically parade through the packhouse to the conference room. When we reach it, Warren opens the door and gestures for my uncle and cousin to step inside ahead of him. He makes eye contact with me, nodding as I pass him and Yorick follows behind me. The Hill children don't come in, but Warren does.

'I can leave if you'd rather have some privacy,' he says in the mind link.

'No. You're family. You're our interim Alpha. You should be here,' I tell him.

He nods, obviously relieved, like he's worried I'll need him here to protect me. The love I feel from all of them settles me and when I sit down across from my uncle and cousin flanked on either side by my mate and his father, I'm ready to face whatever they've come to discuss.

Arman leans forward, his hands clasped on the table in front of him.

"I think it would be helpful if we start with my father telling you why he and your father have such animosity between them. I think it will help you better understand why my father expressed so much anger when you called."

"Alright," I say, turning my attention to Ramin. Arman sits back, letting his father take the lead.

Ramin sighs heavily, then scrubs his hands over his face before sitting forward.

"My sister was beautiful, just like you. She was the pack's darling, but she never let that stop her from becoming a strong and powerful warrior. If anything, the pack adored her more because she didn't expect their admiration, she earned it. She was so good, she earned a spot at the Warrior Academy. You know the one I'm speaking of?" he asks.

"I'm assuming it's the same one that Yorick and I are attending," I say, keeping my tone neutral. I didn't know my mother had gone to the Academy.

Both Ramin and Arman look surprised that we're at the Academy. Then Ramin looks down, shaking his head. "You are very much like Soraya."

He sighs again before looking back up at me. "That's where she met your father, at the Academy. They weren't fated mates, but they became close very quickly."

"That happens at the Academy," Yorick says, thinking of Zach and Piper I'm sure.

"A small group of young Alphas and strong warriors, living together and taking classes together, I'm not surprised. What did surprise me was her coming home one weekend to tell me that she and Arden had decided to become chosen mates. No amount of arguing could talk her out of it."

"Wait, I thought they were in an alliance bond," I say. That's what my father always told me.

Ramin laughs. It's an ugly, angry laugh. "As if I would have ever allied myself with a man like him. The moment their bond was sealed, he began asking for money. I don't know what he did to make Soraya think that he loved her, but all he really wanted was money. Did you know that he got kicked out of the Academy?"

"We found out recently, yes. I never knew he went to the Academy before that," I say. "I didn't know either of them did."

"That was a big blight on his record and his ego, and it was probably the first time Soraya saw through the façade to the real person he was. He came asking for money again, this time for legal fees. He threatened to drag my sister down with him if I didn't pay."

He clenches his jaw. "She was my sister. What was I supposed to do? She had earned her right to go to the Academy. She didn't deserve to be dragged into his nefarious activities. So, I paid for the best attorneys and got him off. He didn't get back into the Academy and Soraya dropped out to return to his pack. That day in court was the last time I saw her," he says, his voice becoming ragged.

I wait while he collects himself. Arman puts a hand on his shoulder, helping his father to steady himself.

"After that, Arden said I had to pay to see my sister. She had no reason to see me, and I had no reason to see her unless he got something out of it," he growls. My stomach clenches. Apparently, my father has always been the way he is. I was just another pawn, a way for him to make money. Goddess, I should be glad he didn't try to sell me off to the highest bidder. He might have if he hadn't been caught embezzling.

"I was angry, furious that he would try to keep me from my sister. I was ready to attack his pack and get her back, but she somehow was able to get a hold of me, and she begged me to stop. She was already pregnant with you, and she didn't want the stress of what was going on between me and Arden to impact her pregnancy. I heard through others that Arden wasn't happy that you were a girl and he got Soraya pregnant again right away. I'm pretty sure that's why she died in childbirth. He should have given her at least a month for her body to heal before getting her pregnant again, but he didn't. She died five months after you were born, their son stillborn. That's what I got from the medical team I paid to give me information about her death. Arden never even called me to tell me she was gone. I never got to say goodbye," he says, his voice ragged as his head drops into his hands.

I sit back, squeezing Yorick's hand under the table as Arman sits forward. "Now you see why there was bad blood between our fathers. And you see why my father, while wrong, jumped to the wrong conclusion about why you were calling yesterday. I hope now, after hearing this story, we can start over. Aunt Soraya was my father's only sibling. I have no other cousins. I, myself, only have one sister. I don't have a lot of family, so it's important for me to get to know the family I do have," Arman says.

'They seem sincere,' I say, opening the mind link to Yorick and Warren.

'I agree,' they say at once.

'Why don't we have lunch in here and we can get to know each other further,' I say.

'I'll go order some food. I need to check on Hacker and Wendy anyway,' Warren says.

I look at my uncle and cousin.

"Would you like to stay for lunch? Maybe we can start to get to know each other better," I say.

Arman smiles his first smile.

"We would love that, wouldn't we Dad?" he says, looking at his father.

Ramin looks at me. "I have let hatred eat at me for nearly two decades. Perhaps it's time to set that aside and get to know Soraya's daughter."

"I'll go order lunch," Warren says, standing up and walking out.

When he steps out, Arman grins at me. "So, you're related to Alpha Quirin through your mate bond. What's that like?"

Chapter 36: Questions and Answers

Yorick

"Before we get to our brother-in-law, I have a question," I say, jumping in before we go down the Quirin rabbit hole. I've been quiet, letting Ramin have his say. I can agree that Cyra's father was a total piece of shit, and I know that if Quirin or anyone ever tried to keep me and our family away from my sisters, it would not go well. So, I can understand his anger and concern that Arden raised Cyra to be just like him. Little does he know that Cyra was just another pawn in Arden's sick and twisted game of life.

"How is Arden's last name Teymoori if yours is Teymoori?" I ask.

Alpha Ramin snorts. "He must have taken our name rather than keeping his own because our name is powerful. The name Castor means nothing. I'm not surprised he took our name."

"How would Alpha Christer and Alpha Stellan have known about my inheritance if I didn't?" Cyra asks them.

"I have no idea. Maybe it was part of the negotiations to get their agreement in the alliance bond," Alpha Ramin says thoughtfully.

"Or maybe, they know the attorney who put the legal documents together. You had to go outside the pack for that, didn't you, Dad?" Arman asks.

"I did. I guess that's another possibility. I'll have to go back and research who the attorney was and which pack he belonged to. It's been nearly twenty years. Soraya decided to give her inheritance to her children when she realized that Arden was possibly going to jail for illegal activities. That day in court, she approached me about moving it over and putting it in her children's names. At the time, I didn't know she was pregnant with you. But the timing fits," Ramin says.

"Why do you think she didn't leave my father?" Cyra asks.

Ramin looks at her with the first softness I've seen since he arrived. "She wouldn't have wanted to risk you. Rejecting him at that time would have made her weak. She wouldn't have risked miscarrying by rejecting him. Maybe he knew that and it's why he got her pregnant again right away. You said he's going to trial for embezzlement?"

"Well, that and basically selling me into an alliance agreement. Stellan is going to trial for the alliance agreement, knowing about my father's embezzlement and not reporting it to the Council, and now he's also been included in the investigation of tampering with birth control," Cyra says.

"Birth control?" Arman asks as dad walks back in with food.

But Ramin figured it out.

"He wanted the other twenty-five million, didn't he?" he asks Cyra.

"I think so. When he came to try and force his mark on me, he said he was going to put a pup in me before he was done," she says, making me growl. She smiles at me, squeezing my hand. "I was on birth control and didn't realize that it was a placebo. It has caused a lot of problems in our pack with older she-wolves becoming pregnant when they thought they were on birth control."

"Thankfully we were alerted to his plan, and we had the Council and the leader of the Alpha Squad on site to deal with him when he arrived," I say.

"Not to mention the retired leader of the Alpha Squad who is now one of our instructors," Cyra says, still watching me.

I pull her hand to my mouth, holding her gaze while I kiss the back of her hand.

Someone, Arman maybe, clears his throat. Obviously, he's not used to the level of affection that my family and I show our mates.

"So, are you pregnant?" he asks.

"We have to check again this weekend. I wasn't when we checked last weekend, but there's a concern that if I wasn't on active birth control when Yorick and I marked and mated, that I could be. If my test is negative again this weekend, Luna Yara wants to check one more time. If the test is still negative after that, I can go back on birth control safely," she tells them.

"You'll let us know, I hope. Not just because you'll get the rest of your inheritance once you're pregnant, but we'd also like to know how you're doing, cousin," Arman says.

"I'd also like to hear the story of how you became co-Alphas," Ramin says as we begin to eat.

"Cyra defeated her father in a battle for the pack," I say proudly.

"Now THAT is a story I want to hear," Ramin says. He's relaxing more and more the longer we talk.

I let Cyra tell the story of what we learned, how we got our friends at the Academy to figure it out, how she challenged her father while Quirin was killing Christer, how Quirin and Kennedy gave us Christer's pack as part of repaying the loan and how they gifted us the land in between.

"So you see, we have a lot going on. Warren has agreed to be the interim Alpha while I continue at the Academy, and he teaches me how to be a leader of a pack since Dad never raised me that way. At the end of this school year, I will hopefully be prepared to take over and run this pack while Yorick takes his place on the Council's C-Squad and runs the pack with me," Cyra tells them.

As she's been talking, they've stopped eating, their eyes have gotten wider, and now they're both sitting back, staring as if they can't believe everything we've been through. When you lay it out like that, it is a lot.

"Oh, that reminds me. I talked to Connor. He said he'll have his warriors build a house for me and Yara here, but he said that's a gift to us, not you. So, he's planning to have his warriors build you a centralized packhouse as his gift to you. He's going to have some plans drawn up this week and he'll send them to you. Once you decide what you want, he'll have them get to work."

"That's amazing!" I say.

"That's too much," Cyra says.

"He's trying to keep up with Quirin," dad says, grinning. "And now, apparently, Henry is put out trying to decide what he's going to gift you in order to keep up with the two of them."

I burst out laughing, then realize that both Ramin and Arman are staring with their mouths open.

"Who are these people?" Arman finally asks.

"Oh, they're my family," Cyra says, making me growl with pride. She's finally accepted that she's not just my mate, but she's part of the larger family.

"Connor is my son and the Alpha heir of my previous pack. Henry is one of our allies and Quirin's adopted brother," my father tells them.

"Suddenly, gifting you pictures of your mother doesn't seem sufficient," Arman says.

"Since I only have one and no one else has any, I'd say your gift is priceless, Alpha Arman," Cyra tells him.

"Please, Alpha Cyra, call me Arman. We're family too."

She looks at him a moment before nodding.

"You really are so much like your mother," Ramin says.

After we finish eating, they bring in the pictures of Cyra's mother. We spend the next couple of hours going through the pictures, laughing at stories that Alpha Ramin tells us about Cyra's mother. My father left after lunch and mid-afternoon, I get a mind link from the gate guard that Hijack is here.

I let Cyra know and after making sure she feels comfortable being left with her uncle and cousin, I head outside to find out why Hijack is here.

I run into him and Yana on the way into the packhouse.

"Hey, is everything okay? We weren't expecting you," I say.

"I contacted your father. I knew this project would be huge, so I came to help," he says.

"I'm going to show him what I did yesterday, Yorrie. And he said I could watch," Yana says, practically bouncing on her toes.

Hijack is contained energy. He doesn't show a lot of emotion, but it always feels like he's a coiled spring ready to snap and do lethal damage at a moment's notice. Yana, on the other hand, is all bouncy, barely contained energy.

"If she starts to bother you ..." I begin.

"Nah, she'll be fine. I hear she's a budding techy and we always need new apprentices," he says.

Yana sticks her tongue out at me.

"Very mature. I expect that from Yvonne, not you, Yana."

"Ugh! You've been Alpha for a week and you're already starting to sound like Connor," she grumbles. "Come on, Hijack. Let's see what a Hijacker does," she says, dragging him off. I'm surprised when he doesn't argue about being dragged away or that he doesn't seem to mind when she begins bouncing beside him again as they walk.

It must be a techy thing.

When I get back to the meeting room, they're all standing and stretching after the long day of sitting.

"Yorick, I've invited my uncle and cousin to stay the night. I was going to give them a tour of our pack lands. Did you want to join us?"

"Absolutely and maybe we'll run into Hacker and Wendy. Then, we can see how the cable is coming along," I say, taking her hand. "Lead the way."

Chapter 37: Yana

Hijack

The space where Hacker set up the security system is small, made smaller by the young girl who is practically bouncing out of her shoes.

"Are you always this excitable?" I ask her.

"This is exciting," she says, peering over my arm to watch. "I mean, don't you think so?"

To me, this work is boring. But I appreciate her enthusiasm, and I want to nurture it, so I don't say that.

"There are many other things that we do that are more exciting," I say instead.

"Like what? Wendy is *always* at her computer working with you guys," she says.

Interesting. Wendy isn't *always* working with me. If she's spending that much time at her computer, then she's spending more time with Hacker than I realized. I already knew he liked her and was probably using this weekend to spend time with her away from me. Which is exactly why I showed up. Wendy isn't eighteen and if we're both interested in her, there's a possibility that she could be mated to one of us. So yeah, I'm here to cockblock that bastard.

"Well, hunting down bad guys is a lot more fun," I say, as I work.

This pup smells a lot like her sister. I've noticed that all the women in the Hill family smell like something out of the kitchen, something warm and enticing, something that smells like home. I've never really paid attention to other families before to see if it's the same, and not having any sisters myself, I can't really compare. The men in this family smell more earthy, like most male wolves do, but the females all have a very attractive scent.

"How do you find them?" she asks. She's pressed so close to me that I can feel her body heat and her head is practically resting on my arm. Her excitement is practically pulsing off her.

"It depends on what they're hiding and how good they are at hiding it. If you're going to continue to breathe down my neck, I'm putting you to work," I say, grinning at her to take the sting out of my words.

"Sorry," she says, scooting back. "But I'll help. Just tell me what you want me to do."

She's eager, I'll give her that. And she's just like Wendy. She absorbs everything I tell her and never once complains about what I ask her to do.

When the last line turns green, she squeals in excitement and throws herself into my arms.

"We did it!"

I'm unused to any display of affection unless it's in the bedroom. I'm certainly not used to young females hugging me excitedly. It takes a second for me to remember that her mother is a hugger and she probably got that from her.

"We did it," I confirm, hugging her awkwardly.

She jumps back, grinning at me. "What's next?"

Hacker's right. We need to keep our eye on this one. She's definitely a techy in the making.

Cyra POV

I let our omegas on the other side know that we need two rooms made up for my family and several more for their warriors to stay overnight. Then we introduced my uncle and cousin to Beta Lewis.

"You have two Betas and two Gammas now?" Arman asks as we walk.

"Two Betas and one Gamma. The other was demoted," I tell him.

"How did that go? Most ranked members don't appreciate being demoted back to warrior status," he says.

"Warren moved him to this side so we can keep an eye on him. He was demoted because he was lazy so other than running his mouth, I don't expect any problems."

As we walk, I see the freshly dug trench on the side of our packhouse leading away from this side toward the other side.

"It looks like he's laying the line so it's closer to the edge of the pack lands," I say to Yorick.

He looks, following the line of the trench. "That's smart. If we ever decide to build anything over here, we won't have to worry about cutting the line for our security system."

"As long as it's not too close to your pack border. You wouldn't want someone sneaking onto your pack lands and cutting the line before your patrols catch them," Uncle Ramin says, looking over the trench lines.

"I know Hacker was mapping it out earlier. That's why he and Wendy were walking the pack lands. Let's go see if he can show us where he's digging the trench compared to where the pack borders are," Yorick says.

We follow the trench which is being dug faster than I expected. When we catch up to them, I can see why. Both Hacker and Wendy are in their wolf forms, digging into the ground and making the job go much faster. As we approach, it looks like they're competing to see which wolf can dig the fastest.

"Not to barge in on your contest here ..." Yorick begins. Wendy's wolf, Dasha, yips in surprise while Hacker's wolf spins, growling and taking a protective stance in front of Dasha.

Yorick raises an eyebrow at him. The hair on his wolf's back goes down and Hacker shifts, grabbing a nearby pair of shorts and pulling them on before wiping his dirty hands on them.

"Hey, you startled us," he says.

"So, I see."

Dasha comes to stand beside Hacker. She doesn't shift, probably because of my uncle and cousin.

"Hacker, this is my Uncle Ramin and my cousin Arman," I say introducing him.

"We spoke on the phone," he says, his tone remaining professional and a bit aloof. My uncle didn't make a good first impression on Hacker.

"We didn't. I'm Alpha Arman."

"Nice to meet you," he says, glancing at me. I nod, reassuring him that everything is good.

"This is Dasha, my sister, Wendy's, wolf. You'll meet Wendy later, I'm sure," Yorick says, introducing her to my family.

"We're showing my uncle and cousin around the pack lands and saw the trench you're digging. We wanted to see the outline of where you plan to lay the cable in comparison to where the pack borders are," I say.

"Ah," he says, walking over to get a tablet that's lying with their clothes.

Yorick's eyes are unfocused and Dasha is looking at him, so I know he's checking to make sure his sister is doing okay. I smile, thinking that he's going to make a wonderful father to our pups someday.

He must catch my thought because he turns and smiles at me.

"Here we are," Hacker says, handing me the tablet. Yorick steps up beside me as Hacker explains where he's laying the cable in relation to the pack borders.

"Hijack looked it over as well. This is pretty standard when you lay cable in pack lands. You want it far enough inside the pack so it can't be tampered with, but far enough away to avoid cutting the lines if you build," he says, reinforcing what Yorick had already guessed.

"Sounds good. Make sure you don't miss dinner," Yorick says.

"We'll stop when it gets dark. That should give us enough time to get back, shower, and make it to dinner before the kitchen closes," Hacker says.

"Howl if you need us," Yorick says, and we continue our tour of the pack lands.

We stop in the central area, showing my uncle and cousin where we want to build our centralized packhouse and where our training grounds are. I watch Yorick sniff the air and walk away, sniffing the ground.

'What is it?' I ask him in the mind link.

'It smells like Hacker and Wendy were sparring. I know she didn't spar with him this morning and their scents are stronger than the others.'

'Is that a problem?'

'I'm not sure,' he says, distractedly.

By the time we get to the other packhouse, it's time for dinner. We introduce my family to Beta Eric and Gamma Elliot and then we show them to their rooms.

"Thank you for giving us a chance to get to know you, Cyra," Arman says. I really do like him. He seems very genuine.

"Yes. I'm glad my son saw the error of my ways and brought me here to meet you," Ramin says.

"Sons are good at that," Yorick says, grinning at Arman.

"That we are," Arman agrees, chuckling.

Ramin rolls his eyes before looking at me again.

"Thank you for giving this old man another chance."

"You're very welcome."

"Tomorrow, perhaps we can talk about me joining you during the trials this week. Your father's, in particular, but I'd also like to see the man who thought he could force his mark on my niece and get away with it," my uncle growls.

"I'd like to be there as well, at least for Alpha Arden's trial. I'd like to see the man who has caused my family so much distress," Arman says.

I look at Yorick who shrugs. "You know mom, dad, and probably most of my siblings will be there. What's a couple more?" he asks.

I shrug. "If you'd like to come, I'd welcome the support," I tell them.

"Then, we'll be there."

Chapter 38: Sparring

Hacker

Last night, Wendy and I got a lot of work done digging the trench for the security lines. We made it a game, and I love her competitive spirit. Her wolf is beautiful and my wolf, Saggio, purred loudly at how beautiful Dasha is. She stood proudly, letting him look her over. Then she'd rubbed her face against his, her wolf showing mine the same affection that Wendy showed me. I'm glad her wolf seems to accept us as much as the woman does.

By the time we got back to the packhouse, showered, and ate dinner, it was late and we were both exhausted. Since Hijack made a point of joining us for dinner, and Yana had followed him like a cute little puppy, I didn't have any time to steal more kisses.

This morning, I sent Sphinx a message in our chat.

Me: See if your father will let you spar with Hijack today.

Sphinx: Why? Why not you?

I love that she'd rather spar with me than Hijack. But this is important.

Me: He's going to realize that something is up if he hasn't already. I want you to prove to him that there's no weakness on our team.

Sphinx: I'm not sure Dad will let me. He's very protective of me.

Me: Defeat him and then tell him you want to spar with someone else. He'll be surprised, but I bet he'll allow it then.

Sphinx: Okay ...

I can feel her anxiety through the chat.

Me: You can do this. Just like we did yesterday. Push past your fear. I have faith in you.

Sphinx: Thanks, Hacker.

Me: Thank me by taking your father down today.

I'm sure if the camera was on, I'd see her rolling her eyes.

I close the chat and get ready to spar. It's always nice to work with a new group of people when you're sparring. There's always something new to learn.

When we get to the sparring field, Sphinx and Yana come to stand beside me and Hijack. Warren and Yorick notice, but they don't say anything until they assign partners. Then they call both girls away.

"You want to tell me what's going on between you and Sphinx?" Hijack says, turning toward me.

I could take his question two different ways, so I choose the easier one.

"I identified a potential weakness that I believe I've now eliminated," I say, nodding at Wendy when she turns to look at me.

She presses her lips together and turns to face her father.

"And you didn't think it was important to tell the rest of the team about this weakness?" he growls.

"Not if I could eliminate it before it became a problem."

"This is about her problems on the sparring field, I take it?" he asks as we get into our fighting positions.

I'm not surprised he knows. We take turns monitoring Sphinx and her activities, making sure she doesn't do anything she shouldn't. Since he's interested in her as well, he would have logged on to watch her spar in the mornings or afternoons just like I did.

"Hopefully after today, we can say 'What problem?' And I notice you didn't say anything to the team either," I say, looking over at her.

"Come on Wendy, you can do this," I whisper.

I watch her attack her father. He gets in three hits before she freezes. He backs off immediately.

Hijack and I begin sparring hard. Because we've both been trained at the Academy for three years, we're evenly matched. But my mind is on Wendy so when he takes me down, I use the opportunity to look over to see how she's doing.

'Come on, come on, come on. You can do this', I think to myself when I see her frozen again. Her father is talking softly to her.

She nods, then looks over at me.

'You can do this,' I mouth to her.

She nods again, and I watch her mouth set with determination.

I get up, but now Hijack is watching her too. We stand slightly away from the other warriors to make sure we don't interfere with their sparring.

Warren tags her once, twice, then three times. I see her start to freeze, then she pushes through it, leaping at her father who is shocked and unready for her attack.

"Yes, Wendy!" Warren shouts happily when she sweeps her legs behind his and takes him down.

She stares at him for a moment then runs and leaps into my arms. "I did it!"

"Of course you did!" I say hugging her tightly.

"Is this what you two were doing out here yesterday?" Yorick says from beside us.

Wendy immediately pulls away from me as I turn to face her brother.

"Your family wasn't pushing her. I did. We needed her to work through her mental block before she comes to the Academy. Her weakness becomes our weakness," I tell him honestly.

"Ready to test your skill against me?" Hijack asks her, as Warren walks over.

"I want to test my skills against one of you," Yana says.

"Let me watch your sister, Yana, then you can take on an Academy third-year and we'll see what you've got," I tell her.

"Come on, Wendy, kick his ass," Yana says.

"Language, Yana," Warren says, but he's watching Wendy.

"Hey, whose side are you on? I let you help me all afternoon yesterday," Hijack says to her.

"Family always comes first, Hijack. Always," she says before beginning to cheer for Wendy again.

Hijack is careful with Wendy, like I was, tagging her hard enough that it hurts, but not so hard that he injures her. When she pushes past her usual fear, I watch the smile spread across her face.

"Nice, Wendy, keep it up," Warren says, watching her closely. Then he turns to me. "Thank you, for whatever you did."

"I just helped her get past her own mental block."

"Yeah, but the rest of us couldn't do it, not even Quirin," Yorick says, watching his sister.

"None of you has trained at the Academy like we have," I say, turning to a very excited Yana.

"Ready to take me on?" I growl in challenge.

"Oh, you're going down, pretty boy," she says, dancing on her toes.

I use the time sparring with Yana to assess her skills. For her age, she is really good. She, like Wendy, will make an excellent addition to the tech team in a few years.

When we're done, breakfast is brought out for everyone. Wendy sits beside me and I gently shoulder bump her.

"How are you feeling?"

"Great. Really great. Thank you again."

"You're part of the team, Sphinx. Everything we do with you, everything you learn, makes you a stronger, smarter, better part of the team."

"I can't wait to start the Academy next year! It's going to be so great!"

"I can't believe I have to wait nearly three more years," Yana pouts.

"You'll probably change your mind by then," Wade, their youngest brother, says.

"Do you find your sisters to be fickle?" I ask him. Being with the Hills is like being with my family. For me, it's easy to fall into the chaos of multiple conversations going on at once. It feels like home.

"No, I guess they're not," Wade says, looking at Wendy and Yana. "I guess I better start thinking about which squad I want to join when I'm eighteen."

"There are other things you can do if you get into the Academy," Hijack tells him.

"Like what?" Yvonne asks excitedly.

For the rest of breakfast, we talk with the younger Hills about the Academy.

"Do you come from a large family, Hacker?" Warren asks me.

"I do. I have three sisters and two brothers," I tell him.

"Older or younger?" Wendy asks me.

"I'm the second child. My brother took over as Alpha and I'm here. The next three are sisters and then I have a baby brother. Well, he's not a baby anymore. He's your age actually," I say, nodding to Wade and Yvonne.

"I'd love to meet him," Wade says.

"And your sisters too. Do they ever visit you?" Yana asks.

"Sometimes. I'll let Sphinx know when they're visiting and if you're here in Yorick's pack, maybe we can come see you."

The rest of the day is spent finishing the trench and laying the cable. Since Hijack and Yana join us, there isn't any time to steal another kiss from my little Sphinx.

However, before we leave, I manage to sneak up to her room to set up her new computer.

"Don't use the other one anymore. Just use this one. This one has layers of protection on it so that when you're working with us, we don't have to be as careful with what you see or have access to," I tell her.

"Okay," she says, watching me.

When I stand, ready to go get my bags and head out, she looks up at me with those sweet green eyes.

I slide my hand into her hair and lean down to gently kiss her. Her response is immediate and she leans into me.

I pull back long before I want to, stroking my thumb over her cheek.

"How would you feel about me talking to your father about taking you out on a real date next weekend?"

"Really?"

"Really. I want to see you again. We can go out to dinner, or to a park, or take our wolves for a run. Whatever you want or whatever he'll allow."

"I'd like that," she says. I can feel the heat of her cheeks under my hand.

"I would too." I look at my watch. "I'd better go find him before I leave. Hopefully he'll agree. But if not, I'll talk to you soon."

"Okay," she whispers.

"Okay," I whisper, leaning in for another kiss.

I groan when I pull away. "If I don't leave now, I won't have a chance to talk to him, and this is better discussed face to face. I'll let you know what he says tonight."

"I'll see you soon," she says, as I step away from her.

"Hopefully very soon," I say, walking to her door before I give in to my desire to kiss her again rather than speaking to her father.

Chapter 39: Saying Goodbye

Cyra

I spent the morning sparring with my cousin. He's very good and we were able to get to know each other even better while we sparred. Afterward, Yorick and I walked around checking in with the pack and making sure we said hello to everyone that Warren told us needed a few minutes with us. Then, we had breakfast with my cousin and uncle. Our time in the pack is limited. This weekend, it was even more so because my uncle and cousin were here.

"I can see you've both got your work cut out for you, spending your weeks at the Academy, and your weekends here while trying to combine two packs into one," Uncle Ramin says.

"Yes, and all while learning how to be good Alphas to a large pack," I say.

"Thankfully, my father was willing to step in to help us. He's already made great strides this past week and we talk to him every night when we're away so we know what's going on over here."

"I would like to apologize again for rushing my judgement about you, Cyra. Being here, seeing what you and Alpha Yorick are doing, has shown me just how wrong I was about you. You are a hard worker, like Soraya was. You have a lot of your mother in you and I'm thankful that history isn't repeating itself. You and your family seem like good people and good leaders, Alpha Yorick. My niece seems very happy."

Yorick turns to look at me, pulling my hand to his lips for a kiss. "Nothing is more important to me than Cyra. Our pack is a close second, but she is the most important person in my life," he says.

"Yes, we noticed the love that your parents have. They are outwardly loving. You don't see that in a lot of mate bonds, even ones where there is true love," Arman says.

"My father never wanted my mother or anyone else to wonder if he loved her. He raised us, all of us, to be that way. We're all very open about our love for each other and our mates. I don't know why people hide it. No one hides their power or strength. My greatest strength comes from my love of Cyra and our mate bond. Why wouldn't I show the world how much I love and adore this woman?" he asks, his eyes never leaving mine.

I smile at my mate, feeling the warmth of his love flow through me.

I get lost in the moment, brought back by Arman clearing his throat.

"Well, we won't keep you today. We know you have a lot of work to do. But I do hope that we can keep in touch and once you have things settled here, maybe at your graduation from the Academy, we can plan to get together again. I'd love for you to meet my mother and sister. Sadiqe is nearly eighteen, so a couple of months younger than you are. As I said, we don't have a lot of family, so I know she'd be excited to meet you and see all the family that you have here," Arman says.

"I'd really like that. I know it's not ideal, but we will have our hands full until we finish the Academy, so it would be better to wait. By then, we should have our new packhouse built and you can see all the changes we've made to the pack," I say.

"And, of course, we'll see you this week in court. Both days," Uncle Ramin says.

"I doubt my father will be happy to see you," I say.

Uncle Ramin smiles a menacing smile. "No, he will not. But if he ends up in jail, which is what it sounds like will happen, he will know that while he may have won the battle of keeping my sister away from me, I have won the war by reuniting with her daughter."

"Just as long as you don't intend to use my mate as a pawn in any revenge you seek over her father," Yorick says firmly.

"I believe Cyra has been used enough in her short life. And I am not Arden. I don't hide behind others. I go on the offensive and I attack head-on," my uncle says.

"Then we'll see you in court," Yorick says.

After breakfast, Hacker lets us know that he's going to finish laying the cable and start getting the systems connected. Hijack, Wendy, and Yana all go with him to finish the project while Yorick, Warren, Yara, and I walk Arman and Uncle Ramin back to their cars.

"If you need any assistance, Alpha Warren, please let me know. I know we didn't get off to a good start, but Cyra is my blood, and I am a retired Alpha as well. I would be happy to come help in any way that's needed," my uncle says.

"Thank you very much for the offer. Right now, the biggest issue is making sure these two packs begin assimilating. Once we have one packhouse, that will be much easier, but I'd like that transition to be easy when the time comes. So, I'm working to create ways for the two sides to spend time together, work together, play together, and get to know each other," Warren says.

"That sounds like a great plan," he says. "Oh, and before I forget, this is for you, Cyra. Please do let us know if you're pregnant. Besides wanting to be a part of your child's life, I'll need to send you the other half of your inheritance," Ramin says, handing me a cashier's check for twenty-five million dollars.

"That really isn't necessary," I tell him and I mean it. We have a plan to repay Quirin's loan. I don't need the money, although it would make our lives so much easier.

"As my son reminded me before we arrived and as he indicated to you, this money is yours by birthright. I'll admit I wasn't happy about giving it to you at first, but now that I've gotten to know you, I'm very pleased to know that it will go a long way toward helping you rebuild your pack. I also know my sister will rip me to shreds when I see her again in the Moon Goddess' realm if I kept this from you. So please, do an old man a favor and take this money. I look forward to visiting you in the future and seeing all the things that having it have allowed you to do to improve your pack."

"Thank you," I say.

We wave goodbye, then turn to Yara.

"Ready to come take your test?" she asks.

"Yes," I say, nervous and excited. I can feel that Yorick is as well.

"Can you deposit that tomorrow, Warren?" I ask, giving him the check.

"I will. Do you want me to pay off the loan to Quirin right away?" he asks.

"Yes, but I'd also like to invest like we planned on doing. I know we haven't come up with a number yet, but as soon as we have it, I'd like to start sending that money to him to invest for us. Just because we have money, doesn't mean we shouldn't find a way to make more money for the pack," I say.

Chapter 40: Negotiations

Cyra

I look at Yorick. "We haven't really had a chance to talk about it, but I'd like to consider taking that second check and putting it aside as an inheritance for our pups. Then the money we make on our investments could be used for the pack."

"Oooh, I like that idea. Let's see, we'll get another twenty-five million when I get you pregnant, so, we could have twenty-five pups and they could all get a million dollars when they come of age," he says, grinning at me. Warren snorts and I hear Yara mumble about Yorick being passionate just like his father.

"Maybe let's start with a more manageable number, like twelve," I laugh.

"Deal! And once we reach twelve, we'll renegotiate," he says, still grinning at me.

I shake my head, laughing as Warren kisses his mate and heads to the packhouse while we continue toward the pack hospital.

Once we get there, Yara has me pee in a cup and then draws my blood. "Just a reminder, even if you don't have a positive pregnancy test today, I'll want to test you next weekend. If both tests are negative, then we can start you on birth control. If you're negative today, you'll need to continue using birth control while having sex for the next week. Let me go process this and I'll be right back," she says.

As soon as she leaves, Yorick comes to stand in front of me where I'm sitting on the table.

"So, twelve to start, huh?" he says, pushing my legs apart so he can step between them. He pulls me against him, and I wrap my legs around his waist.

"That seems a bit more manageable than twenty-five. We'd need to build another packhouse just for our family," I say, watching his eyes glint with excitement.

"I would be okay with that. And, if you're like Kennedy, you could have four in one shot. Then you'd only be pregnant three times and we'd already be at our twelve," he says, as if having quadruplets is an everyday occurrence.

"I want you to live your dreams, Yorick. I want you to become part of the C-Squad. If we have quads or even triplets, that's going to be hard. Let's see how it goes. If I'm not already pregnant, let's not plan to start having pups until we're done with the Academy or maybe even a bit longer."

"My dreams include a big family with you, Cyra. C-Squad is work, work that I'm sure I will love. But you are my life. Our future family is my life."

"Fine," I say with mock surrender. "Keep me pregnant for twelve years," I sigh.

"That's the spirit," he says, growling as he kisses me, pulling me tightly against him.

'For the record, I'm good with twenty-five pups,' Rina says in the mind link while we're kissing.

'I would give you hundreds, my love,' Thad purrs back.

'Not hundreds,' Yorick and I say together, laughing as we pull away from our kiss.

When Yara walks back in, I can tell by the disappointed look on her face that it's another negative pregnancy test.

"We'll test again next week, just to be sure," she says.

I'm not sure why I feel disappointed. I hadn't intended to have a pup this soon, but honestly, with Yorick, I want one. I want his pup growing in my belly.

'I do too. I wish it would have happened, but it doesn't seem like it has. While I really want that pup now, I agree we should wait,' he says in the mind link. I can feel his disappointment along with Rina's and Thad's.

"We can always change our mind at any time," I tell him out loud.

"I know. Come on, we have a lot of work to do before we head back to the Academy tonight," he says, lifting me off the table and putting me on my feet.

We spend the rest of the afternoon working with the pack and Warren. When Hacker and Hijack return, they shower and have dinner, then Hijack says goodbye before heading back to the Academy. Hacker shows us how the security system works, what to do if an alarm goes off, how to switch between quadrants, and everything else we need to know about the system.

"This is incredible! Thank you so much," I say.

"You're welcome."

"We're going to head out in about an hour, does that work for you?" Yorick asks him. He checks his watch.

"That's perfect, I'll meet you down here."

We spend our last hour with Warren, making a plan for the week. We've just finished our meeting when Hacker knocks on the door.

"Ready?" Yorick asks him.

"Almost. Alpha Warren, may I speak with you?" he asks.

"Of course."

Since it doesn't seem like he needs us, Yorick and I go to our room to get our bags and put them in the car. When Hacker walks out, he's got a huge grin on his face.

We say goodbye to the family and even Hacker joins in. I'm a bit surprised when I see him hug Wendy and even more surprised when I hear him whisper that he'll see her next weekend.

The moment we get in the car, Yorick starts.

"Why will you be seeing my sister next weekend?" he asks.

"Your father agreed that I could take her on a date," he says, looking very pleased about that. "And before you go all big brother on me, your father has already reminded me that Wendy is underage. I've assured him that I will respect that. But your sister is amazing, and I can't wait to spend more time with her."

Yorick is quiet on the ride back to the Academy. He still holds my hand and still pulls it to his lips to kiss every once in a while, but he doesn't say anything. Through our bond, I can feel him processing how he feels about Hacker dating Wendy.

Finally, as we pull into the parking lot at the Academy, he speaks.

"You did help her with sparring. She responds to you in a way that she didn't respond to us. I appreciate that, and I'm sure my father does as well. Just be careful with my sister. You've seen our family in action, you know how much we love each other, and you know what we do to those who hurt the ones we love," he says, parking the car and turning to look at Hacker.

"I do. I have nothing but good intentions with your sister," he says.

"Good. Then I guess we'll be driving together again next weekend?"

"No, actually. I want to take your sister out to dinner, and I'll need my car for that. But I wouldn't say no to crashing in your pack for a couple of nights."

"I'll think about it," Yorick grumbles before getting out and getting our bags.

Chapter 41: Protection

Lila

I feel sick to my stomach. I couldn't eat breakfast. Alpha Warren noticed I was distracted in warrior training and pulled me aside.

"Lila, we'll all be in court today. You won't be alone. Why don't you plan to ride with me and my family? I know Cyra and Yorick will be waiting for you, but this way, you'll be surrounded by pack members when you arrive," he said.

"Okay," I say.

When we get ready to leave, Wendy comes up and squeezes my hands. "I know it's scary. I was terrified when I went in front of the Council. But it helps to have someone you trust standing beside you. Yorick and Cyra will be there to support you and so will we."

"Thank you."

Luna Yara pulls me into a hug. It's so unexpected that I nearly burst into tears.

"You're going to be okay, sweetheart. What are you afraid of?"

"What if he doesn't accept my rejection?" I whisper.

"The Council can force him too, Lila. If they put the force of their command behind it, he won't have a choice. Are you second guessing your rejection of him?" Alpha Warren asks.

"No. No, he lied to me. He used me. I could never trust someone like that. I just ... he doesn't know that I'm the one who warned Alpha Cyra."

"He probably does by now. He'll have his own legal representation, and they will have reviewed the evidence that was presented to the Council. He may try to intimidate you, or say something cruel, but the Council will also put a halt to that. Remember, you did nothing wrong. You are as much a victim in this as Cyra is," he says.

I nod, realizing that while Luna Yara has continued to have her arm wrapped around me, their pups have all moved closer, as if cocooning me in their protection.

"Thank you," I say, swiping at a tear that escaped.

The ride to court was mostly quiet. Alpha Yvonne asked who was coming to court. I found out that Alpha Cyra and Alpha Yorick's classmates, the ones who visited us when Alpha Cyra defeated her father, are all coming to court. Apparently, Alpha Quirin is coming which makes me even more nervous, and Alpha Connor is coming too. We only spent a day with him, but he seemed nice. Cyra's uncle and cousin are coming. Some other Alpha, Alpha Henry, is apparently visiting his mother's pack and won't be in attendance, but his father will be.

"That's a lot of people," I say, surprised that so many people who weren't directly related to what happened with Stellan will be here today.

"He threatened our family," Alpha Wade says.

"No one threatens our family," Alpha Wendy says.

"Yes, Alpha Quirin was very clear about that," I say, shivering as I remember how violent Alpha Christer's death was.

"We may not be as vicious as Quirin, but we still protect our own," Alpha Yana says.

I wonder if it's an Alpha thing, or if it's just this family. Alpha Christer and Stellan didn't seem to have this level of loyalty to each other. I mean they worked together to try and get Alpha Cyra's pack lands, but that was more about status and money, not love. This family has a lot of love for each other.

I've been around the Hill children in the pack the last few days. There, they are easy-going and relaxed, even playful. However, when we step out of the car in front of the courthouse, every one of them is all Alpha. They are here for one reason. To let Stellan know he messed with the wrong family.

Once again, they surround me as we walk up the steps, engulfing me in their protection as if I am also part of their family. I guess as a pack member, that love and protection extends to me. It makes me feel safe in a way I haven't for a long time.

As we walk up the steps, I see Alpha Quirin and his Luna, Kennedy. Standing beside them are Alpha Connor and a woman I haven't met. I assume that she's Alpha Connor's mate since his arm is wrapped around her.

"Lila, how are you feeling?" Alpha Connor asks as we walk up. He's a lot like his father and Alpha Yorick. He's intense without being overbearing, unlike Alpha Quirin who is just terrifying.

"Nervous," I say, honestly. My hands are shaking and I'm sure all of them can hear my heart that feels like it's going to beat out of my chest.

"Yorick and Cyra are inside, but we waited for you," Alpha Connor says.

"Thank you."

"Hey, wait for us!" I hear a woman's voice behind me. I turn and see Piper walking up. "Hey, Lila," she says.

"Hi, Piper."

We say hello to their other friends, Zach, Chase, and Landon, and then we all walk into the courthouse together. As we walk into the courtroom, I am once again surrounded by protection. This time, it's the older Alphas who are encircling me. As scary as Alpha Quirin is, I feel safer knowing that I'm also under his protection.

I smell him the moment I step into the courtroom. Stellan is already here. Because I'm surrounded by so many people, I can't see him, but I know he's here.

"Where's Henry?" Alpha Connor asks quietly.

"Visiting his mother's pack," Alpha Quirin growls softly. I'm not sure why that's a bad thing, but when Alpha Connor looks at him, something passes between them.

"We'll talk later," Alpha Connor says. Alpha Quirin just grunts.

Inside there's an older couple already sitting in the seating area. Based on the aura coming off the man, I'm guessing these are Alpha Henry's parents. Seated beside them are the two men who came to the pack over the weekend, Alpha Arman and Alpha Ramin.

Everyone begins saying hello when Alpha Cyra and Alpha Yorick come up to us.

"Lila, you need to come sit with us," Alpha Cyra says.

As everyone parts to let me through, my eyes lock with Stellan's. His eyes burn anger and his lip curls in a sneer of disgust.

I blink when he's blocked by Alpha Yorick who puts his body between us.

'Don't let him get to you,' he says in the mind link.

'We're right here with you,' Alpha Cyra says.

I nod and take a deep breath before following them to the front of the seating area on the opposite side of where Stellan and his attorney are sitting.

Alpha Yorick keeps his body between me and Stellan until we're seated. Alpha Yorick sits on one side of me and Alpha Cyra on the other.

There are three people standing in front of the Council's bench in a triangular formation and several military looking people standing around Stellan. I don't think I've ever been so intimidated in my life.

When the Council files in, they take their seats and one man steps forward.

"I see we have a full house here again today. I guess I shouldn't be surprised since this involves a mate of one of the Hills. For those of you who don't know me, I am Councilman Edward."

He goes through the other council members, introducing them to us.

Chapter 42: Stellan's Trial

Lila

My palms are sweating and I'm clutching my hands so tightly in my lap that my knuckles are white. Alpha Cyra reaches over and gently covers my hands with hers.

"Alpha Stellan, please step forward," Councilman Edward says.

When he passes, he makes sure to glare at me. I don't look up, but I can feel the heat of his anger.

"Alpha Stellan, you are facing three charges in this courtroom today. First, you had knowledge of another Alpha's embezzlement and kept that information from the Council. You then used that information to force an alliance bond with Alpha Arden, using his daughter as collateral in the agreement. Alpha Cyra was underage at the time and unable to give her consent, therefore making the agreement illegal in the eyes of this courtroom. Second, you are charged with knowingly and intentionally using information about Alpha Cyra's inheritance to gain access to her inheritance for your own gain. You are charged with attempting to force your mark on Alpha Cyra against her will and threatening to rape her to complete the bond in order to obtain that inheritance money. Third, you are charged with tampering with a supply of birth control that was delivered to Alpha Cyra's pack. This tampering has caused multiple unwanted pregnancies in older she-wolves, putting them and their pups at risk. How do you plead?"

"We plead not guilty on all counts, Councilman," his attorney says.

"Fine, let us start with the first one. Knowledge of Alpha Arden's embezzlement," he turns to the triangle of people standing off the side, waiting to be called upon. "Tracker?"

"Councilman ..." she begins, then outlines the process of how the money was tracked. The other two, Hacker and Hijack, also speak to their roles in acquiring the information they found. A recording of the conversation between Alpha Arden, Alpha Christer, and Stellan is played, clearly outlining not only his knowledge of the embezzlement, but also Stellan's suggestion of the alliance bond.

I grip my hands even more tightly together. I was such a fool.

When Alpha Cyra is called upon, she steps forward and states what happened when the alliance bond was presented to her and that she wasn't given a choice in the process.

'It wasn't your fault,' Alpha Yorick's voice filters into my head.

I look up at him. 'You didn't know. He used your mate bond against you. Don't blame yourself. You're not stupid. You were in love, and you trusted your mate.'

I nod my head at him as Alpha Cyra returns to sit beside me, putting her hand over mine.

'I completely agree with Yorick. You didn't know and when you did, you told Piper so she could warn me,' she says in the mind link.

I nod again, taking a deep breath. Stellan may hate me, and while my wolf, Bree, is howling at his betrayal of us, my Alphas believe me and have faith in me.

I tune back in just in time to hear the Council give their verdict of Stellan's knowledge of the embezzlement and alliance bond.

"This court finds you guilty of your first charge."

"THAT'S INSANE!" Stellan roars.

One of the military men steps forward, putting a hand on Stellan's shoulder. He pushes it off, but two more step up, restraining him.

"Calm down, Alpha Stellan, or you will be removed from this courtroom," Councilman Edward says, his voice booming around the small space and making me jump.

I don't know why Stellan is surprised. The audio very clearly identified him and his role in what happened.

Stellan finally settles. The military people release him, but they don't step back, ready to jump in again if he gets out of hand.

"Your second charge is knowingly and intentionally using information about Alpha Cyra's inheritance to gain access to that inheritance by attempting to force Alpha Cyra into an unwanted mate bond. Blaire McIntosh, please step forward."

Stellan immediately turns to glare at me. When I stand, Alpha Cyra stands with me and steps forward. The Councilman looks at her.

"Alpha Cyra, you will be called when we're ready to hear your information."

"I am Lila's Alpha, that's the name she goes by. I am here in a supportive role for her. Alpha Stellan is her fated mate and while their bond was never completed, standing against her mate is difficult for her."

He turns and quietly talks to the other council members before turning back.

"We'll allow it. Warrior Lila, please tell us your knowledge of what happened and how you ended up having information about Alpha Stellan's plan to gain Alpha Cyra's inheritance," he says. I notice his voice is kinder with me than it was with the others.

I feel support being pushed into me by both my Alphas, Alpha Warren, and all their family members.

"As Alpha Cyra said, I am Stellan's fated mate. For the longest time, I didn't know what was going on. Stellan told me that it was Alpha Cyra who insisted on the alliance bond, and he was trying to get out of it so we could be together. I believed him. It wasn't until one of Alpha Cyra's Academy mates called me, telling me about Alpha Cyra finding her fated mate and not wanting the bond that I started to ask more questions. I realized that Stellan never really answered my questions and would distract me with ... intimacy. Then, one evening when I was asking him questions, he said his brother, Alpha Christer, needed to speak with him. I followed him and hid outside Alpha Christer's office. That's when I realized that Stellan had been lying to me. Alpha Quirin had bought the loan and was calling it. Alpha Christer didn't have the money to pay for it, so Stellan told him he was going to the Academy to force Alpha Cyra into the mate bond. That's when he said he would get the money to pay the loan. I didn't know what any of it meant, I just knew that I'd been lied to and I needed to inform Alpha Cyra. I still had Alpha Piper's phone number, so I called to tell her to warn Alpha Cyra."

The Council asks me a couple of questions about where I was hiding, how no one had seen me, and I explained that they were too worried about Alpha Quirin coming to attack the pack to notice me.

"Is there anything else, warrior?" the councilman asks me.

I glance at Stellan, seeing that his chest is heaving with his anger.

"I want to reject him as my mate. I don't want him. He lied to me and he used me," I say, my voice quivering.

"No, Lila!" Stellan snarls. "I won't accept it."

Councilman Edward ignores him, and I watch the military team step closer, grabbing hold of Stellan again.

"If you want to reject him, Ms. McIntosh, this council will assist you. Say the words to reject your mate," he says.

"Don't you fucking do it, Lila! Don't you fucking dare! You're mine! Do you hear me! You're mine! You'll always be mine."

Alpha Cyra reaches out to take my hand, gripping it tightly, but she doesn't say anything.

I take a deep breath and look up at the councilman so I don't have to look at Stellan.

"I, Blaire Lila McIntosh, reject you, Alpha Stellan Mc-Donald, as my mate."

I feel the pain slash through me as Bree begins howling in pain.

"I told you I wouldn't accept it," Stellan snarls. When I glance at him, he looks nearly feral. He has started to foam at the mouth in his fury.

"ACCEPT IT!" Councilman Edward booms again, this time his aura pushes out, hot and heavy. I yip at the pressure and pain of it.

Alpha Cyra wraps her arms around me and then Alpha Yorick is there, scooping me into his arms, his wolf purring at me to ease the pressure of the councilman's aura.

I hear Stellan fighting, his wolf snarling against the command.

"I ... Alpha. Stellan. McDonald ..." another snarl. "Accept your rejection."

His wolf, Dolph, howls in pain. I expected to feel terrible pain, but as the councilman's aura recedes, I smell one of my favorite scents in the world. It's the scent of beef stew, the stew that I love to eat on a cold winter night when I'm snuggled in a blanket in front of a fire. It's my comfort food.

I hear a deafening growl behind us and Alpha Yorick spins around, still holding me in his arms.

The man steps out of the seating area into the aisle, his chest panting as he sniffs the air, then looks right at me.

"MATE!"

My eyes go wide as Bree howls happily in my head.

"Mate," I say.

I hear Stellan scream "NO!" behind me, but I barely notice, mesmerized by the man in front of me.

Chapter 43: Unexpected but Wanted

Landon

What a fucking asshole. Guys like Stellan make me glad I'm not an Alpha. Thankfully, I know plenty of Alphas who are good people and the ones in this seating area who are all here to support Striker, Aphrodite, and Lila are perfect examples of that.

"How the fuck did that guy not realize he'd be caught? They have it recorded." Nickname asks quietly, leaning toward me.

"Agreed, what a douchebag. He's not worthy of his Alpha title."

I watch as Aphrodite stands in front of the council and makes her statement. I'm really impressed with her. She's come a long way in a few months. She's gained so much confidence in herself. She's another Alpha who is worthy of the title.

We walked in with Lila and Striker's family. She and Piper have talked before and I saw her at the pack when we sparred with them, but I've never spent any time with her. The poor woman's heart is going to give out if it doesn't slow down.

I'm really glad when Aphrodite stands with Lila in front of the council. Even from here I can see her hands shaking. I feel for her. The mate bond is sacred. It shouldn't be taken for granted or used the way Alpha Asshole used it against her.

I watch as Stellan continues to try and use it against her, telling her he won't accept her rejection. There is some low-level growling in our area of seating, me included. He doesn't deserve Lila or anyone after what he's done.

When she says her part of the rejection, I get a whiff of my favorite scent, strawberries and bananas. I don't mind them separately, but when you put them together, fucking delicious.

My wolf, Osman, stands up and begins prowling in my head.

'Buddy, what's up?'

'I'm not sure. Something is about to happen.'

Well, yeah. This asshole is about to lose the gift that the Moon Goddess gave him because he didn't take care of her like he should have.

When Alpha Asshole still refuses to accept the rejection, Councilman Edward's aura pushes out across the entire courtroom. Unlike the others here, I'm not an Alpha, so his heavy aura affects me more than the others. I am held captive by the aura. I know Lila feels it too because she yelps and Aphrodite wraps her arms around her. When that doesn't seem like enough, Striker leaps up to hold her in his arms.

Osman begins fighting against the restraint, not liking being held down.

'Hold on, Osman, this is temporary,' I say, trying to console him.

He ignores me, snarling against the restraint of the councilman's aura. A moment later, Stellan accepts Lila's rejection, and the scent of strawberries and bananas fills my nose.

Osman practically goes wild in my head, snarling against the restraint that is keeping him from her, our mate.

The moment the restraint releases, he pushes forward, leaping out of our seat and snarling viciously, wanting to get to our mate.

He lifts his nose in the air and takes a deep whiff of her scent. Then he looks right at Lila, still in Striker's arms, and I feel the connection.

"Mate!" he growls before I can stop him.

I watch as her eyes go wide, a look of shock on her face.

"Mate," her wolf says, but Lila is forward enough that it comes out as a question.

I hear Stellan scream from behind her. He begins thrashing, trying to get to her. I'm not sure how he breaks away from Raptor's team, but he does, lunging for my mate.

Osman steps past Striker and Lila, snarling and pulling our fist back before smashing it into Stellan's face, sending him flying backward into Raptor who slaps cuffs on him.

"You gave up your right to her the moment you betrayed the gift that the Moon Goddess gave you. She is mine now and I won't make the same mistake you did," I snarl at him.

"Get him out of here!" the councilman says as Raptor and his team drag a screaming and bleeding Stellan from the room.

I turn around to see Lila still staring at me with wide eyes. She's still in Striker's arms and Osman growls at him to let her go.

"I'm her Alpha, Osman. I was just protecting her. You know I'm mated to Rina," Thad tells him, setting Lila on her feet.

Osman pulls her to us, burying his face in her neck. "Mine!" he growls loudly.

"LANDON!" Striker's voice is sharp. "You saw what just happened here. Get hold of your wolf and go talk to your mate."

He's right. While Osman only cares that we finally found our mate, I know that Lila has been through a lot and we need to take this slowly.

I pull him back and look at her, brushing the hair out of her face. She still looks like a deer in headlights.

"Will you come talk with me?" I ask her softly.

She nods and I smile happily. She's at least willing to talk. I tuck her under my arm and begin leading her out of the courtroom.

"Nice punch, Just Landon," Alpha Quirin says, grinning as we pass.

"He threatened my mate, Alpha," I say to him.

"And we definitely don't allow that," he agrees with a growl.

"You know Alpha Quirin?" she asks as we walk out of the courtroom. It's the first thing she's said since her wolf called mine her mate.

"Yes. We sparred with him when he was in Striker and Aphrodite's pack," I tell her.

"Whose pack?"

"Oh, sorry, that's right. You wouldn't know them by those names. They're nicknames that our friend Zach gave Yorick and Cyra. Well, Striker is a codename given by Raptor and Steel, two elite fighters," I tell her as I lead her out of the courthouse. Then, I turn to look at her. "But I don't want to talk about them. I want to talk about you."

She looks down, clasping her hands together. "You were in there. You know what he did. You don't want me."

"I absolutely do want you. I'm ready to put my mark on you right this minute."

"You don't mean that," she whispers.

I pull my phone out of my back pocket and without looking away from her I hold it between us.

"Siri, where is the nearest hotel to my location?" I ask, watching her eyes go wide again. "You have beautiful eyes," I murmur.

"The nearest hotel is one point two miles from your current location." Siri responds.

"Perfect, we could walk there."

"Any hotel around here is going to be expensive," she says.

"I don't care, you're worth it. We can get to know each other, order room service for lunch and dinner, and when you're ready to accept me, I'll leave my mark, right here," I say, running a finger over her marking spot. Her body shivers in response.

"Hey Hercules, they called an end to today's trial because of that mess. Are you and Lila returning to the Academy?" Nickname calls out.

"I'm going wherever you're going," I say to her.

"But you have school."

"I'll call them and let them know I'll miss tomorrow. They weren't expecting me today. You are more important and after everything you've been through, I don't want there to be any miscommunication about how much I want you. I want my mark on you. I want you to be mine."

She looks at me for a moment, and I hold her gaze. Then, she smiles a soft smile.

"A hotel sounds good," she says. "But I don't have any clothes."

"If everything goes the way I'm hoping it does, you won't be needing them," I growl softly, watching her body shiver in response.

"We're staying in town. I'll see you guys tomorrow," I call out to my friends.

"She didn't eat this morning, Landon. Make sure you feed her," Alpha Warren calls out.

"I'll take care of her, Alpha," I say, finally looking away from her to my phone, hitting the walking directions to the hotel.

"Ready, beautiful?" I ask her, holding out my arm to her.

"Ready."

Chapter 44: Lunch

Cyra

"Well, that was unexpected," Yorick says.

"Serves that asshole Stellan right!" Wendy says as we watch Landon walking away with Lila.

"He'll be good for her," Piper says quietly to me.

"Yes, he will," I agree.

"Who wants to get some lunch?" Luna Yara asks.

Since none of us need to be back at the Academy today, we all agree to go to lunch. However, my uncle and cousin decide to go back to their pack.

"We'll be back on Thursday for Arden's trial," Uncle Ramin says.

"Thank you for being here today. It means a lot to me," I tell them.

"I'm glad we could be here," Uncle Ramin says. He hugs me. Unlike Warren's hugs, I can tell he's unused to physical displays of affection. Arman's hug is a bit warmer, but still not as warm as the hugs I get from the Hill family.

We say goodbye to them and head to the same café we went to the last time we were here. Hacker and Hijack join us again, much to the excitement of Wendy and Yana, who begins peppering them with questions while we walk.

I'm surprised that Hijack tolerates her exuberance. Maybe it's because she's asking him questions about how they followed my mother's money trail and got the recording that sealed Stellan's guilt. I notice that Hacker doesn't make any outward movements toward Wendy, but his hand continues to brush against hers and every once in a while, as we walk, their fingers lock together for just a moment.

"So, what's the deal with Henry?" Connor asks Quirin.

"Yeah, why isn't Henry here?" Wendy asks.

"He went to his mother's pack, searching for his mate," Quirin says, but the look he gives Connor says there's more to it than that.

"Bad idea," Connor says softly.

'I'm confused. Why is that a bad idea?' I ask Yorick in the mind link.

'He's looking for a chosen mate. He's coming up on his thirty-third birthday and he's starting to feel the need to take a mate and have pups,' he says.

'But what if she's younger than him? Quirin and Kennedy have quite an age gap. She's young enough to have given him a lot of pups,' I say.

'Yes, which is what Quirin keeps trying to remind Henry of. I get the impression that Henry thought that Kennedy would be his mate. I thought he was waiting to see if Wendy was his mate, but now it seems he's lost patience with waiting.'

"He did offer to come today and for your father's trial, but I told him we were good," Warren says.

"You should have told him to come. He's not that fucking old," Quirin growls.

"Henry's not like you, Quirin. He has wanted his mate from the moment he turned eighteen. Even I remember that. You never wanted a mate, you just wanted me," Kennedy says, grinning up at her mate.

"You're damn right. And you are worth every minute I waited for you," Quirin growls, scooping her into his arms and making her laugh. He somehow manages to carry her and kiss her with utter abandon without tripping or falling until we get to the café.

"He really should wait," Wendy says quietly.

"Maybe he'd listen if you told him," Quirin huffs.

"I doubt it. He doesn't come by as often as he used to," she says.

Connor snorts. "Yes he does, you're just always busy at your computer."

"Really?" she asks.

"I told you! You are *always* at your computer, Wen," Yana says.

"Is that so?" Hijack asks, looking between Wendy and Hacker.

'Oh boy. Is that going to be a problem?' I ask Yorick.

'It's not my problem as long as they don't make it a problem for Wendy,' he says.

"I'm just trying to make sure I'm prepared for the Academy next year! Plus, there has been a lot going on with Cyra's father and Stellan. I'm taking advantage of everything the Tech Team is teaching me. Speaking of, why didn't Tracker join us?" she asks. I can tell she's trying to divert the conversation.

"Raptor took a sharp elbow jab to the jaw from Stellan. I think I heard his jaw crack," Hijack says.

"It did," Hacker says. "That's how Stellan was able to lunge at Lila."

"Who were the other two guarding Stellan?" Zach asks.

"Intrigue and Venom. I'm sure Raptor is going to rip them a new one for letting Stellan get past them."

"He didn't get very far," Chase says.

"He got close enough that Landon punched him. Their job is to make sure that doesn't happen. They're the Alpha Squad for a reason," Hacker says.

"I think sometimes they become complaisant in the courtroom. It's easy to think you have one person contained with three guards in such a small environment. I'm guessing they'll be running tight formation drills again by tomorrow," Hijack says.

"Have you ever run those drills?" Yana asks, making sure she sits beside Hijack so she can continue peppering him with questions. I notice that Hijack made a point of sitting beside Wendy, so she's flanked by him on one side and Hacker on the other.

"In my first year, yes. But after I made the Tech Team, I began running different drills with them," he says.

"Like what?" Yana asks.

"I was going to wait until this weekend, but since we have some time, we can talk now," Warren says, drawing my attention away from Hijack.

"What's up, Dad?" Yorick asks him.

"Beta Lewis approached me after you left. He apparently wanted to talk with you this weekend but with your family there, he didn't think it was a good time. He wants to retire. He's your father's age, Cyra, and he doesn't have any heirs, just two girls who are already mated. He feels that Beta Eric, being younger, is a good choice for Beta, especially if you're going to combine the packs. Before I speak to Eric, I wanted to talk to you, see if you wanted me to have the conversation with him or if the two of you want to have it," he says.

I look at Yorick. "What do you think?" I ask.

"I think we should talk to him. I think he'll be excited at the opportunity, but it means a lot more work for him over the next year while we're away and we work to combine the packs. Let's plan to talk to him this weekend while we're there," he says.

"And that reminds me, I have plans drawn up for a new packhouse. I'll have them sent over to the two of you tonight," Connor says.

"Thank you, Connor. Your gift is very generous," I say to him.

He grunts, glaring at Quirin who grins, but doesn't look away from the conversation he's having with Piper and Wade.

"You know, we're going to end up with that same problem with Gamma Elliot, and we don't have the back up in Christer's old pack anymore," I say to Yorick.

"You're right, he's older, although not as old as Lewis, I don't think," Yorick says, looking at his father for confirmation.

"He hasn't approached me, but he never took another mate after his mate died. He only has the one daughter who is also mated. So, yeah, you're going to need a Gamma," Warren says.

"Maybe ..." I begin.

"No!" Quirin says. When I look up, I see he's focused on our conversation. I realize he was talking to me. "I need a Gamma more than you do," he growls.

Yorick begins laughing. "Lila is terrified of you. She'll never agree to moving to your pack, Quirin. Too bad."

"Oh! Landon and Lila as Gammas? What a great idea! Although do you think Landon would want a ranked position?" Piper asks.

"I'll plant the seed, but now that he has Lila, he won't want a position on Alpha or Beta squads and the C-Squad position is mine," Yorick says, grinning.

"Why is she terrified of Quirin?" Yvonne asks.

"She watched him kill her Alpha," I tell her.

Yvonne looks at Quirin, who watches her, waiting for her reaction.

"Yeah but, once you're under his protection, all that violence is used to protect you," she says.

Quirin winks at her. "Yes, it is."

"Not everyone was born under Quirin's protection, Yve. Lila never had that and her first interaction with Quirin was when he was in feral mode. There's a reason Quirin's name is known and feared by all the packs," Yorick says to her.

She shrugs. "I guess. Well, I'd be happy to be your Gamma, Quirin."

"I'd be happy to have you, Yvonne. Can you grow up a little faster?" he asks, making her giggle.

After lunch, we head back to the Academy and use the free afternoon to study hard, getting caught up on everything we've missed lately.

On Wednesday, Landon and Lila return to the Academy, both sporting brand-new mate marks.

"Congratulations!"

We all rush to congratulate them. Lila blushes sweetly while Landon hovers over her protectively, grinning proudly.

"Is Alpha Nevaeh around?" Landon asks.

"Her office, I think," Yorick tells him.

"Good. I need to speak with her, then I'd like to talk with the two of you about joining your pack. I know it's a bit sudden, but ..."

"Actually, it aligns perfectly with something we want to talk to you about," Yorick says, interrupting him.

Landon frowns. "Alright. Let me speak to Alpha Nevaeh and then we can talk. Lila and I are going to see my family this weekend so I can introduce her and let my parents and Alpha know that I'm going to join her pack. But the following weekend, we'd like to spend at your pack. We stopped by on the way here for Lila to get some things, but I'm hoping that Alpha Nevaeh will agree to letting Lila stay here during the week and then we can do what the two of you are doing and return to your pack on the weekends."

"What a wonderful idea," Yorick says, pulling me against his side.

Landon frowns again but takes Lila's hand. "I'll find you when we're done."

"Sounds like a plan," Yorick says. I can feel the excitement in him.

When they walk away, Yorick turns to me. "Perfect. While we're learning how to run a pack, Landon and Lila can learn how to be Gammas from Elliot. It's a win-win all the way around. And since they won't be there this weekend, we can talk to Elliot about his retirement plans and see if he likes the idea of training his successor."

I slide my hand into his hair. "Everything is coming together, isn't it?"

"I promised you a beautiful life, and I intend to give it to you, my beautiful, amazing, wonderful mate."

"I can't wait," I say, before he leans in to take my mouth in one of those passionate kisses that I can't get enough of.

Chapter 45: Gamma Position

Y orick

When Landon and Lila return from talking to Alpha Nevaeh, we're all at dinner. They join us and while Lila is obviously shy about being in this new environment, it helps that both her Alphas and her mate are here as well.

"Alpha Nevaeh said Lila can stay at the Academy during the week as long as it doesn't impact my studies," Landon says excitedly.

"And she's giving me a job here so I can stay on campus and make some money. I'll be cleaning the dining room after breakfast and lunch. It will give me something to do, and I can help Landon pay for the Academy," Lila says sweetly.

"The Academy is paid for already. Keep your money," Landon says, kissing the side of her head.

"It's our money now, though, right?" she asks. I haven't spent a lot of time with Lila. Cyra and I haven't been able to spend a lot of time with any of our new pack members, but it infuriates me that Stellan took advantage of a woman who is this sweet and kind. Her innocence would have made her an easy target, but as an Alpha and her mate, he should have felt the need to protect her, not exploit her.

Landon growls softly. "Then we'll start saving for that pup you're going to give me."

She blushes a bright shade of pink and giggles. "Okay."

When everyone is done eating, I ask Landon and Lila to stay behind to talk to Cyra and I about our Gamma position.

"So, obviously with Lila and I being mates, I want us to be part of the same pack," Landon begins.

"That's a done deal. Neither Cyra, nor I, have any problem with you joining our pack," I say and Lila sighs in relief. I didn't realize she was worried that we might say no.

"We can make it official whenever you're ready, which I assume will be after you return from your visit to see your family this weekend," Cyra says.

"Yes. Obviously, I want to show off my mate," he says, pulling Lila into a side hug and kissing her temple. "But

I need to let my Alpha know that I'm leaving his pack for hers. It's the right thing to do."

"I agree," I say.

"Thank you. Now, you had something you wanted to discuss?" he says.

"Yes. As you know, Cyra and I are working to combine our two packs into one. We've demoted one Gamma, leaving us with two Betas and one Gamma. One of our Betas has spoken to my father about wanting to retire," I say.

"Not Beta Eric?" Lila asks quickly.

"No, he's much too young to retire. We're going to meet with him this weekend to discuss him taking over as Beta for both sides while we combine the packs. But our remaining Gamma, Gamma Elliot, is also older and probably thinking about retirement. I wanted to know if you'd be interested in taking over that position. It wouldn't be until you'd finished the Academy, of course, but Cyra and I plan to speak with him this weekend about training his successor. We'd like that successor to be you, both of you," I say, including Lila. "You could do what Cyra and I are doing. Attend the Academy during the week and then learn how to be a Gamma on the weekends until you graduate."

He blinks at me, then looks at Lila, before looking back with a frown on his face.

"Have you spoken to Alpha Quirin?"

I narrow my eyes at him. "Yes. Why?"

"Well, he called me this morning. I didn't even know he had my number. I called him back while we were on our way to your pack to get Lila's clothes. He asked me if I'd be interested in his Gamma position," he says, making me growl.

Cyra stifles a laugh beside me.

"I think I'm starting to understand why Connor gets so annoyed with Quirin," I growl before focusing on Landon. "What did you tell him?"

"Honestly, the same thing I'm going to tell you. A lot is happening very quickly for me and Lila right now. I'd like to have the weekend to think about it. Lila has some trepidation about joining Alpha Quirin's pack and until I met Lila, I'd been hoping to earn a position on one of the elite fighting squads."

He turns to look at Lila. "But my priorities have changed now. I have Lila and I want to be with her. I want to have a family with her and create a life together. I thought I could take a warrior position in your pack, but now I have not one, but two offers for a Gamma position. I don't know anything about being a Gamma, but it's an opportunity that I never thought would be available to me."

"You'd be great at it," Lila says, beaming at her mate.

"You would too. It's not just me who would become a Gamma, Lila. That's why I'd like to talk about it this weekend." He smiles as they look at each other. "But I can already tell that my mate feels more comfortable with the idea of staying in her pack and becoming the Gammas there."

"YES!" I whisper yell, pumping my fist.

"That's not a yes from me. Not yet. But Lila's comfort and happiness are my number one concern," he says, stroking her cheek.

I know what it's like being newly mated. Hell, Cyra and I are still technically newly mated, and I can barely keep my hands off her. So, I know that it's time to wind down this conversation and let them be together.

"Think about it. We'll approach Gamma Elliot this weekend about his plans for retirement and training a successor without mentioning any names. When you get back from your weekend, let us know what you've decided."

"Thank you, Alphas," he says.

"We're not your Alphas yet," I tell him.

"But you will be after this weekend," he says, standing and saying goodbye before leading Lila to their room.

"You know, it's a lot funnier when Quirin is undermining someone else," I grumble.

Cyra chuckles and takes my hand. "Come on, Alpha. Why don't you come burn off that frustrated energy on me and then we need to go to bed. We have court again in the morning."

I can tell my mate is nervous about tomorrow, about facing her father in court. So, I do what she's asked. I take her to our room and make her come until the only thing on her mind is me. Then I make her come long and hard over and over so that when I finally pull out of her, she snuggles against me and falls right to sleep.

In the morning, we meet up with our friends for breakfast. They're coming to support us at court once again. Unlike Stellan's trial, they didn't have a role in taking down Alpha Arden, but they were there to witness Cyra defeating her father to take possession of the pack.

This time, Lila is able to sit in the seating area with Landon. When Alpha Ramin and Alpha Arman walk into the courtroom, rather than sitting toward the back like they did for Stellan's trial, they sit right behind Cyra and I, making sure that Alpha Arden will see them.

Cyra and I greet my family and wave at the tech team who is once again stationed in their triangular formation between the defense table and the council chairs.

When they announce that Cyra's dad is coming in, we turn to sit.

He walks in with the Alpha arrogance that I've come to expect from him. I reach out and take Cyra's hand as his eyes find her. He sneers at her, but her chin goes up and while I can feel her sadness at his reaction through the bond, I can also feel her resolve. She's not going to let him hurt her anymore. I feel my family pushing their support toward my mate and for the millionth time in my life, I'm so thankful for the family that I was born into.

When his gaze passes over me, I don't look away, but it doesn't linger, as if I'm not worth his time. However, it stops right behind me, and he erupts into a thunderous snarl.

"WHAT THE FUCK ARE YOU DOING HERE?"

From the corner of my eye, I see Alpha Ramin finger wave at Arden, a victorious smirk on his face.

"Hello, Arden. I told you we would meet again some-day."

Chapter 46: Arden's Trial

Cyra

I shouldn't be surprised that my father still thinks he's won. How did I not see his arrogance? I guess I needed to see what a *real* father, a *real* man, a *real* Alpha looked like in order to see the difference. If all you've ever known is your father, Christer, and Stellan, you don't realize that not all Alphas are created equally. But now I see my father clearly, and he does not measure up. Not even close.

I watch my uncle taunt my father. It doesn't surprise me. After everything I've heard, Uncle Ramin has a lot of reasons to hate my father.

Today, unlike Stellan's trial, Raptor and his two squad members have a tight handle on my father.

"You will settle down now or I will cuff you," Raptor snarls. I can see the lingering bruise on his face from where Stellan broke his jaw two days ago.

My father sneers at my uncle, turning his glare to my cousin who looks enough like my uncle that it's obvious who he is, before turning back to me.

"I've barely left the pack and look at you, already associating with the dregs of society," he sneers.

"That's rich, coming from the man who embezzled money, then sold his daughter to pay his debts," I say.

I can see the shock on my father's face. I didn't raise my voice. I didn't have to. The only time I've stood up to my father was when I challenged him for the pack. He obviously didn't think I'd changed enough to stand up to him now. He's about to find out just how strong his daughter really is.

Yorick squeezes my hand, and I feel his mind caress mine. I can feel all of them, the entire Hill family, pushing their encouragement and support into me through our family bond.

The Council is announced and we stand, watching them file in before returning to our seats.

"Alpha Arden Teymoori ..." Councilman Edward begins.

"I'm changing my name back to Castor. The court will address me as such," my father demands.

Councilman Edward raises an eyebrow. "Is that your legal name?"

"Not yet. The paperwork is still in process. That ... woman is no daughter of mine and I will not share her last name," he says, glaring at me. Honestly, I'm thrilled. My name will be changing to Hill anyway, but my father using Teymoori leaves a blight on our family's name that I know they wouldn't want.

"Well, until it's your legal name, we won't be using it in this courtroom," Councilman Edward says and I have to hide a smile. My father isn't used to not getting his way.

"You are charged with two crimes, embezzlement and forcing your daughter into an alliance bond when she was underage. How do you plead?"

Unlike Stellan, my father is arrogant enough that he didn't get an attorney, so he's representing himself.

"Not guilty."

"Alright then, we'll start with the embezzlement," Councilman Edward begins.

"Any money that was ... misplaced in the company holdings has been repaid. Those charges should be dropped immediately," he growls.

Councilman Edward looks at him a long moment. "Interrupt me again, and I will have Raptor muzzle you. You will not speak until you are asked to do so," he says, his voice cold as ice. "YOU are not in charge here, Alpha." He stares at my father a moment longer before turning to the Tech Team.

"Tracker, your team found the money trail. I know you explained this in a previous court case, but for the purposes of this trial, could you and your team reiterate what you found and how you found it," he says.

The Tech Team goes through it again, their words almost verbatim from Tuesday.

When they're done, Councilman Edward turns back to my father. "Whether or not that money was repaid, you did, in fact, knowingly and unlawfully take that money for your own purposes."

He turns to look at the council members behind him. Almost immediately, he turns back. "This court finds you guilty as charged."

"HOW DARE YOU!" my father snarls.

I watch Councilman Edward nod at Raptor. Quick as a whip, he slaps a solid, yet malleable strip of something over my father's mouth, fastening it behind his head. The device allows my father to breathe through his nose, but it completely covers his mouth.

We can all hear the sound of silver sizzling against my father's skin a moment before the smell of singed flesh reaches my nose. I squeeze Yorick's hand. I had no idea the council meant that they would truly muzzle my father.

"You were warned, Alpha," Councilman Edward says.

It looks like my father is about to try and speak, but the sizzling sound increases before he stills. It doesn't stop him from growling, but it does keep him quiet.

"You are also charged with forcing your daughter, Alpha Cyra, into an alliance bond."

The recording is played again, then Councilman Edward looks at me.

"Alpha Cyra, will you step forward please."

I do, feeling the heat of my father's glare. I don't look at him. I face the Council.

"I know your statement was made in another trial earlier this week, but for the sake of this one, would you please reiterate how you came to be a part of an alliance bond between your pack and Alpha Christer's?"

I go through it all again. When I'm done, he thanks me.

"Councilman, may I address Alpha Arden?" I ask.

"You may."

I turn, facing my father. I can see the burn marks around the edges of the muzzle where it is surrounding my father's mouth.

"I used to think that all Alphas were like you. I used to think that you were a good father and a good Alpha. Now I know better. You were a terrible mate, a terrible Alpha, and a terrible father. How could any man keep his mate away from her family to try and extort money from them? How could any man sell his own child to pay for his sins? Only a selfish man would do those things. Only a man not worth the title of Alpha would do that. You don't want me as a daughter? Well, I have news for you. I don't want you as a father."

I gesture to where the Hills are sitting. "I have a family now, a *real* family, a *loving* family. Every one of these people is here today because they love and care about me. They are here to support me," I say, chuckling humorlessly.

"They, this family that I have because of my mate bond, are here to support me because the man who should have cared for me, who should have loved me, used me as a pawn in his sick and twisted life. I'm ashamed to be your daughter. I'm glad you're changing your name. Mine was changing anyway now that I'm mated to Yorick, but now the Teymoori name can continue without the disgrace of your sins attached to it. You should be ashamed of yourself and yet, you stand here as arrogant as always. From today forward, you are not my father, and I am not your daughter. You will never see me again after today. I want nothing more to do with you," I say, finally turning away and nodding to the council before returning to my seat.

Yorick stands and opens his arms for me. I walk into them, feeling both incredible sadness but also like a huge weight has finally been lifted off me.

"Alpha Arden, the court finds you guilty of forcing your daughter into an unwanted mate bond. For your crimes, you are hereby stripped of your Alpha status and sentenced to life in prison."

When I step away from Yorick, and turn to sit again, I see my father still watching me. No, it's not my father, it's Caesar, his wolf.

He whines at me, then turns to the council, whining again.

Councilman Edward looks at him then at me. "What is the name of Arden's wolf, Alpha Cyra?"

"Caesar, councilman."

"Caesar, do you wish to speak?"

He nods.

"I will warn you, if you say anything inappropriate in this courtroom, you will be muzzled just like your human."

He nods again.

Councilman Edward nods to Raptor who takes the muzzle off him.

Caesar turns to me and Rina pushes forward.

"Daughter, no name change will ever change the fact that you are mine. I may not have wanted to submit to you in a battle for the pack, but I never wanted my human to treat you so poorly. He and I have been at odds for years. You deserve the best in this life, and I hope you find it with your mate. No matter what Arden says, I will always love you."

"Thank you for that, Caesar," Rina says softly. I can feel her sadness at her father's words. Caesar, at least, still cares for us. I didn't know that he and my father were at odds.

Yorick pulls me into a hug, pressing his lips against the side of my head while Raptor and his group lead my father out of the courtroom.

We get ready to stand but Councilman Edward stops us.

"We still need to complete Alpha Stellan's trial. We can do that today, or we can finish it next week. Which do you prefer, Alpha Cyra?"

I feel exhausted after what just transpired between my father and I, but I also know that taking another day off from the Academy will be difficult for all of us.

"Could I have an hour to settle and then we can resume with Stellan's trial?" I ask.

The Councilman looks at the time. "Why don't we break for lunch. If we return here at one o'clock, that will give you an hour and a half. Will that work for you, Alpha?"

"Yes, that works. Do you need Lila here? I'll have to call and have her come back."

"Yes, I think it would be good for her to be here, just in case we need to speak with her again. Let's plan to meet at one-thirty then, to give Ms. McIntosh time to get here."

"She completed her mate bond with Landon. She's Lila Reed now, Councilman," I tell him.

He smiles. "I'm very glad to hear that. And I'll make sure that Alpha Stellan is brought in with handcuffs so we don't have a repeat of Tuesday."

"Thank you," I say.

When I turn back, I see that my family, the Hills, and our friends are all waiting for me.

"You did great, my niece," Uncle Ramin says.

"Thank you." He doesn't offer to hug me, and I'm not surprised. It's not who he is. But right behind him, Warren opens his arms for me.

I don't hesitate, I walk into them, feeling his entire family, my family, wrapping themselves around me, hugging me tightly and embracing me in their love.

This is what family should be.

Chapter 47: Staking his Claim

Lila

When Landon received the call that we were needed in court, I was terrified. He felt it immediately and took my face in his hands.

"You're not going in there alone. You're mine. He can't take you from me. He's done a lot of stupid things in his short life, and Alpha Cyra may disagree with me, but taking you for granted was the stupidest thing he could have done. How could anyone not love and treasure the beautiful woman that you are. And I don't just mean on the outside. I mean you *are* the most beautiful woman I've ever seen, but you're just as beautiful on the inside. So fucking gorgeous and all mine."

He presses against me until my back hits the wall. "I mean, what sort of man doesn't want to know that his mate is ticklish right here," he purrs, stroking his fingers over the part of my waist that makes my body shiver.

He's watching me as he touches me, his eyes getting dark. "What sort of man doesn't want to hear his mate catch her breath when he strokes his thumb over the swell of her breast," he says, doing just what he said and eliciting that gasp from me.

"What sort of man doesn't want to see his mate's eyes darkening with desire when she knows he's about to bring her pleasure?"

I know my eyes are dark. I can feel Bree pushing forward just as I can feel my arousal beginning to pool between my thighs. Landon affects me in ways that Stellan didn't. Maybe because I know he wants me, all the time. He can never get enough of me, and he doesn't bother to hide that desire and need. He lets it flow freely through our bond, letting me know how much I'm wanted. It's a heady thing, being wanted by a man as passionate as Landon.

He was very clear with me our first night together. He wants everything; me, love, passion, a life that we build together, pups, a family that continues to grow as we grow older. He laid out a beautiful future for me, the kind I've always dreamed of. I know we haven't been together long, but I have no doubt that he meant every word he said that night. And if his desire for me is any indication of how much he wants a family, we'll have one very soon.

He leans in, running his nose across my jaw to my ear, kissing the spot just below my ear before nibbling on my earlobe. My body shivers so hard that I have to cling to him to steady myself.

"I want you to smell like me when we enter that court-room. I don't want any question from that asshole that you are mine. I want my scent all over you," he growls.

I nod, unable to speak, as his words and the heat of his body pressed against mine begin having the desired effect.

"Glad we're in agreement," he whispers, then pulls my shirt over my head. I pull his shirt from his shorts, needing him with a desperation I've only ever felt with him. Un-willing to waste time unbuttoning his shirt, I rip it open, hearing the buttons ping on the floor where they land.

He chuckles, before reaching into my shorts and ripping them off. "Two can play that game, baby."

He's so fucking strong. I love it.

He begins purring as he hears my thoughts. He kicks off his shorts then slides a hand between my thighs.

"Already soaked for me," he growls, pulling his head back just enough to watch as he expertly strokes my clit in just the right way to make me come hard and fast.

I cry out as he croons at me. "That's my girl. Come undone for me. You're so fucking beautiful."

"I need you inside me," I whimper.

"Yes, you do," he says. He puts his arms underneath my thighs, lifting me up so he can line himself at my entrance.

I wrap my legs around his waist as he slowly slides me down his length forcing me to feel him stretch and fill me.

"Mine!" he growls.

I gasp, my body quivering with need and desire.

"We don't have a lot of time, baby. We need to get going. So I'm going to need you to let go and just feel. We're not leaving here until my baby has had at least three more orgasms. I want to fill you completely. I want everyone in that courtroom to smell me on you," he growls possessively as he begins thrusting into me.

The next orgasm comes hard and fast again. He knows I love it when he's possessive. It's what Stellan never was, not until the end. But with Landon, he's not shy about being possessive. I know he wants me, and I know he means it when he says he wants everyone in that courtroom to know I'm his.

As I cry out from the force of my orgasm, I lift my chin. He immediately begins sucking and nipping at my throat, making me whimper. I love submitting to him. He makes me feel precious and special when he wraps his love and protection around me. That feeling has me shooting off again.

I feel him follow me, his body jerking with his own release. In the past, that was all there was. Stellan was one and done. But not my man, not this incredible, strong, passionate man. He continues thrusting through his orgasm growling against my throat until he's hard again.

"Got a couple more for me, baby?" he growls, his voice deep. That's another thing that is very different. His wolf, Osman, is always close to the surface when we're together and he calls Bree to come forward. It makes everything between us so much more intense. He's everywhere, in my mind, my body, and my soul.

"Always," I moan. He's already pushing me back up to the edge of bliss.

I look at my mate, this man who has very quickly become my whole world, who promises to make all my dreams come true. I slide my fingers into his blond hair grabbing hold of it as I watch him.

"I love you so fucking much," I say.

"I love you, my sweet, sexy mate."

I kiss him just as the next orgasm hits, crying out against his mouth. He devours my cries, dominating my mouth, and pushing me through this orgasm and right into another one.

This time, he falls off the cliff with me, draining himself inside me.

He slowly brings us down, still kissing me, somehow using his mind to caress mine while his hands hold me up.

'I love you. I love you. I love you,' he says, over and over in my mind.

I can do nothing but open myself to him, letting his love flow through me. It's so beautiful, so wonderful, that I feel tears prick my eyes. I didn't know love could feel like this. So absolute, so unquestioning, so perfect.

When he sets me on my feet and slides out of me, I can feel the evidence of our love making dripping down my thighs.

"Let me just clean up a bit and we can go," I say.

He stops me, holding my gaze. "I said I want you to smell like me."

I know my eyes go wide. "There's smell, Landon, and then there's reek."

"Call it what you want. I don't want any question that you're mine. Please don't clean up. I promise we can shower together when we get back," he says grinning at me.

"The whole courtroom will smell me," I say.

"And? Are you embarrassed to be mine?" He asks it playfully, but there's enough hurt in the question to make me stop.

"Never. I am so proud to be your mate," I say, cupping his cheek in my hand. "Never, ever doubt that."

He smiles, leaning forward to press a quick kiss to my lips. "Good, then we agree."

In truth, I don't mind. Well other than practically wearing a neon sign that says we've just had sex. I love that he wants his scent all over me. I love that he's claiming me so publicly.

I get dressed and we make our way to the courthouse. When we arrive, everyone is standing outside, waiting for us. As we walk up, all heads turn to us.

"Damn, Just Landon. That's Alpha level possessiveness right there," Alpha Quirin says, making me blush.

"Or Gamma level," Alpha Yorick says, glaring at Quirin. "I know what you did."

Alpha Quirin just shrugs. "I was already at a disadvantage. I just leveled the playing field," he says, winking at me.

I blink. Did the fierce Alpha Quirin just wink at me?

Landon chuckles. "We haven't made our decision yet."

"Just ... keep your options open. You should come visit my pack. You've met my mate. You won't find a better woman or Luna," he says.

"Agree to disagree," several of the other Alphas say at once.

Alpha Quirin grins at me, pulling his mate to him and kissing the top of her head.

"Mine is the best," he mouths to me. Who is this man?

"Don't worry, Lila. If you don't want to be Quirin's Gamma, I've already offered," Alpha Yvonne says.

"As I said, grow up faster, Yvonne! I don't want to wait five more years for a Gamma," he grumbles.

As we walk inside, I feel like I've somehow entered the inner sanctum of this group of Alphas and Lunas. Maybe it's because two of them want Landon as their Gamma ...

'They want both of us, baby,' he says in the mind link.

I lean over and kiss his cheek. It's nice having someone in my head, making sure I'm okay.

'Right, because I'm just chopped liver over here,' Bree grumbles, making Landon snort.

'I do agree with you though. It feels like we've been pulled into the group. It feels good to me. Does it feel that way to you as well?' he asks, wanting my opinion as always.

'It does. It feels really good.'

'Good. I like the idea of becoming Gammas. We just need to decide on a pack. We could go visit Alpha Quirin's pack if you'd like. We'll talk about that more this weekend as well.'

'Okay,' I say as we walk into the courtroom. We find our seats and thankfully Piper doesn't seem to mind sitting beside me.

"Damn Hercules. Maybe try leaving a little of *her* scent on her next time," Zach murmurs as he passes us to sit beside Piper.

"It's not my problem if your nose isn't good enough to smell her. I smell her just fine."

"I'm pretty sure that's her scent on you," Chase says as he passes us to sit on Zach's other side.

In just a couple of days, I've realized that this group of friends is very close. They tease each other mercilessly, but they are there at a moment's notice if they're needed. It's like they've created their own little family at the Academy, another family that I get to be a part of because of my amazing mate.

Landon hasn't let go of my hand and the moment Stellan enters the courtroom, he squeezes it, reminding me that I'm safe.

Stellan's eyes meet mine, his nose twitching. I watch his lip curl, and he snarls loud enough to make the chairs rattle on the floor in the front of the courtroom. The three guards hold him tightly this time.

"Mine," Landon says proudly and arrogantly, before turning and taking my mouth in a passionate, dominant kiss. I hear the scuffle, but Landon doesn't stop until he's ready to.

When he finally pulls away, I feel breathless.

"Was that really necessary?" the leader, Raptor, asks.

"It absolutely was," Landon says, completely unapologetic.

Chapter 48: Stellan's Sentencing

Piper

Jealousy. There's no other word for it. I'm jealous. I mean, I'm happy for Lila. I really am. She's great and what she did for Cyra was incredibly difficult. It says a lot about her integrity and honor.

But when she and Landon walked up and her scent was smothered with his, I felt a spike of jealousy. I'm not proud of it, but there it is.

'We'll find our mate one day, Piper. And when we do, he'll want the world to know we're his just as much as Landon wants everyone to know that Lila is his,' my wolf, Fallon, says.

'I shouldn't be jealous, Fallon. It's beneath us,' I say.

'Wanting our mate is an acceptable reason to be jealous.' My wolf, she's always the voice of reason.

I watch as Stellan loses his shit while Landon practically devours Lila beside me. By the time Landon releases her, the Alpha Squad has forced Stellan to his knees. I don't feel bad for him. He did this to himself and from everything that I know about Lila, she deserved a much better mate than Stellan.

When he's done, Landon wraps his arm around Lila and smiles smugly at a panting Stellan. Seriously, what did he think was going to happen? That Lila would just wait for him after everything he did to her? He gives Alphas a bad name.

When the Council files in, they try to get Stellan's attention. When he doesn't respond, Raptor puts his hand on Stellan's head and forces him to turn to face the council.

"Alpha Stellan, I see we're still having problems today. We'll make this quick. After hearing the testimony of Lila McIntosh, now Lila Reed," he begins and Osman, Landon's wolf immediately begins purring loudly just as Stellan's wolf begins snarling. Landon shuts Osman up, but not before Councilman Edward gives him a brief look.

Then he turns to Stellan.

"She is mine!" Stellan snarls.

"Geez, dude. Get a grip. You lost," Zach murmurs beside me.

"Idiot," I say.

"Alpha Stellan, keep talking out of turn and I will have Raptor muzzle you. It wouldn't be the first time today we've had to muzzle someone who couldn't control themselves," Councilman Edward says.

"Osman, stay quiet. I don't want them muzzling you," Lila says quietly, putting a hand on Landon's chest. Osman very, very quietly purrs his appreciation at his mate before she shushes him.

Councilman Edward continues. "As I was saying, we heard the testimony of Lila Reed earlier this week. The Council was also notified by Alpha Nevaeh about Mrs. Reed's notification and the concern that you were going to try to force your mark on Alpha Cyra. You were remanded into custody later that night by the leader of the council's Alpha Squad, Raptor, and the previous leader of the Alpha Squad, Steel. The Council finds you guilty of your second charge, knowingly and intentionally attempting to force Alpha Cyra into a mate bond to gain access to her inheritance."

Alpha Stellan remains on his knees, panting with his anger, but he doesn't say a word. I wonder if he saw Arden returning to prison with burn marks on his face.

"For your third charge, you are charged with tampering with a supply of birth control that was delivered to Alpha

Cyra's pack causing multiple, high-risk pregnancies in older she-wolves."

Once again, he turns to the Tech Team. "Tracker, your team was able to identify and locate the delivery truck in question?"

"Yes, Councilman," she says, going through how she tracked the delivery using the truck's GPS system. She also stated that the company had cooperated completely with her request for information and she provided the information to Saber from C-Squad.

"Saber, please come forward," Councilman says.

I hadn't even seen her enter the back of the courtroom. She's incredibly quiet. I'm surprised her code name isn't Stealth.

She steps up in front of the council and explains her involvement, the information that she obtained in Yorick and Cyra's pack, and how they hunted down the delivery driver.

Councilman Edward looks at another military person standing beside the bench and nods. I don't know this person, but they are obviously part of one of the council's elite squads.

"Do you know who that is?" I whisper to Zach.

"Beta Squad, don't know his name," he says. I know Zach is vying for the Alpha Squad, especially now that Yorick has plans to join C-Squad.

The Beta Squad member leads a man out of the back. Instantly, Stellan begins snarling.

"You fucking asshole!"

"Christer is dead and you're on trial. I'm not going down with you. You promised no one would ever know. I lost my job, and my mate is considering rejecting me because I helped you. So, fuck you!"

"Damn," Chase murmurs. "No honor among thieves."

"Richard James, please step forward," Councilman Edward says.

We listen as the man, Richard, explains how Stellan came up with the idea to switch the birth control in the shipment with placebos. He stated how he met with Stellan and switched out the birth control pills before delivering them to Yorick and Cyra's pack. His testimony follows along with what Tracker and Saber already said in their testimony.

"Thank you. Because of your cooperation, your sentence in these crimes will be reduced. You will be placed on probation. Bane will take you to get processed out. Do not miss meetings with your probation officer or we will see you again in this courtroom."

"Thank you, Councilman," he says, walking off with the Beta Squad member.

I turn to look at Zach. 'Bane,' we mouth at the same time. He shoulder bumps me as we both grin. There's a reason we've remained sex partners. We enjoy each other's company and we care about each other, just not in the same way that mates do.

Councilman Edward turns to look at the rest of the council. It's only a moment before he turns back around.

"Alpha Stellan, we find you guilty of tampering with birth control and putting older she-wolves and their pups at risk of premature birth or death. You have been found guilty of all three charges brought against you. The Council has unanimously agreed that from this day forward, you will be stripped of your Alpha status ..."

Stellan begins snarling and fighting against Raptor and his team. Raptor is obviously over it and slams Stellan against the floor, putting his knee to his back and leaning on him to hold him in place.

Once he's contained, Councilman Edward continues. "You are ordered into custody and will remain in prison for the rest of your life."

"Just kill me," he says, his voice breaking.

"Take him away," Councilman Edward says.

When Raptor drags him to his feet, he turns once more, looking at Lila. I reach out instinctively to take her hand.

"Lila, please," he begs.

"You made your choices, Stellan, and I've made mine. Goodbye," she says, her voice strong and steady.

I squeeze her hand, so proud of her strength.

Stellan begins howling as they drag him from the courtroom.

"Good for you, Lila," I say as the council leaves the courtroom.

Osman begins purring loudly again, making Lila blush as Landon pulls her into his arms. I hear him murmur about how he's going to show her just how happy her words made him later, and I feel that flare of jealousy all over again.

"Ready to head back to the Academy?" I ask Zach and Chase.

"Yeah, let's say goodbye. This week has put us behind and I could use the time to study," Chase says.

"Hey, you okay?" Zach asks me quietly.

"Yeah. I'm good," I say, smiling. It's a fake smile and Zach knows me well enough to know it, but thankfully, he doesn't push.

As we say goodbye, Alpha Quirin reminds me again that I'm welcome in his pack anytime.

"I need to reach out to Vivienne. She's gone rogue again, but maybe a pack like yours would work for her."

"Rogues are my specialty. Let me know," he says.

"Thanks, I will."

We say goodbye and head back to the Academy. Zach isn't the only one vying for a position on the Alpha Squad and if I'm going to defeat him for the one position avail-

able, I'm going to have to work my ass off for the rest of
the school year.

Chapter 49: Excitement and Concern

Yorick

After Stellan's court hearing, Cyra and I went back to campus.

"It's done. It's finally done!" she says.

"Good, now you can relax. You haven't been sleeping, you haven't been eating, I can feel how upset you've been all week. I don't like my mate being so stressed."

"There was no way around it, Yorick, you know that. But now, it's done. Now we can focus on our pack, our studies, getting you on the C-Squad, and starting our lives together."

"Mmm, I like the sound of that," I tell her.

Since I know she's been overly stressed this week, I tuck her beside me on our loveseat while we study. But the next day, she still wakes up feeling queasy.

"Baby, you have to relax," I murmur in the morning, still holding her against me in bed.

"I know. I thought I would feel better today, but maybe it's going to take a couple of days. So much has happened so quickly," she says.

We get through our Friday classes, then say goodbye to Landon and Lila, wishing them a good visit with Landon's family.

"I expect good news when you return on Sunday," I tell him.

Landon just laughs. "We're going to talk. Hopefully, we'll have a decision by then, but I won't rush Lila. A lot has happened to her in a short amount of time."

"I understand and I respect that, having my own mate who has had a rough week," I tell him.

We say goodbye and are heading to our car when I hear a familiar voice calling out to me.

"Striker!"

I turn, seeing Hacker jogging over to us. "Hey, I was just wondering if you'd given any more thought to me staying the night in your pack this weekend?"

Honestly, I'd pushed the thought of having the man, who is taking my sister on a date, staying at my pack, under the same roof as my sister, so far out of my mind that I'd completely forgotten about it.

I hear Cyra chuckling beside me.

"Fine. One night."

Hacker grins excitedly. "Great! Thanks! I'll see you tomorrow then!" he says before jogging off.

"Why do I feel like that was a huge mistake?" I grumble.

"It wasn't. He's not going to do anything stupid. First, he knows your family would kill him. But second, it's important that he maintains a good relationship with Wendy since she'll be on their team next year. I thought it was telling how he said that any weakness of hers is a weakness for all of them. If he does something to put a rift between them, it weakens their team. He loves what he does. I don't see him doing anything to jeopardize that," she says.

"Always the voice of reason!" I say, kissing her before we get in the car.

We haven't had a lot of free time, but Connor did send over the packhouse specifications for us to look at this week. Cyra and I decided on the ones we wanted and as we drive down the road toward her father's old packhouse, we pass the centralized area where we want our new packhouse to be. I'm shocked when I see that Connor has already started breaking ground. It must have happened today because he didn't say anything about it when we saw him in court yesterday.

I pull into the area, stopping beside a bunch of trucks and machines. Cyra and I get out excitedly, seeing my father ahead of us.

"Dad!" I call out.

"Hey, Yorick. Hey, Cyra. Connor wanted this to be a surprise," he says.

I look around, realizing they've already dug out and framed the foundation of the packhouse.

"We pour the concrete tomorrow and then we have to let it set before they can start building," my dad says.

I wrap my arm around Cyra, pulling her against me. I can feel her excitement, as strong as mine.

"This is incredible. I can't believe everything is falling into place," she says.

"Obviously, we can't spar here for a while. They've taken over our sparring area, and it will be too loud once they start construction. So, I have the different sides alternating. We'll spar on the west side tomorrow and the east side on Sunday. I'm looking at other areas where we can create a joint sparring ground temporarily. We can be near here in the morning, but afternoon training will be more difficult with the construction going on," my father says.

After we talk to the construction manager, Cyra and I get back in the SUV. I call Connor, thanking him again for this gift.

Dad and Cyra spend the evening going through the pack's financials, while I spend time with pack members, checking in and making sure everyone is settled.

Over dinner, Cyra and I announce the results of court this week, letting everyone know that Alpha Arden and Alpha Stellan were both found guilty and will be spending the rest of their lives in jail. I'm thankful that no one seems upset by this.

The next morning, Cyra once again wakes up feeling nauseous.

"We're going to see mom," I tell her.

"I know. We have our final pregnancy test before she puts me on birth control. Honestly, it seems ridiculous to even bother. If I was pregnant, I'd know by now."

"Well, mom will insist and since you're not recovering from the stress of this week, I want her to look you over. Life isn't going to slow down for us, Cyra. I want to make sure you stay healthy."

"Have I told you that I love you?" she asks, grinning up at me.

"Only twice today. I'm feeling a bit unloved," I say grinning, and making her laugh.

At breakfast, I ask my mom if she can see Cyra sooner rather than later.

"I'm worried about the stress that she's been under, mom. She's been off all week, not sleeping well, not eating well. I just want to make sure that everything that happened this week isn't causing problems that we don't know about," I say.

"Of course. Why don't we go right after breakfast," she says.

"Thanks, Mom," I say, feeling relieved. I know if there is something wrong with Cyra, Mom will figure it out.

I let Dad know that we're going to see mom first thing, then he and Cyra can get to work while I go visit the other side and check in with Beta Eric.

"Is everything alright? I noticed she wasn't herself at warrior training this morning," he says.

"The stress of the week has really gotten to her. I just want to make sure I don't need to force her to rest more. She's not bouncing back after everything that happened this week."

"It was a lot. If there's a problem, your mother will find it and fix it," he says confidently.

"I know. That's why we're going now. And Dad, if Cyra needs rest, I'm going to force her to take the weekend off."

"Understood," he says.

After talking to my father, I get Cyra and we walk to the pack hospital together.

"Stop worrying, Yorick. I'm fine," she says.

"Of course you are," I say, not feeling nearly as confident as I'm forcing myself to sound. I'll feel better hearing that she's fine from my mother.

We go through the usual process of Cyra peeing in a cup, then while my mother takes her blood, she begins asking Cyra about her symptoms.

"She's not sleeping. She's not eating as much as she used to. She wakes up feeling nauseous every morning, at least she has nearly every day last week," I say, watching Cyra closely.

My mother stops and looks at me.

"What?"

"Is your name Cyra?" she asks me.

I open my mouth, looking at my mate who grins at me.

"No," I grumble.

"Now that we have that established, *Cyra*," she says, stressing her name, "why don't you tell me how you're feeling."

Cyra lets her know that this past week was very stressful for her. She's been feeling run down and tired, more than normal, and she has struggled to eat, feeling nauseous, especially in the mornings before court.

"Rina, how are you feeling?" my mother asks Cyra's wolf.

"The same, Luna. My human and I have struggled this week. Seeing our father, hearing what he said, it was very difficult emotionally."

"I definitely understand that. I'm going to run some extra tests to check your iron, your adrenal glands, and a couple of other things that could be causing your fatigue. I'll be back in a few minutes," she says.

When she leaves, I take Cyra's hand.

"Yorick, I'm not dying. I'm just tired."

"And nauseous," I insist.

She reaches out to cup my face. "Would you be able to eat if your father said those horrible things to you?"

I shake my head, leaning in to press my lips to hers. "No. But you handled it beautifully. You were so strong. I'm so proud of you."

My mother is back more quickly than I expected and she drags a machine in with her.

"Mom? What's going on? Is Cyra sick?" I ask her, my fear for my mate spiking as Thad pushes forward.

My mother chuckles, turning to look at us.

"No son. She's not sick. She's pregnant."

Chapter 50: A Beautiful Life

C yra

Pregnant?

"You said I'm pregnant?" I ask. I was confident that I *wasn't* pregnant because of my two negative pregnancy tests.

"Yes, you are," Luna Yara says, smiling at me.

I look at Yorick, huffing out a small laugh. "We're going to have a baby?"

I watch that beautiful, sexy smile spread across his face.

"We're going to have a baby," he growls, then he leans over my belly. "Do you hear that baby? We know you're in there now," he says, making me laugh. I slide my fingers through his hair as he leans his face against my stomach. Thad begins purring loudly as if calling our baby to him.

Luna Yara chuckles. "You're going to have to give me some space, Thad. I want to see if Cyra is following the Hill tradition of having multiples on the first go."

My mind immediately begins spinning with everything that this means. Yes, things are more settled, but Yorick and I have so much that we still need to accomplish in the next year. A pregnancy is going to add to that already. A pregnancy of multiples would make it even more difficult.

"We'll make it work. And now, more than ever, I know the C-Squad is for me. I want to come home to you and our pup every night," he says, stepping back and giving Luna Yara the space she needs.

She explains what she's going to do with the ultrasound machine, then she squirts some gel on me and begins running the wand over my stomach. We hear the heartbeat almost instantly.

"Is that my baby's heartbeat?" I ask, as Yorick reaches out to squeeze my hand. Both of us are glued to the monitor that Luna Yara is looking at.

"There it is right there. See that?" she asks.

"Yes," I whisper, feeling overwhelmed with excitement.

"That's your baby's heart. He or she has a strong heartbeat."

She studies the image, clicking buttons. "You're bigger than I would have expected. But Cyra was probably close to having a positive pregnancy test last week," she murmurs to herself.

"This is your baby's head," she says louder, obviously speaking to us this time as she rolls the wand over my stomach. "Looks like there's just one baby in there."

She continues rolling the wand over my stomach, clicking buttons and taking measurements. "Probably a good thing since Kennedy is pregnant again, too," she murmurs.

"Kennedy's pregnant again?" Yorick asks.

Luna Yara turns and looks at us. "Oh, did I say that out loud?"

"Yes," Yorick says, chuckling at his mother. She always seems so surprised that she mumbles out loud.

"Yes, she is. She's having triplets this time," she says, shaking her head and laughing. "She calls it the 'Christer effect'. I just think her mate is very passionate."

'I'm thankful that we're not having triplets,' I say in the mind link to Yorick. But he's frowning.

"I'm passionate," he grumbles.

"I'm sure you are. You are your father's son. But you've been very busy, Yorick. You and Cyra, both. One pup is probably good for now."

He turns and looks at me, determination burning in his eyes.

"Next time, we're having multiples."

I laugh. "It's not a competition."

"It's starting to feel like it," he grumbles. "If passion is rated by how many pups you give your mate, I'm damn sure filling you with pups next time."

"I'll just be happy if our baby is healthy," I say, taking his hand.

"Fine. Happy, healthy baby this time. After we graduate, multiples," he insists.

I laugh, cupping his face in my hand. "I'll give you as many pups as you want."

He growls possessively. "You've seen my family. Mom and Dad had seven of us, Connor and Madison have five, and now Quirin and Kennedy are going to have ten. If we're going to keep up, we'll need to have several multiples."

"Madison is pregnant again, too. Just one this time," Luna Yara says. "Did you want to know the gender of this pup?"

I'm still reeling from Yorick's proclamation that we're going to have multiple pregnancies with multiple pups. While the thought is a bit terrifying, the idea of how he's going to put those pups in me is very exciting.

"Do you want to know?" he asks. I can feel his excitement. He's dying to know.

"Yes," I say. It doesn't matter to me if we know, but I can tell Yorick wants to announce it to everyone as soon as possible.

"You're having a little boy," she says, smiling at us.

I didn't care either way. I just wanted to have a healthy baby. But for some reason, knowing that I'm going to have a little Yorick running around makes everything feel more real and more special.

"I'm having a little Yorick," I say, my voice tight and my eyes burning with tears of joy.

"Yes, you are," he growls, leaning in to kiss me.

Yorick is always open about his love for me. He always pushes his love through our bond, but it feels even more powerful in this moment, as if I've just made him the happiest man in the world.

'You have,' he growls in the mind link. 'I am so fucking happy that you're carrying my pup. My son,' he says, not releasing my mouth.

When he finally pulls back, I realize that Luna Yara left to give us some privacy. There's a towel on my stomach so I can wipe off the gel.

"You know this is going to make everything harder this year, right?" I ask him.

"You know we're going to make it work, right?" he counters. "Nothing is too much for the two of us to over-come. Look at how much we've already worked through.

Look at how much is happening in our lives. Is it a lot? Yes. Will I be crazy protective and overbearing? Absolutely. Will we make it work? You're damn right we will. Why? Because I promised you a beautiful life and I intend to give it to you. And do you know what's going to make that life even more beautiful?"

"What?" I ask grinning as I watch my mate becoming more and more excited.

"Pups. Lots and lots of pups," he growls before taking my mouth in another dominant, possessive kiss filled with love and the promise of a perfect life together.

Wendy POV

I'm so excited for my date tonight. I've changed into and out of every outfit that I have in Yorick's pack. I wish I had the dress that I know is currently in Connor's pack, but oh well.

I hear the chat ping on my computer. I rush to it, hoping it's Jude. Instead, it's Hijack.

Hijack: Hey Sphinx. I have a project I'm working on. I wanted to know if you'd like to sit in and watch tonight.

Shit. He must not know about my date. I've felt the tension between him and Hacker when it comes to me. I also know that we're all going to be part of the same team next year, so I don't want to cause any problems between them.

Me: I can't tonight. But if you're still working on it to-morrow, I'd love to watch.

It takes a moment before he responds.

Hijack: Got a hot date?

Shit, shit, shit! What do I say?

Me: Just some things going on around here. Cyra and Yorick found out they're having a baby boy, so the pack is celebrating.

It's not a lie. I just won't be here for most of the celebration.

Hijack: Ahh, tell them I said congratulations.

Me: I will. Have a good night.

Hijack: You too.

I close the laptop, knowing that sometimes the guys turn on the camera when we're talking. I've learned that cameras are dangerous when you aren't monitoring them. Anyone with enough skill can hack into your computer and see you. As exciting as the work we're doing is, it's also made me aware of how creepy some people can be.

'Hacker is here, Wendy,' my father's voice says in the mind link.

'Thanks, Dad.'

I take one more look in the mirror before walking to the top of the stairs. My eyes lock with his. He's wearing a blue button-down shirt that brings out the color of his eyes and khaki dress pants. I didn't know it was possible for him to look better than he usually does, but wow! He looks great.

"Hey beautiful," he says as I walk up to him.

"Hi," I say shyly.

"Your dad tells me that the pack is celebrating Striker and Cyra's pregnancy. Did you want to stay and celebrate with them?" he asks.

"I already congratulated them. They'll probably still be celebrating when we get back," I say. I'm excited to go on this date, my very first date. I know this is a big deal for my brother and Cyra, but I really want to go on this date with Jude.

"I won't have her out too late, Alpha," he says to my father.

"Bye, Daddy," I say, hugging him.

"Bye, sweetheart," he says, hugging me then looking at Jude.

"I'm trusting you with one of my greatest treasures. Don't make me regret it."

"I'll keep her safe, sir," he says as I hug my mother good-bye.

"He's such a respectful young man," my mother murmurs. I don't bother answering her. I know she wasn't talking to me.

Instead, I step back and take Jude's hand.

"We'll see you later," he says, before we walk out to his car. He opens the door for me, and I slide inside. The car smells like him, like cedarwood and leather. It's a rich masculine scent that makes my body feel strange and tingly.

When he gets in the car, he takes my hand, pulling it to his lips.

"Ready?"

I nod excitedly. "Where are we going?"

"There's a restaurant about thirty minutes from here. It's on a big lake. I thought we could have dinner and maybe walk around the lake afterward."

"That sounds wonderful," I say.

He leans over and presses his lips to mine, gently teasing my lips with his.

"Mmm, I've missed that all week," he says, before putting the car in gear and heading off the pack lands.

I was worried that we'd run out of things to talk about or that Jude would get bored with me since I've led a pretty sheltered life. But instead, the night flies by. Dinner was amazing. He'd requested a table that overlooked the lake. The restaurant had lights that twinkled on the water, giving it a magical glow. We talked about our families and laughed at silly things that have happened in our family. Then we walked around the lake, just talking and holding hands. When we'd made our way back to the restaurant, he stopped, gently caressing my cheek before kissing me again.

He took his time, as if he was savoring the kiss and my taste. I let him lead the kiss, leaning into him and enjoying the feel of his strong arms around me, the heat of his body against mine, and his masculine scent and taste.

When we pulled apart, we were both breathless.

On the drive back to the pack, he'd stolen a kiss every time he stopped at a light, making me laugh when he'd slow down, just so he'd catch the light.

When we got back, he walked around to open the door for me, helping me out of the car.

"I had a really good time tonight, Wendy."

"I did too."

"Maybe we could do this again next weekend?" he asks, bringing my hand to his lips and kissing my knuckles while waiting for my answer.

"I'd love that."

"Excellent. It's a date."

Epilogue 1: Making it Work

Yorick

Four Months Later

Life has been as difficult as Cyra and I expected it to be. Our pace is grueling, made more so because of Cyra's pregnancy. Alpha Nevaeh has been incredible, working with us to make sure we didn't fall behind in our studies. I know it's a lot harder for Cyra, her body has changed a lot over the past few months and even after the nausea ended, she still suffered with more fatigue than usual.

However, being excluded from sparring has allowed her to become more knowledgeable of the pack's management. While I attend sparring class every day, pushing myself harder and harder to ensure a place on the C-Squad,

Cyra uses that time to work with my father. It's amazing to me what she's learning and how quickly she's picking it up. I see it in her discussions with me each night when we talk about our day, but I also see it in our afternoon classes. She has more insight than I do about how the things they are teaching us could impact a pack.

When we spoke to Alpha Nevaeh about Cyra's pregnancy, we were worried about what would happen once Cyra delivered. We know she'll miss at least a week of school, but once she's back, what do we do with the baby? We can't leave our child unattended while we take afternoon classes. Knowing that we'll still have four to five months of classes after she delivers, it was a real concern, not only for Cyra but for me as well. I didn't want her pregnancy to interfere with her ability to achieve her goals.

The answer to our problem surprised us. The instructors all agreed that they would help us during afternoon classes. If they aren't teaching the class, they are willing to watch our pup for us. It's a half day, five days a week, but it gives the instructors a little extra money, and we know that if anything should happen, we're right there.

The packhouse is nearly complete. That has been a blessing for more than one reason. The timing of Cyra's pregnancy gave us an opportunity to design our Alpha floor the way we wanted it. Knowing we would have a pup right away, we included an adjoining door to the room next to ours so we can have a nursery while our pups are young.

Beta Eric has also been able to design his floor for his future mate and pups, and in what I consider my first and best win against Quirin, Landon and Lila have been able to design their own floor, having chosen to become our Gammas.

That had been a huge weight off our shoulders. The transition of the pack to Beta Eric had been easy. He was already a Beta and those who were used to Beta Lewis knew he was ready for retirement. Gamma Elliot was thrilled to have an exit strategy and since Lila isn't attending classes at the Academy, she and Elliot spend time together every day on video chat while he teaches her the ins and outs of being a Gamma. Much like me, Landon always gets a proud look on his face when Cyra and Lila begin talking about the pack and what's going on. The two of them work well together and are already starting to make decisions for our pack.

And since Lila is now pregnant too, it's a good opportunity for our mates to have someone to talk to while they navigate their first pregnancy. Alpha Nevaeh has moved Cyra, Landon, Lila, and I to a quieter part of the Academy. That way our pups won't keep the other students awake and the students who are up late partying won't keep us and our pups awake.

There was one other thing that we've done that was very important to me and even more so to Cyra. It occurred to me during Arden's trial, but with everything going on with the pregnancy, needing to make arrangements for continuing classes, making arrangements for Landon and Lila to start training as Gammas, it had taken longer than I wanted to approach the subject with Cyra.

When I did, she began crying. She tried to blame it on pregnancy hormones, but I know it meant a lot to her. So, about a month ago, we made it official. We both changed our last names to Teymoori-Hill, hyphenating our names so the Teymoori name could continue through her bloodline.

When we'd told her uncle and cousin that she was pregnant, they had asked if they could come see us after the baby is born. Cyra and I have made a point to call Alpha Arman weekly on our way back to the Academy so that we can stay in touch and build a stronger bond with them. We've started conversations about an alliance agreement and when they come for our pup's birth or our graduation, we'll sit down and finalize the agreement. I'm letting Cyra handle that because, honestly, she's the real Alpha of our pack. She tells everyone that we're partners, and the pack calls both of us Alpha. But the reality is, she's doing everything besides training our warriors. Neither of us mind, though. We both know my path is leading me elsewhere, at least for now, and hers is to lead our pack.

I watch her rubbing her large belly as we pack for our weekend home. I step up behind her, putting my hands on my son as Thad begins purring loudly. She leans back against me, letting Thad's purr ease her aches and our son's restlessness. She's very close to her delivery date. I'm hoping that when we see my mother again this weekend, we can decide if Cyra stays behind to have the baby or if she thinks Cyra has another week. Neither of us want her to deliver our pup at the Academy. I'm sure Dr. Johnston would be fine, but she's not my mother. I'd feel a lot better if mom or even Kennedy were to deliver our pup. However, since Kennedy just delivered her triplets, all three boys, a set of identical twins and a fraternal triplet, she won't be participating in any deliveries for a while. Quirin was absolutely thrilled, although I heard that Kennedy had to yell at him again about passing out. Goddess, I hope I don't pass out when it's Cyra's time.

My son shifts against my hands, and I gently rub Cyra's stomach.

"He's so big! He obviously takes after his father," she groans.

"I'll take that as a compliment," I growl in her ear.

She grins, her eyes remaining closed. "It was meant as one. But this pup is running out of room. How the hell did Kennedy carry four?"

"They didn't go full-term. Just like the triplets were born before our son, her quads were born a bit early as well."

"How are Kennedy and the pups doing? Have you talked to her? Your father said the delivery was easy."

"I haven't talked to her, but I figured we could ask mom when we see her this weekend. I think she's only leaving Quirin's pack to come check on you and Lila."

"Well, that and the other pups that have been born recently," she says.

That has been another blessing in our pack. I've heard my mother's mantra all my life about no one dying in her hospital. But when it's your pack members, when it's during a delivery for a pup a she-wolf never intended to have, when both the mom's and baby's lives are on the line, her words mean so much more. All four of our older pregnant she-wolves had harder than normal pregnancies. Two nearly lost their pups, and one nearly died during delivery. It was only my mother's expertise that saved them all.

Because the council was keeping tabs on those females, ready to add involuntary manslaughter to Stellan's charges if any of them died, they knew it was my mother's skill as a doctor that saved them. Now, they are practically begging her to become an instructor at the Academy. They're willing to open an entirely new school of medicine for her to lead.

I didn't think she'd consider it, knowing how busy she stays in all our packs, but Hacker, who is still dating Wendy and coming to our pack nearly every weekend to see her, mentioned whispers about one of the council members retiring. Because he's dating Wendy, I'm getting a bit more of the inside track of what goes on at the council. The rumor is, they're looking at my father to take the vacant seat on the council. If he does, that would mean he and mom would be spending more time in the city, making it a lot easier for her to work at the Academy.

As we do every Friday on our way to the pack, we talk about what we need to accomplish over the weekend. We definitely want to see how the packhouse is coming along. The kitchen should have been installed this week and if so, we should only be a couple of weeks away from being able to move the pack into the new packhouse. Everyone is really excited about moving now that they've been watching the packhouse being built. The pack has become more cohesive and the need to combine our two packhouses into one has intensified. It will be so good to have everyone together in one place.

I keep my eye on Cyra after we arrive. She's quieter than usual and she's been rubbing her stomach almost constantly since before we left the Academy. I notice my mother pulling her aside before dinner. Because I know that she's more uncomfortable than normal, I go see if everything is okay.

"Why don't we just go check on your mate, Yorick. If she's this uncomfortable, she could be in the early stages of labor. We'll see how things are going. If it's too soon, we'll let you sleep in your bed tonight and we'll check again in the morning."

I take Cyra's hand, walking with her and mom to the pack hospital. I can feel Cyra's nervous excitement. But when my mom checks her, she says it's not time yet.

"This looks like the early stages of labor, but since your contractions aren't strong or consistent yet, I'm going to send you back to the packhouse. If anything changes overnight, wake me up. Otherwise, we'll check you again in the morning. But I'm pretty sure you won't be going back to the Academy on Sunday, Cyra. It's almost time," Mom says excitedly.

Because I know she's uncomfortable, I order food to be sent to our room and I spend the evening helping to ease my mate's discomfort. I make sure that everything is ready for our little pup. This packhouse isn't set up the way we've set up the new one, but we have everything we need for our pup's first month until we can move to the new packhouse with our built-in nursery.

Mom said sex could help initiate the birthing process, so before we go to bed, I lay behind my mate, sliding inside her and gently teasing her into an orgasm. Afterward, I held her as Thad purred, lulling her to sleep. Once her breathing leveled out, I followed her into sleep.

"Yorick, wake up," Cyra's anxious voice has me jolting awake.

"What's wrong?"

"It's time," she says.

"Are you sure?"

"Yes. It's time."

I help her out of bed and almost immediately, she doubles over, clutching her stomach. I quickly scoop her into my arms.

'Mom!' I say, pushing my voice into her mind.

'Yorick?' Annika asks sleepily.

'Wake mom, Annika. Cyra's in labor.'

'We'll be right behind you.' I can feel her waking my mother, so I disconnect the mind link and focus on my mate.

My mother reaches the pack hospital immediately behind us, looking awake and ready to deliver my pup.

After talking to Cyra and getting her settled, my mother agrees that she's in labor.

It's hours later, hours of pain that I wish I could take from my mate, but this is something that I can't help with. I can only be here with her, supporting her while she pushes and delivers our pup.

It's just before sunrise when my son makes his appearance. My emotions overwhelm me as I cut the umbilical cord, looking at the beautiful baby boy in my mother's hands. She shows him to Cyra before taking him to wash him off and check him over.

I turn to my mate. "You're so perfect. You did so well." My voice is tight with the extreme emotions that I'm feeling, my own and Cyra's.

I kiss my mate, tasting her tears. Then, I kiss her tears away just as Mom brings our son and lays him in Cyra's arms.

"Have you decided on a name?" she asks.

We did. Just like with Cyra's last name, we wanted our son's name to follow her Persian heritage.

"Mom, meet our son, Alpha Cyrus."

Epilogue 2: Mate

Henry

"Tell me again why we're stopping at the Academy, Henry?" Justine asks from the seat beside me.

I've spent the last several months courting her, getting to know her, and deciding if she would be a good fit for my pack as my chosen Luna. I had hoped to find my fated mate, but as the years have gone by, the feeling that I'm running out of time has increased. And it's not just me. If my mate is close to my age, her child birthing years are limited. The Alpha in me is feeling a powerful need to create an Alpha heir and to create one soon.

I met Justine when I went back to visit my mother's pack several months ago. She's in her late twenties and has yet to meet her mate. We hit it off right away and before I left, I made plans to visit again the following month.

I did, and once again, we had a wonderful time together. The following month, I came back and stayed for a week, taking Justine away for a few days so we could spend some alone time together. While we don't have the fireworks that my brother and the Hills seem to have with their mates, Justine and I both agreed that we are compatible in all aspects of our lives. She is anxious to settle down and start a family and she loves pack life. She already has the skills to be a great Luna so, after multiple visits, I've decided to bring her back to my pack for a visit. If all goes well, I'll mark her and make her my Luna officially.

"I am very delayed in signing an alliance agreement with Yorick and Cyra Teymoori-Hill. I've been a bit busy," I say, grinning at her. She blushes a sweet pink and I stroke my knuckles over her cheek.

"Cyra just had their pup a couple weeks ago, so my plan to see them then was put on hold. I know they're both back at the Academy, so I want to stop by now and get this done. It's a formality, but an important one. Plus, it will give me a chance to introduce you to them and for me to meet their pup."

I've already met Quirin and Kennedy's triplets. I didn't stay long during that visit. Q has been very vocal about his disagreement with me taking a chosen mate. But he and I aren't the same. He never expected to find his mate. I've always wanted mine. I thought for sure it was Kennedy.

It felt like we would have been perfectly compatible. I'm happy she and Quirin are together, she makes him happy and he's a better man because of her, but I've always wanted a woman just like her; sweet, kind, generous of heart, and loving.

Justine checks all those boxes.

"I hope they like me. The Hills seem very important to you," she says.

"They are. They are as much my family as Quirin is. I've talked to Connor. His pack is closest to mine. He's invited us over for dinner in a few days. I know it might be a lot for you, meeting so many people, but I want you to know what it would be like for you if we were to accept each other as chosen mates," I say.

We've spoken about it more than once. This trip, bringing her to meet the pack and my family, is the last box I need to check. If she fits in well with everyone, then it's a done deal for me. Quirin will be the hardest to convince, but I'm counting on him loving me enough to accept my decision, even if he doesn't agree with it. I get it, the love he has with Kennedy, hell, the love all fated mates share, looks incredible. I did want that, but I have to think about the future of the pack. Justine is a perfect complement to me and we're very compatible. We will have a lovely, peaceful life together.

"Alpha Yorick and Alpha Cyra are the ones who were recently in court, right?" she asks.

"Yes, it was a big issue with her father trying to force her into an alliance bond because he had embezzled money. He's in jail now and the man who schemed to get him to sign the alliance bond is also in jail."

I do feel bad that I wasn't there for those court appearances. I heard from Connor that the first one became a total shit-show with Stellan being rejected and his mate finding her second chance immediately afterward. Even now the thought has jealousy eating at my insides. That woman, Lila, was blessed with two fated mates and she's only in her twenties. I'm thirty-three and haven't met mine.

For a while, I had intended to wait for Wendy, to see if she was for me. I've always been drawn to the Hills. When I didn't find my mate at a young age, I hoped that I'd find her in their family. But, after talking with Hijack, and seeing how excited Wendy is about going to the Academy, I realized that her path and mine are not the same. I don't want to take her dreams away from her. If that's her path, she should follow it and see where it goes. I need a Luna, someone who can be happy standing at my side and running the pack with me. Over the last several months, I've realized that's not Wendy. Even Yana, the next youngest in the family, is showing a penchant for technology and is already talking about wanting to follow in Yorick and Wendy's footsteps by going to the Academy and becoming part of the tech team.

It was time for me to face reality, so I did.

I hadn't expected to meet someone in my mother's pack. I'd gone more as a fishing expedition to see what other she-wolves were out there and if there were ones who were interested in being my mate more than being a Luna. Justine hadn't flirted openly, she hadn't tried to sneak into my bed or promised to make all my dirty dreams come true. She'd just been herself. She'd asked about me, my pack, my family, and we'd talked about hers as well. It had been slow, we'd taken our time to get to know each other, and now it is time for the big test, the final test to show that she is meant to be my Luna.

When we pull into the Academy's parking lot, I get out and sniff the air. There are a lot of scents here. I swear I catch hints of Cyra's and Yorick's scents, but there are so many scents in the air that it's hard to narrow them down.

Tyrus, my wolf, sits up, sniffing the air.

'Can you find them, buddy?' I ask him as I walk around the car to open the door for Justine.

'No ...' he says, distractedly.

When Justine stands, I press my lips to hers. "They're going to love you," I say.

I can feel how nervous she is. I'm sure it's a combination of meeting new people and knowing how important the Hills are to me. If for some reason they don't like Justine, I'll have to really consider my decision to take her as a chosen mate. But I know they'll love her. She's just like the Hill women. She'll fit in perfectly.

I grab the papers out of the back of the car, then take her hand. I follow the signs for the entrance to the Academy and step inside. The scent of food and lunch preparation hits me first, burying the scent of everything else for a moment.

There's a large room that must be the dining hall on the left, but I see students walking up from the right. I turn, leading Justine with me as Tyrus lifts his nose in the air and sniffs for Cyra and Yorick.

I catch Yorick's bamboo scent a moment before I hear him.

"Hey stranger!"

I smile, happy to see my friend. Tyrus, rather than sitting down in my head, continues to pace.

'What's up, buddy?' I ask him, but I'm distracted by Yorick pulling me into a hug.

All the Hills are huggers. It's uncommon in the were-wolf world, but with their family, it works.

"Yorick, this is Justine," I say, introducing her, then looking at Cyra and the baby she's holding in her arms.

"Hello, Alpha Yorick," Justine says.

"Hey Cyra," I say, walking up to her and looking at their little pup. My own need to start a family flares in my gut. I grit my teeth. I refuse to be jealous of my friends' happiness. "And this must be little Cyrus," I say.

"Oh, he's beautiful. Hello, Alpha Cyra, I'm Justine."

"It's nice to meet you, Justine," Cyra says, smiling at Justine before looking back at her little bundle.

"I think he looks just like Yorick, don't you?" she asks me.

"Well, you both have dark, wavy hair, so it could go either way," I chuckle. Cyrus has a head full of dark hair.

"So, you're finally here to sign that alliance agreement with us? I was beginning to think we were going to be the only family you didn't sign with," Yorick says, joking.

At that moment, I catch the scent, the scent that Tyrus has obviously been searching for. He growls possessively, stepping forward as the scent of warm pumpkin pie fills our nose. It's my favorite scent in fall. It reminds me of changing leaves, cooler nights, fireplaces, and heartier, richer foods. It's everything I love about fall, my favorite season.

Yorick pushes Cyra behind him and turns, giving me my first look at the gorgeous red-head in front of me. The woman smells like home and is holding the hand of a man with dark hair.

He, intelligently, pulls his hand out of hers and steps back as I snarl at him. "Mine!"

"Don't you dare!" the red-head growls at me, taking a step in front of him. "Don't you fucking dare growl at him, while you have a woman clinging to your arm like she belongs there!"

I jolt, turning to look at Justine beside me. In that moment, I'd completely forgotten about her.

I open my mouth to say ... I don't even know what I would say, but the red-head, my mate, beats me to it.

"Let me guess. You're Alpha Henry, right? The man who couldn't wait to find his fated mate, so he's been out searching for a chosen mate. The man who couldn't wait to find me. That's you, right? Well, I see you've found her. Congratulations," she snarls.

"I can explain," I begin.

"Don't bother. I, Alpha Piper Conley ..."

"Piper no!" the dark-haired man behind her says, grabbing her arm.

"He's made his choice, Zach, and it wasn't me." I can see the hurt in her eyes, hear it in her voice. Tyrus howls in my head, unwilling to let our fated mate go.

She turns back to look at me, anger and determination flashing in her eyes.

"I, Alpha Piper Conley ..."

Before I can think about it, I rip my arm out of Justine's grasp and slap my hand over Piper's mouth, pulling her body against mine when she begins to fight me.

"No! I refuse to allow you to reject me," I snarl at her.

I realize in that moment that there's a reason I'm not mated to a Hill, not mated to someone like Justine. Just like Quirin needed a woman who is soft and gentle to ease his anger and hate, I need a woman who will light a fire in me, someone who will make me burn for them.

And this angry, hurt woman in front of me is exactly that kind of woman.

Shit, what the fuck have I done?

*This story will continue in The Pack's Luna.

About the author

C ooper has been a lover of paranormal romance since reading her first dragon book, Dragonflight, by Anne McCaffrey. Like most binge readers, she has been known to stay up until the early morning hours to finish a book that she can't put down. She strives to bring that same level of enjoyment and excitement to her readers.

You can follow Cooper's books and updates on her website at authorcooper.com, or find her on Facebook at Cooper's Pack or Instagram @coopersgreedyreaders.

Cooper lives in Florida with her husband and four dogs.